ADDIE BELL'S
SHORTCUT
TO GROWING UP

✳

addie BELL'S SHORTCUT to growing up

jessica brody

delacorte press

Text copyright © 2017 by Jessica Brody Entertainment, LLC
Jacket photograph copyright © 2017 by Ericka O'Rourke
Jacket illustrations and lettering by Alyssa Nassner

randomhousekids.com

Educators and librarians, for a variety of teaching tools, visit us at RHTeachersLibrarians.com

Library of Congress Cataloging-in-Publication Data
Names: Brody, Jessica, author.
Title: Addie Bell's shortcut to growing up / Jessica Brody.
Description: First edition. | New York : Delacorte Press, [2017] | Summary: "Seventh grader Addie Bell can't wait to grow up. Her parents won't let her have her own phone, she doesn't have any curves, and her best friend, Grace, isn't at all interested in makeup or boys. Then, on the night of her twelfth birthday, Addie makes a wish on a magic jewelry box to be sixteen . . . and wakes up to find her entire life has been fast-forwarded four years!"— Provided by publisher.
Identifiers: LCCN 2016004515 | ISBN 978-0-399-55510-7 (hardback) | ISBN 978-0-399-55512-1 (ebook)
Subjects: | CYAC: Growth—Fiction. | Friendship—Fiction. | Wishes—Fiction. | Magic—Fiction. | BISAC: JUVENILE FICTION / Social Issues / Friendship. | JUVENILE FICTION / Social Issues / New Experience. | JUVENILE FICTION / Humorous Stories.
Classification: LCC PZ7.B786157 Ad 2017 | DDC [Fic]—dc23

The text of this book is set in 12-point Candida.
Interior design by Trish Parcell

Printed in the United States of America
10 9 8 7 6 5 4 3 2 1
First Edition

For my mom, who taught me how to stay young
(even if it's just at heart)

CONTENTS

ADDIE BELL'S SHORTCUT TO GROWING UP

POWER-SMOOTHIE BLENDER BRAIN

You know how every street has at least one crazy person living on it? Well, on our street, it's Mrs. Toodles.

Of course, that's not her real name. Mrs. Toodles is a nickname. Her real name, according to the dusty piles of old catalogs stacked in her living room, is Theodora Philippa Beaumont-Montgomery. But who has time to say all that? I'm not sure where the nickname came from. It's just what everyone on Sherwood Drive has always called her. But it's very fitting. She looks and talks exactly how you would imagine someone named Mrs. Toodles to look and talk.

She's got long silvery hair that she wears pinned up inside a hat so tiny, sometimes I wonder if she stole it off a doll. And there are always these little wispies flying out of it, as though even her hair is trying to escape her crazy mind. She has pale blue eyes framed by layers of wrinkly skin, and she wears all her jewelry at once. She says it's because someone is bound to steal anything she doesn't have on her.

My parents told me she has something called dementia—a disease that mixes up your mind so you can't tell what's real and what's not. That's how Mom explained it to me once. Now every time I overhear someone on the block talking about Mrs. Toodles's "condition," I can't help but imagine all her thoughts getting jumbled around in a blender like the ingredients of one of Mom's disgusting green power smoothies. (Mom is still trying to get me to drink those, by the way, but I don't trust anything the color of pond scum.)

I feel sorry for Mrs. Toodles. She never had any children of her own, and her family is all dead. I don't think she has a lot of friends either. I never see anyone come to visit her. As far as I can tell, I'm the only friend she's got. I go to Mrs. Toodles's house at least once a week because she tells the best stories of anyone around and she always serves me lemonade and cookies. The lemonade is from a package and the cookies are from a tube, but they're still pretty yummy.

I'm supposed to go over there tonight because it's Thursday and I always visit Mrs. Toodles on Thursdays, but I'm running late. I told her I'd be there at five o'clock. It's now 6:02 and I'm knee-deep in a pile of sweaters, leggings, and dresses that are all completely unwearable. I'm searching for the perfect birthday outfit for school tomorrow and it's *not* going well. It doesn't help that I'm turning twelve in exactly five hours and fifty-eight minutes and I still have to shop in the kids' department. Mom swears that any day now I'll get my growth spurt, but my body apparently never got that email, because I'm still short and scrawny and embarrassingly flat.

To be honest, it's kind of hard to get excited about a birthday when absolutely nothing has changed. I mean, sure, it's great to be another year older (I thought I'd be eleven for the rest of my life!), but where's the evidence? Where's the proof? Not in my chest, that's for sure.

It also doesn't help that I'm the youngest person in my class. The cut-off birthday for starting kindergarten was September 15 and I just barely made it with a birthday on the fourteenth, so everyone is older than me. A fact that's painfully obvious whenever we have to line up by height and I'm always at the end.

When I catch sight of the clock on my nightstand and realize how late I am, I abandon my search for the perfect outfit—it was hopeless anyway—grab the plastic bin that I keep on the bottom shelf of my closet, and make my way downstairs. But as I pass Rory's room at the end of the hallway, I notice the door is half ajar, which is strange because my sister *never* leaves her door open even the slightest bit. She's sixteen and in her supersecret spy phase, where no one is allowed to know anything about her business, least of all me.

I swear, with the amount of effort that goes into keeping everyone out of her room, you would think she was deciphering enemy launch codes in there or something.

Rory even takes baths with her bathing suit on, something I only know because I once accidentally walked in on her while she was in the bathtub. She yelled and yelled until I left with my arms covering my head, like I was running from a grenade explosion. I actually believed she might throw a shampoo bottle at me.

Later, after she'd calmed down, I asked her why she wore her bathing suit in the bathtub. She said it was because of pervy Peeping Toms like me who come barging into the bathroom when people are trying to take baths. I tried to argue that I wasn't a pervy Peeping Tom, that it was just an accident, but her mind seemed to be made up on that.

I slow down and try to get a glimpse through the cracked door of Rory's bedroom. This is a very rare occurrence: being able to steal a peek into my older sister's bedroom when she's not home. I'm careful not to actually *touch* the door, though, in case she decides to dust it for fingerprints later.

The room is a mess. You can barely see the top of her dresser because it's covered with expensive makeup and her clothes are strewn everywhere.

I let out a sigh. If I had cool clothes like Rory, I would take better care of them. I wouldn't just leave them in heaps on the floor. And what I wouldn't give for just *one* of her eye shadow palettes. I'd even settle for a stupid tube of lip gloss. But no. My parents have a strict no-makeup-until-high-school rule. The last time I tried to go to school with just a smidgen of mascara on—praying that my mom wouldn't notice—I got grounded for three days.

That's the difference between being (almost) twelve and being sixteen. Sixteen is infinitely better.

My sister is popular and gorgeous and shops in the juniors department and has a car and a cute Boyfriend of the Week who takes her on dates to exciting places like the Human Bean (the coffee shop in town where all the teens go). And then there's me. A freckle-faced, frizzy-haired, flat-chested loser who hangs out at home and plays board games with my parents while my dad, the King of the World's Most Random Facts, drones on about the secret unknown history of Monopoly.

I bound down the stairs two at a time and take the shortcut through the living room to the front door. Mom hates it when I pass through the living room with shoes on because it's supposed to be kept extra clean for when we have extra-special guests (which we never have).

"I'm going to Mrs. Toodles's house!" I call out as I shift the plastic bin I'm holding under one arm so I can prop open the door.

"Did you just walk through the living room with your shoes on?" Mom calls back.

"No!" I lie, and slip through the door before she comes out of the kitchen to check.

Despite her power-smoothie blender brain, Mrs. Toodles is still my favorite person on Sherwood Drive, and I always look forward to visiting her. She reminds me of an old queen forced out of her kingdom who now roams the countryside looking for people to worship her. She's quirky and funny and eats the strangest combinations of foods. Last week during my visit, she chowed down on a cucumber and peanut butter sandwich. It smelled disgusting, and I spent the whole visit breathing through my mouth. But it's totally worth it because every time I come over, I get to hear one of her amazing stories. My favorite is the one about the little girl who stole the witch's bread from her oven and the witch turned her into a goat. Or the one about the boy who had special blocks and built a tower that went all the way to the sky, only to find it was too cold up there, so he knocked them all down.

I love the way her eyes light up when she gets to the magic parts. And how her voice rises and falls, like she's singing the story instead of telling it. I used to think they were real stories about real people. But now that I'm twelve—or will be in five hours and fifty-three minutes— obviously I know better.

Mrs. Toodles lives three houses down, between the Lester family and the Tucker family. The Tuckers have a son my age—Jacob—who is in my class but who I try to avoid at all costs because he's super-immature and likes to make fart noises using various parts of his body. Plus, he kind of smells. Although I suppose he doesn't smell any worse than the other boys in my class. What is that about, anyway? Do seventh-grade boys just *not* bathe?

When I get to Mrs. Toodles's house, she's standing on her front lawn, explaining to Mr. Tucker, Jacob's dad, that one of the other neighbors killed her cat by drowning it in her pool.

Mrs. Toodles doesn't have a cat.

She doesn't have a pool either. Her backyard is pretty much just dead grass and one lonely pear tree that, according to her, hasn't borne fruit since 1982.

"And the police refuse to investigate," Mrs. Toodles is lamenting to poor Mr. Tucker, who looks really eager to return to his house. He probably just came out to get the mail or something and then got roped into one of Mrs. Toodles's long-winded stories. "Because they said Whiskers had only been missing for twelve hours."

Chances are, Mrs. Toodles saw this storyline on an episode of some crime drama. She sometimes confuses her real life with what she sees on TV.

I decide to save Mr. Tucker from his misery. I set the plastic bin on the grass and announce myself. "Hi, Mrs. Toodles!"

Mrs. Toodles turns around and instantly brightens

when she sees me. "Mademoiselle Adeline!" she trills. Mrs. Toodles is probably the only person who calls me by my full name—one of the many reasons I like her.

She straightens her tiny hat, walks over to me, and pulls me into a hug. Over her bony shoulder I see Mr. Tucker give me a grateful wave and hurry into his house.

As I hug her back, I inhale her familiar scent—lemons and baby powder. "Happy birthday!" she sings, and then releases me.

"Thanks, but it's not until tomorrow."

She taps my nose with her index finger. "I know." Then she tilts her head and stares at me like she's just noticing me for the first time. "My, my, you're growing like a bamboo shoot. Turning into a proper young lady."

I frown. "No, I'm not."

She says this every week. But I think it's actually because *she's* shrinking, not because *I'm* growing. In fact, I have proof. I measure myself against the doorframe of my bedroom daily and I haven't grown an inch in months. Still a meager four foot six inches, which, by the way, is the average height of a ten-year-old. I looked it up.

She squints at me, like she's examining a questionable piece of brisket the butcher is trying to sell her. "Are you sure?"

Desperate to change the subject, I grab the plastic bin from the grass by my feet. "Here you go, Mrs. Toodles. Fifty. Just like you asked for."

She flips off the lid and gasps in delight when she sees what I've placed inside.

The bin is filled to the rim with empty toilet paper rolls.

"Adeline!" she squeals, pinching my cheek. Then she grabs the bin from me and cradles it affectionately in her arms like she's rocking a baby. "You are such a sweetheart! I will treasure these dearly."

Now, before you go thinking that she is like *really* crazy—getting all excited about a bunch of toilet paper rolls—I should explain that Mrs. Toodles likes to make Christmas ornaments out of them. You'd be amazed at how many things you can craft from a tube of cardboard. So I go around the house and collect the empty rolls for her. Not the most glamorous job in the world, I know, but it makes her happy.

"Come on inside, dear. I made doodersnickles!"

I try not to laugh as I follow Mrs. Toodles into the house. She obviously means snickerdoodles, but she often mixes up letters in words just like she mixes up fact and fiction.

She places the bin on the dining room table and disappears into the kitchen to get the cookies and lemonade. I glance around the cluttered house. It looks the same as always. Like she's never thrown away anything in her entire eighty-nine years of life. She swears she needs every single thing in this place, but I can't imagine what use she has for ten brass candlesticks, three lampshades without lamps, seven giant cat figurines, five old-fashioned telephones that aren't even plugged in, or a needlepoint sign that says HOME, SWEET GNOME with a picture of a tiny red gnome in front of a mushroom-shaped house.

In the five years that I've been coming over here, nothing has ever changed. Which is why the mysterious object sitting on the dining room table next to my bin of toilet paper rolls immediately grabs my attention. In fact, for some strange reason, I'm unable to tear my eyes away from it.

That definitely wasn't there last week. Is it new? Or was it just hiding somewhere else?

I step over a knee-high stack of old catalogs and approach the table. Upon closer inspection, I see that the mysterious object is actually a jewelry box. A very *old* jewelry box. The gold legs are sculpted in the shape of elegant dragons. The lid is encrusted with hundreds of tiny gems. The dark blue sides are painted with hundreds of pale white stars. And finally, set inside the lock in the front is a brass key with a single starburst on the top.

It's probably the coolest thing I've ever seen in this house. Most of the stuff in here is just junk. But this. This is special. I can tell just by looking at it.

I reach out curiously to lift the lid, and that's when I hear something. A breathy, far-off sound. Almost like a woman singing. I hastily shut the lid and the noise stops.

Mrs. Toodles emerges from the kitchen carrying a tray of cookies and lemonade. She moves at about the pace of a snail on crutches, and I can never tell if it's because she's really old or she's just so weighed down by all the jewelry she wears. Her armful of bracelets jangles as she places the tray on the table.

"Aha," she says knowingly, glancing at the jewelry box. "I see *la Boîte aux Rêves Cachés* is already calling to you. That is an excellent sign."

Of course, I haven't the foggiest idea what she's talking about. I just started taking French this year, but all we've learned so far are the days of the week and how to order a ham sandwich.

It's not unusual for Mrs. Toodles to randomly mix in French words with the English ones. She was born in France and moved to the United States when she was young, so she used to speak French all the time. Now it just comes out in bits and pieces, like the rest of the stuff in her smoothie brain.

"What is it?" I ask, somehow managing to rip my gaze away from the jewelry box. But even as I do, I can still feel it there. The way you can feel someone watching you.

Ever so delicately, Mrs. Toodles lifts the blue-and-gold box and holds it protectively in her wrinkled, ring-adorned hands, like she's guarding an injured baby bird. "Sit down, Adeline," she says with a twinkle in her eye. "I have a very special story to tell you tonight."

MAGIC
IN THE HEART

"Did you know," Mrs. Toodles begins with her usual whimsical flair, "that I am a distant relative of the Starlit Lady?"

She's sitting at the head of the table like always, and I'm sitting next to her, stuffing snickerdoodles into my mouth and washing them down with gulps of sugary powdered lemonade.

Wide-eyed and speechless, I shake my head. Mrs. Toodles has never actually been *in* any of the stories she's told me.

"The Starlit Lady," she goes on, clutching the mysterious jewelry box in her lap, "or *la Dame Étoilée* in French, was a very powerful witch hired to be the personal mystic for the queen Marie Antoinette. Do you know who Marie Antoinette is?"

I nod. "Rory watched a movie about her once. She had a lot of shoes."

Mrs. Toodles lets out a raspy laugh. "That she did.

She was a young, frivolous queen who had many luxuries and many servants who worked for her. But *la Dame Étoilée*—the Starlit Lady—had to be kept a secret from the rest of the French court."

"Why?" I mumble with my mouth full of cookie.

"Because she was a witch. And people in the eighteenth century didn't take kindly to witchcraft. But after the death of Queen Marie Antoinette, the identity of the Starlit Lady was discovered and she was convicted. They executed her and burned her cottage to the ground. All of her belongings were destroyed." Mrs. Toodles's eyes fall to the box in her lap. "Except for *this*."

Involuntarily, I draw in a sharp breath.

"It's called *la Boîte aux Rêves Cachés*," she goes on. "The Box of Hidden Dreams. It was rescued from the Starlit Lady's cottage by her daughter and has been secretly passed down from mother to daughter for centuries. My grandmother received it on *her* twelfth birthday. My mother received it on *her* twelfth birthday. And I received it on mine. But since I didn't have any children, I've been waiting for someone to give it to."

Her gaze rises from the box and lands on me.

I blink in surprise. "Me? You want to give it to me?"

Mrs. Toodles nods once and I feel a lump form in my throat.

"But why?" I croak.

Mrs. Toodles makes a *tsk, tsk* sound and beckons me to lean in closer to her. I do.

"Because you," she whispers, glancing suspiciously over her shoulder even though we're the only two people in the house, "are a believer."

She leans back, looking mighty proud of her confession. "I knew it from the first day I met you. I saw it in those beautiful green eyes of yours."

I am tempted to remind her that I have blue eyes, but I resist. It doesn't really matter. It's not like the story is true. It's not like *any* of Mrs. Toodles's stories are true. The woman thinks her neighbor drowned an imaginary cat in an imaginary pool. Clearly, she's not really a descendent of some eighteenth-century mystic.

"You," she goes on, "have magic in the heart."

I can't help but smile at the compliment. "But why magic?" I ask. "Why do I have to have magic in my heart?"

She lets out an indignant snort, as though the answer to my question is obvious. "Because the Box of Hidden Dreams won't work if you don't."

"Won't work?" I repeat. I can feel curiosity bubbling up inside me like water coming to a boil. Even though I know it's not real, even though I tell myself over and over again that (almost) twelve is too old to believe in stories like this, I can't help but lean even closer and ask, "What does the box *do*?"

Mrs. Toodles flashes me a mischievous grin and bends forward until our foreheads are touching and I can see deep into her crinkly blue eyes. "Oh, Adeline, you silly girl," she says mysteriously. "It grants wishes."

STARFISHES
AND ONION BREATH

The next morning my alarm goes off at six a.m. I groan and press Snooze, pulling the pillow over my head. I'm so tired. I didn't sleep well last night. I tossed and turned for hours thinking about the story of the Starlit Lady.

Every time I closed my eyes, I could hear Mrs. Toodles's voice in my head, like a ghost wandering the halls, reciting the same thing over and over.

"It grants wishes."

Before I went back home for dinner, she handed me the box. "All you have to do is write your birthday wish on a piece of paper and lock it inside with the key," she said, her eyes twinkling. "The Box of Hidden Dreams will do the rest."

Then she stood up, grabbed the cookie tray, and casually walked back into the kitchen like nothing had happened. Like she hadn't just dropped a huge bomb right into my lap.

I stood in silence for a long time, staring at the box and thinking over the things she had just said. An executed witch? A magic jewelry box?

Obviously, this is just a story, I told myself. *Obviously, none of this is actually true. Obviously, the box doesn't really grant wishes.*

But then, a moment later, as I was making my way to the front door, Mrs. Toodles emerged from the kitchen again, pulled me into a hug, and whispered something into my ear. Her voice was suddenly different than it usually is. Less whimsical and childlike. More serious. "Whatever you do," she said to me, her words warm and urgent against my ear. "Whatever you choose to wish for, be sure to hide the key in the safest place you can think of. If you lose it, your wish will be locked inside the box forever."

My alarm clock rings again. I kick the covers off my legs and drag myself out of bed, yawning repeatedly. Why do we have to go to school on our birthdays? It should be illegal or something. We don't have to go to school on George Washington's birthday or Martin Luther King Jr.'s birthday. So why should we have to go on our own?

My best friend, Grace, is lucky. She was born in the summer. She never has to go to school on her birthday. Although one year, when she turned nine, she insisted on having a science-themed party and we all had to do science experiments in her kitchen. I thought that was a waste of a perfectly good summer birthday because it was basically the same thing as going to school.

On my way to the bathroom, I catch sight of the blue-and-gold jewelry box on my dresser and stop, staring at it intently. *La Boîte aux Rêves Cachés,* Mrs. Toodles called it. The Box of Hidden Dreams. For some reason, it almost feels like it's . . . like it's . . .

Calling to me.

Oh, no. Am I going crazy, too? Is this what it feels like to lose your mind? Is dementia contagious? I grab the box and stuff it in the bottom drawer of my dresser, giving the drawer an extra bump with my foot to make sure it's fully closed. Then I continue into the bathroom to get ready.

I still haven't figured out what I'm going to wear. It's my birthday, remember, so this is a big decision. After I hem and haw in front of my closet for twenty minutes, Mom finally comes in and picks something out for me.

It's a blue-and-white striped dress with a giant glittery starfish on the front.

Not exactly what I had in mind for my big day, but I can't really argue because everything I did have in mind for my twelfth birthday would require me to grow eleven inches, magically sprout boobs, and raid Rory's closet, all of which are virtually impossible.

So I guess I'm stuck with the starfish dress.

My hair is a whole other fiasco. The problem with

having curly hair is that there's really not much you can do with it. The problem with having curly hair that's *also* uncontrollably frizzy is that there's absolutely *nothing* you can do with it, apart from tie it up in a bun with about a million bobby pins to keep the flyaways in check.

I stare at my reflection in my bedroom mirror and let out a groan. Between the aquatic apparel, the uninspired hairstyle, and the hundreds of freckles on my face (that I can't cover up because of the whole no-makeup-until-high-school policy), I might as well just tape a sign to my chest that says HAPPY BIRTHDAY, LOSER.

Or I might as well just go back to elementary school, where I belong.

I grab a pencil from my desk and stand with my back against the frame of my bedroom door, marking the spot where the top of my head meets the wood.

When I step back, it's just as I suspected.

Not even a centimeter taller.

"Addie!" Mom calls from the bottom of the stairs. "We're late! Get a move on!"

With a sigh, I grab my blue-and-white polka-dotted backpack and hurry downstairs to face what I'm already expecting to be the worst birthday in history.

❋

Grace and I were supposed to be born a week apart. Our mothers met in childbirth class, so technically Grace and I have known each other since before we were born, which is probably why we're such close friends now. The only reason Grace is a summer baby is because she was born premature, while I was born exactly on my due date. Mom says that's when my punctuality streak ended, because now I'm pretty much late for everything.

Dad is already gone when I get downstairs, which is pretty typical. He leaves for work every morning at 6:30 on the dot. Mom is just finishing her moss-colored power smoothie when I emerge into the kitchen.

"Happy birthday!" she trills, holding out a bagel wrapped unceremoniously in a paper towel.

"A bagel?" I say. "On my birthday?"

"That's what happens when you run late," Mom replies. "If you had gotten down here earlier, I could have made you something special."

"Maybe if I had a dog to take care of, I'd be more motivated to get out of bed in the morning."

Mom gives me a look. "Nice try."

I grab my bagel and sulk all the way to the garage. I'm not sure why I thought the dog argument would work today when it hasn't worked the past three hundred times I've tried it. I have no idea why my parents are so against the idea of having a dog. No one in the house is allergic, and I already promised to feed it and walk it and do all the things that need doing, but for some reason, they still refuse.

I climb into the backseat of Mom's SUV and stare

down at the sad little breakfast in my hand. The bagel isn't even toasted. And it's onion flavored. I hate onion flavored. I prefer plain. Or sesame. Onion will only give me bad breath, but I'm starving, so I take a bite anyway, vowing to find someone with mints the moment I get to school.

The middle school bus passes by our house super-early, so I only take it on the way home. In the mornings, my mom and Grace's mom take turns driving us to school. Today is Friday: our day to drive. When we pull up, Grace is waiting in front of her house. She's holding a white sweater in her hand, which I find strange because she's already wearing a sweater.

"Happy birthday!" she tells me as she gets into the car. "I got a very strong clothing vibe this morning. I thought maybe you'd need this." She tosses me the extra sweater.

Sometimes Grace and I can read each other's minds. It never happens when we're trying; it always comes randomly. Grace normally wouldn't believe in that kind of stuff. She's extremely scientific and usually has to have physical proof of something before she'll buy into it but for some reason, she believes in this. Maybe because it happens so often, it's hard to ignore. Maybe that's proof enough for her.

Gratefully, I take the sweater and throw it on over my embarrassing starfish dress. It's not a total makeover, but it's definitely an improvement. I'm just starting to feel a little better about my ensemble when Grace turns to put on her seat belt and I catch sight of the super-awesome braid she has in her hair this morning.

Grace is a braiding master. She comes up with all sorts of elaborate designs. Today her long, sandy-blond hair is swept into a messy side braid that starts at the crown of her head and swoops down over her shoulder. I reach up and subconsciously touch my plain brown bun, suddenly remembering why I was in a bad mood to begin with.

Not that I'd have the patience to do a braid like that. I'd probably just mess it up and then quit. Grace is super-patient and meticulous. It's why she's a better trumpet player than I am. We both started lessons in the third grade, but she's already four levels ahead of me. The band teacher says I need to practice my scales more, but scales are so incredibly boring. I'd much rather just play a song. Except you can't really get good at a song until you learn your scales, so there you have it.

As Mom pulls away from the curb, I see Grace's little sister, Lily, coming out the front door to wait for the elementary school bus. Lily is eight and always driving Grace crazy. She's really cute with her pigtails and glasses, but I suppose I might think differently if she were my sister and always deleting my shows from the DVR without asking and eating the last of the good cereal.

Still, I wave to her and she grins wildly and waves back.

"I'm so excited for tonight," Grace says. "I have so many ideas of things to do!"

Every year on our birthdays, Grace and I have slumber parties. We always have regular parties with lots of people on the weekend, but it's been our tradition since we were five to spend the actual night of our birthdays together. Just the two of us.

"Oh my gosh!" Grace exclaims, jumping up and down as much as her seat belt will allow. "We definitely need to work on our dance routine. I have some new ideas for the breakdown section that I think you'll like. And then obviously we'll do the sleeping bag obstacle course. That's a given. Oh, and I found this really amazing new friendship bracelet design I want to try and . . ."

Grace is rambling now. Even though I'm smiling and nodding, I'm not really listening anymore. I don't know what's wrong with me. Normally, the mention of one of our epic slumber parties is enough to pull me out of any bad mood, but not today. Maybe it's because of the lack of sleep last night, but for some reason, hearing Grace list all our usual slumber party activities is making me kind of tired. But not like sleepy tired, like mentally tired. I mean, we've been doing the same activities for years now. Doesn't she want to try something new?

My mom must sense my bad mood, because after

turning off Grace's street she puts on my favorite Summer Crush song, "Best Day Ever," in an effort to cheer me up. And I guess it kind of works, because a moment later, Grace and I are dancing in our seats, singing along at the top of our lungs, "Between you and me, I know this will be the best day ever! Ever! Ever!"

ADDIE AND THE TERRIBLE, HORRIBLE, NO-GOOD, VERY BAD BIRTHDAY

Okay, Berrin Mack, the lead singer of Summer Crush, is so totally wrong. This is *not* the best day ever. In fact, this might be the worst birthday in the history of birthdays.

First, I'm late to math class because Asher O'Neil, a stupid boy in my class, decides he wants to pretend to be a bull in front of my locker. He keeps snorting and ramming me like I'm a matador with a cape whenever I try to get close. Eventually, I give up and go to class without my books, which of course the teacher yells at me about.

Then, at the end of second period, when we line up at the door to be excused, Teddy Rucker lets out a huge belch, which all the boys think is really funny. I pull the collar of my dress over my nose and try not to throw up from the horrible smell. Did he eat rotten pickles for breakfast?

In science class we have to do a lab experiment, and instead of following the directions in the textbook and pouring the chemicals into the beaker in the order speci-fied, I figure it would just be easier and quicker to dump them all in at once. I'm a big fan of shortcuts. My philoso-phy is: If there's a quicker way to do something, why not just do it? Grace calls this laziness. I call it basic efficiency. For instance, why take the stairs when the escalator gets you there faster? Why clean your room when you can just shove everything in the closet and be done with it?

Apparently, though, there are a few things in life this philosophy doesn't apply to. Like science experiments. Which becomes evident a few minutes later when the beaker—filled with what can only be described as a thick fluorescent orange goo—explodes in my face.

Fortunately, I'm wearing safety goggles.

Unfortunately, I fail the experiment.

And now Grace's beautiful white sweater is covered in neon slime.

Also, today I have gym, which means I have to wear my gym clothes. I hate my gym clothes. All they do is show off my scrawny legs, which are still covered in embarrassing blond hair because my mom says I'm too young to shave them.

As I change clothes in the locker room (shorts and a baggy T-shirt to cover up how pathetically flat I am), I can't help but glance across the aisle at Clementine Du-mont. She's talking to one of her friends about some super-romantic movie she saw last weekend while she pulls her long, blond hair into a messy bun on top of her head. If I tried that kind of hairstyle, I would probably look like a Muppet.

"And the guy in it was so hot, I was practically sweating," she tells her friend.

The other girl sighs. "Oh my gosh, I *have* to go see that."

Clementine nods. "It's even better if you can go with a guy. Perfect date movie." She grabs a red hoodie from her locker and zips it up over the sleek black sports bra that she doesn't just wear to look sporty. She actually *needs* it. Clementine hit *her* preteen growth spurt three years ago. And her parents clearly don't have a no-makeup-until-high-school rule, because she's been wearing eye shadow, mascara, and lipstick since the fifth grade. *And* her legs are shaved. Sometimes I look at her and wonder if she's really twelve, because she looks more like sixteen. I even heard a rumor once that she's dating a freshman in high school who she met in the food court at the mall, which, considering the selection of boys at this school, is a very wise choice.

I would ask her if the rumor is true, if we actually, you know, hung out. Which we don't. Because we have basically *nothing* in common. What would we even talk about? She wears eyeliner and flirts with boys in malls. I still have slumber parties and make friendship bracelets.

That's probably why, when I finally get to lunch, I'm not really in the mood to listen to Grace list more tired, childish ideas for our sleepover tonight. I'm so eager for a distraction, I'm actually *grateful* when Jacob Tucker approaches our table. Normally, I try to steer clear of Jacob Tucker because of the whole smelly-boy issue.

"Hi, Addie," Jacob says, sidling up to us with his hands behind his back. He looks a little sheepish and embarrassed and his face is turning a strange shade of red.

"Hi, Jacob," I reply warily.

A strand of unwashed dark hair falls across his pudgy, round face and he blows it away with a quick breath. "I . . . um . . . heard it was your birthday. So I brought you a present."

He pulls his hands from behind his back and I see that he's holding a can of my very favorite kind of soda: Grape Crush. I'm so surprised by the kind gesture that I let out a little gasp.

How did Jacob Tucker know I like grape soda?

And where did he get it?

They definitely don't sell soda at school and Grape Crush can be hard to find. Most supermarkets don't even stock it. Mom usually has to drive to the next town to buy it for me.

"Wow, Jacob," I finally bring myself to say. "Thank you so much. That was really sweet of you!"

He shrugs, his face growing redder by the second. "It was nothing. I hope you like it."

I eagerly take the soda from his hand. Jacob takes a

step back and watches me closely as I pry my fingertip under the tab and pop the top.

The soda explodes out of the can like a broken fire hydrant, spraying all over my face and clothes. Some of it even squirts up my nose.

I scream and drop the can. It continues to spurt and gush everywhere, rolling around on the cafeteria floor like it's been possessed by an evil spirit.

That's when I hear the laughter. It's coming from the next table over, where a bunch of seventh-grade boys are cracking up and giving Jacob fist bumps.

"How long did he shake that thing?" one of the boys asks between hoots of laughter.

"Like twenty minutes!" another one replies.

I scowl and grab a wad of napkins from the dispenser on the table, doing my best to wipe off Grace's sweater, which is now covered in both neon-orange slime *and* grape soda.

Happy birthday to me.

EVERYTHING ABOUT EVERYTHING

*U*gh.

Why are middle school boys so immature? Rory's boyfriends would never do something so atrocious. That's because Rory's boyfriends are all in high school. They're practically men. Meanwhile, I'm stuck with these insufferable *boys* who think tricking a girl into spraying grape soda up her nose is the funniest thing in the world.

By the time the bus drops me off at home, I'm ready to call it quits on the whole birthday thing. "I'm just going to hide in my room until I'm sixteen," I tell my mom when I walk through the door. "Which, in case you're wondering, is in exactly one thousand, four hundred, and sixty-one days."

Mom looks up from folding a pile of laundry and frowns. "Wow, that *is* a long time. I guess I'll have to call JoJo's and cancel our reservation for your birthday dinner tonight. Too bad. I was really looking forward to some jalapeño-and-pineapple pizza."

Oh, right. I forgot we were going to my favorite restaurant tonight. And jalapeño-and-pineapple pizza does sound pretty good.

"Fine," I say grudgingly as I head for the stairs. "I'll come out for that. But that's it!"

❋

At six o'clock, Dad knocks on my door and starts singing, "When the moon hits your eye like a big pizza pie, that's your birthday!"

I roll my eyes and push past him down the hallway. "Dad. Don't sing."

"Did you know," he asks, undeterred, as he follows me, "that the average American eats around twenty-three pounds of pizza every year?"

"Fascinating," I mumble as I head down the stairs.

Dad is obsessed with this podcast called *Everything About Everything*. It's basically two guys who talk for forty-five minutes about totally random stuff. Dad thinks it's the most interesting thing on the planet and has basically made it his life's mission to educate the rest of us.

When we all pile into the car to go to JoJo's Pizza, I'm surprised to see that Rory didn't bring a date to my birthday dinner. It's pretty rare to see her by herself.

"Where's . . . ?" I start to ask, but then realize that I don't remember Boyfriend of the Week's name.

"Henry," she finishes grumpily. "Mom said he couldn't come."

Mom turns around in the passenger seat to shoot Rory a look. "It's your sister's special day. Not date night."

Rory crosses her arms and stares out the window. "Whatever. At least he won't have to listen to Dad talk about Tupperware all night."

"Hey!" Dad says defensively from the driver's seat. "Henry seemed really intrigued when I told him how Earl Tupper was able to use his chemistry background to literally reshape the future of plastic."

"No, Dad," Rory corrects him. "He was just being polite."

"Really?" Dad sounds genuinely disappointed.

"Really."

I have to admit, I'm relieved that Henry isn't allowed to come tonight. He's pretty much the cutest guy I've ever seen in person, and I don't want to have to worry about how frizzy my hair looks or whether or not I have pizza cheese running down my chin. Even though I changed out of my sparkly starfish dress and Grace's slimed sweater, I still feel far from glamorous, and being around Rory's boyfriends just reminds me of how very *un*cool I am.

✳

JoJo's Pizza is not a fancy kind of place, but it's still my favorite restaurant. I like the extra-thick crust and the honey they give you to dip it in. And they have the best root beer floats in town. Probably because they make their own root beer.

"So!" the hostess says excitedly as she leads us to the booth. "I hear someone is celebrating a birthday tonight!"

I shoot Mom an evil look and whisper, "I told you not to tell them. Now they're going to sing."

"The singing is the best part!" she tells me.

"No," I disagree. "It's the most embarrassing part."

"You always used to love it when they sang. Remember, they bring out the big cowbell and the kazoos?"

I shudder at the very thought. "Yes. Exactly."

Mom just chuckles. "Fine. I'll tell them not to sing."

The hostess leads us to a booth. I climb into one side with Mom, and Rory slides into the other with Dad. The hostess sets a napkin-wrapped silverware set in front of each of us and then hands menus to Mom, Dad, and Rory.

At first I'm confused, wondering why I don't get a menu, but then she sets a large paper place mat in front of me, and a box of crayons.

"Enjoy your dinner!" she chirps before walking away.

I hear Rory snicker from across the table. Curiously, I study the place mat in front of me. "What's this?" I ask to no one in particular.

But as soon as the question is out of my mouth, I catch

sight of the horrifying words printed across the top of the paper.

Children's Menu
(For our diners 10 and under)

Hot tears spring to my eyes but I immediately blink them away. I don't want Rory to see me cry.

Mom chuckles. "I wish people thought *I* was younger than my age."

"Well, at least the bill will be cheaper this way," Dad says, laughing.

"It's not funny!" I cry, and everyone looks at me in surprise. "This whole birthday has been a disaster and you're all making jokes!"

"Addie," Mom says in that tone that tells me she thinks I'm being overly dramatic. But I'm not. If she only knew what I've been through today. "It's a simple mistake. If you want a regular menu we can—"

"I don't want a regular menu! I just want to go home! You don't understand! None of you do!"

"Addie," Dad says soothingly.

"Just forget it!" I jump out of my seat and run from the booth, wiping furiously at my wet cheeks. But the tears are falling faster than I can swat them away.

THE YETI
FORGETTI

If I were sixteen, I could just get in the car right now and drive myself home. But since I'm still only twelve, I have to sit on a bench outside the restaurant and wait for my parents to drive me home. Because there's no way I'm going back in there. I can never show my face at JoJo's Pizza again!

I expect to see my entire family come rushing out the front door to make sure I'm okay, but only Mom makes an appearance. She sits down next to me on the bench with a sigh.

"For the record," she says, "I don't think you look ten."

"You don't count," I reply grumpily. "You're my mother."

"That means I count double!" she jokes. I know what she's trying to do. She's trying to cheer me up. It won't work.

"I hate this," I say, kicking at a rock on the sidewalk. "I'm a year older but nothing has changed. Strangers still think I'm a little kid. You won't let me wear makeup or shave my legs or have a cell phone when like every kid in my class has one. I still have all these annoying freckles on my face—"

"I like your freckles," Mom interjects.

"They're babyish. Just like my name."

"Do you want us to start calling you Adeline?" Mom asks hopefully, like this will make everything better.

"I want to be turning sixteen. Not twelve."

Mom laughs and puts her arm around my shoulder, pulling me close to her. I want to scoot away because I'm afraid someone I know will walk by and see me sitting here cuddling with my mother, but I'll admit, it feels kind of good. "There are no shortcuts to growing up," she says. "That's just one of the things in life you have to do the hard way."

I huff in response.

"Why are you in such a hurry to grow up, anyway?" she asks. "You haven't even given twelve a chance yet. Maybe you'll like it."

"I doubt it," I grumble.

"C'mon." Mom nudges my shoulder. "Let's go back inside and have some pizza."

"I'm not hungry anymore."

"Hmm," Mom says thoughtfully, tapping her chin with her finger. I immediately notice the mischievous twinkle in her eye. "If I can't cheer you up, then there's really nobody else to call."

Now I do scoot away, glancing uneasily around for witnesses. Thankfully, the parking lot is empty. "No. Mom. Don't. Don't do it. Not here."

"Don't do what?" Mom's voice grows deeper, more like a growl.

"Mom," I beg. "Please. Someone might see."

"You must pay a toll to the Yeti Forgetti." Her voice has completely transformed now. There's no turning back. I try to stand up but Mom grabs me, pulls me back, and starts tickling me everywhere. Under my armpits, on my belly, under the backs of my knees. I shriek with laughter. "Mom! No!"

"Who is Mom?" she bellows in her bigfoot voice. "I don't understand this word."

I'm giggling so hard I can't even breathe. "Yeti Forgetti! Stop!"

She tickles me harder. "The Yeti Forgetti can't stop."

I scream and wiggle out of her reach, rolling right off the bench onto my feet. Mom stands and lowers into a crouch, ready to attack. I run. She sprints after me, all the while never losing her deep monster voice. "The Yeti Forgetti needs more tickles!"

Five minutes later, we're both out of breath and ready to go inside for pizza. By the time I sit back down at our booth and smell the mouthwatering jalapeño-and-pineapple pie waiting for me at the table, I've almost managed to forget why I was so upset.

TOO OLD
FOR TEA PARTIES

Grace arrives for the slumber party about ten minutes after we get home. She's right on time, which is typical. Of the two of us, she's definitely the punctual one. I don't think I've ever seen her late for anything.

"I'm saving your present for the party tomorrow," she announces as soon as she walks into the kitchen.

"Is it a puppy?" I ask hopefully.

"No," Mom and Dad say in unison, and I scowl at them.

Grace giggles. "It's not a puppy. And I'm not telling! You're going to love it, though! I picked it out months ago!"

Mom brings out a small cake—she's making cupcakes for tomorrow's party—and I blow out the candles. I don't bother making a wish this year. Mom already said I wasn't getting a dog and that's been my wish for the past six years, so what's the point?

After we gobble down our cake, Grace and I say good-night to my parents and head outside to the Hideaway.

The Hideaway is a playhouse in the backyard that my dad built for Rory and me when we were little. He's a con-tractor, which means he builds big houses all the time. So building this smaller version of a house was no big deal. Rory decided early on that she was too cool to play inside a playhouse, so Grace and I moved in and made it our own. We call it the Hideaway because it's the only place where we can really hang out alone, without par-ents and sisters spying on us. Of course, I never worry about Rory spying on *me*. She couldn't care less what I'm doing. But Grace's little sister, Lily, always wants to hang out with us.

We run down the stone path through the yard and bound up the front steps. The Hideaway is a pastel yel-low house with white trim, white shutters, and a white wraparound porch. Mom says it's Victorian style, like the old houses in San Francisco. There's a small chalkboard sign that rests inside the front window. Right now it says GRADDIE DANCE STUDIO (which we got by mashing our two names together) because lately we've been using the play-house to choreograph dance routines to our favorite songs. Last summer it said GRADDIE'S BUTTERCUP BAKERY because we decided to start a cupcake business and the Hideaway was the hub of our operations. Over the years the sign has also said GRADDIE'S TEAHOUSE, when we turned the house into a tearoom, and even DOLLY DAY CARE, when we were really young and used the house as a day care for our dolls.

Grace and I decorated the Hideaway ourselves. The walls are covered with pictures of Summer Crush. There are four posters of the entire group—Berrin, Donovan, Maddox, and Cole. And then one poster of my favorite member—Berrin—and one poster of Grace's favorite member—Cole. There's also a small round table in the corner, a huge clothing rack against the back wall where we keep all the dance costumes we've collected over the years; and a cabinet full of dishes, stuffed animals, extra blankets, old Barbie dolls, and friendship bracelet string.

Grace rolls out her sleeping bag on the pink carpet directly under the poster of Cole and lies down, gazing up at it. "Do you believe the rumors that Cole and Berrin don't get along?"

I plop down on my own sleeping bag. "Of course not. It's just haters trying to stir up trouble. I read that they're all best friends and hang out even when they're not on tour together."

"What do you think they do when they hang out?"

"Go out to dinner," I reply knowledgeably. "Berrin's favorite food is sushi."

"I hate sushi," Grace says, scrunching up her nose.

"Me too," I agree. "It smells like . . ."

"A fish tank," we both say at the exact same moment. Then we point to each other with open mouths and cackle like old ladies. It's what we always do whenever we say the same thing at the same time, which happens a lot.

"So," Grace says, rolling onto her stomach. "What do you want to do first? Work on our new routine? Make friendship bracelets? Build a sleeping bag obstacle course?"

I let out a sigh. "I don't know."

"We haven't had a tea party in a while!"

I fight back a groan. "Grace. C'mon."

"What?" she asks and sounds like she really doesn't understand what's wrong with that idea. "It'll be fun."

I rub at the small scuff in the carpeting next to my pillow. There's a dent in the wood floor underneath to match. I remember when we made that dent. It was the summer we decided to use the Hideaway as a library and loaned out our books to the neighborhood kids. We tried to move a giant bookshelf from the house and it ended up falling over and damaging the floor. "Don't you think we're a little old for tea parties?"

Grace stares blankly back at me. "The queen of England has tea parties and she's like a hundred."

I look over at the plastic floral teapot sitting on the table in the corner. It was part of a whole set that Grace got me for my seventh birthday, but that was a long time ago. My mom now uses the sugar bowl to hold loose change in the kitchen and only two of the cups and saucers remain. I have no idea what happened to the rest of them. Grace and I haven't actually used the teapot for tea parties in more than three years. Now we use it to leave secret messages for each other. When I was bringing my stuff out here after school, I found she had hidden a happy birthday message inside. I don't know when she did it, but that's kind of the point.

"Maybe we could work on our English project," Grace suggests. We've been studying retellings in English class. That's when someone takes an old, outdated story and transforms it into something new and shiny that people can relate to again. The assignment is to retell any story in any format we want. As soon as Ms. Mailer said we could work in pairs, Grace and I immediately reached for each other's hands.

"But it's my birthday," I point out. "Why would I want to do homework on my birthday?" I can tell from Grace's slightly injured reaction that I was a little too bratty when I said that, but I'm sorry. All her suggestions so far have been really lame.

"I thought that sounded like fun," Grace defends. "Maybe we can make a movie and our movie studio could be called Graddie Productions!"

I shrug. "What story would we retell?"

Grace's eyes light up with an idea. "Ooh! How about doing a modern-day retelling of a fairy tale!"

I immediately perk up at the suggestion. Grace always has the best ideas for school projects. But then, a second later, just as I'm making a mental list of my favorite stories, I think about what would happen if we showed up to school with a fairy-tale movie. We'd get laughed at for sure. Clementine Dumont would never do anything so immature.

I quickly change my smile to a grimace. "A fairy tale? Seriously?"

"What?" Grace asks, sounding offended. "What's wrong with fairy tales?"

"For starters, we're not seven."

She crosses her arms. "Fine. What story do you want to retell?"

I think about the conversation I overheard in the locker room today between Clementine and her friend. They were talking about some new romantic movie that's out in the theaters.

What's the most romantic story ever?

My eyes open wide. "*Romeo and Juliet!* We could re-tell it in modern times with a music video! It would be so awesome."

Grace's expression looks like she just drank sour milk. "No."

"Well, it's better than doing *Snow White*," I mutter.

"I never said it had to be *Snow White*. It could be something cool like *Rapunzel*."

I shake my head adamantly. "No."

"Okay," Grace mumbles, tugging at her earlobe. It's what she does when she's nervous or uncomfortable. "Let's just forget about the school project for now."

"I know something we could do tonight," I say, jumping up to my knees.

"What?"

"Rory is getting ready for a school dance right now. When she leaves, let's break into her room and try on all her makeup!"

Grace giggles but rejects the idea quickly. "No way. If she finds out, you'll be dead. And I kind of like having you around."

I laugh, too. "Okay, well, when Henry comes to pick her up, let's sneak into the back of his car and spy on them at the dance!"

The light in my best friend's eyes goes off like someone hit a switch. "Why?" she asks, and I don't miss the subtle hints of repulsion in her voice.

"Because it would be fun," I snap, causing Grace to flinch. I sort of feel bad for getting so defensive but to be honest, I'm kind of frustrated with her. Would it kill her to grow up a little bit and try some new things?

"But what if we get caught?" she asks.

"So what?"

"So, that doesn't sound fun at all."

"Aren't you curious what a high school dance is like?"

Grace fidgets with the edge of her pillowcase. "I guess. Maybe a little. But we'll find out eventually, right? You know, when we're in high school."

"But I want to know *now*."

Grace bites her lip in response.

"Well, it sure beats making friendship bracelets," I sneer.

She looks shocked. "I thought you liked making friendship bracelets."

"Yeah," I admit. "Maybe when I was like nine."

"What are you saying?" she asks, and now I hear the defensiveness in her own voice.

I pick at some dried green paint on the wall. It's from two years ago, when Grace and I tried (and failed) to paint a jungle mural. "Nothing. I'm just getting tired of doing all this immature kids stuff."

"So you think *I'm* immature?"

I just shrug, but apparently that's enough for Grace to get really mad.

She leaps to her feet. "What's going on with you?"

I blink in surprise. "Me?"

"Yeah, *you*! You used to be fun. You used to want to do fun things."

I cross my arms over my chest. "I guess I'm just growing up faster than you."

Grace's fists clench at her sides. I can see her face starting to turn red like it does when she gets really upset. "If growing up means becoming totally boring, then I think I'll stay the way I am!"

I snort. "If I'm so *boring,* then why are you even here?"

I feel kind of bad about that last part. Grace looks like she's about to cry.

"I don't know!" she screams, and then begins hastily rolling up her sleeping bag.

I expect her to stomp out right then. She certainly looks ready to stomp out. But instead, she just stands there, staring at me. I think she's waiting for me to stop her. Maybe she's waiting for an apology.

Guilt suddenly punches me in the stomach. I shouldn't have said those things. But I'm still all riled up from everything that's happened today. I open my mouth to tell Grace I'm sorry and that I didn't mean what I said, but apparently I'm taking too long, because she says, "Since you're so grown-up and mature, then maybe you should celebrate your birthday all by yourself!" And then she really does stomp out.

She slams the door so hard behind her, the little chalkboard falls out of the windowsill and lands with a thud by my feet.

SEALED WITH A KEY

Grace's mom came to pick her up an hour ago. I watched her drive away from my bedroom window, trying to convince myself that it didn't bother me. That I didn't need Grace to have a fun birthday. But I've never been very good at convincing myself of things that aren't true.

So I lie in bed and continue to feel guilty instead.

I toss and turn, trying to fall asleep, but it's no use. I can't get comfortable. I left my sleeping bag and my good pillow in the Hideaway because I didn't want to wake up my parents by dragging them through the house. When Mom finds out that Grace left early because of something I did, there are going to be lectures. I'm going to have to listen to Mom drone on about the *right* way to treat guests and the *wrong* way to be a friend.

After another hour of feeling wretched and being unable to sleep, I decide to call Grace. I get up and tiptoe

46

into the hallway to grab the phone from the charger and carry it back to my room.

Grace's mom won't let her have a cell phone until high school either. It was some kind of pact our mothers made a few years ago, thinking it would be easier on both of us if neither of us had one. For some reason, Grace doesn't seem to mind all that much, while I, on the other hand, pretty much consider it child abuse.

I start to dial Grace's home phone number, but halfway through the digits, I catch sight of the time on my alarm clock.

It's after midnight.

I don't think Mrs. Harrington would be too thrilled about getting a call at this hour.

I quickly hang up and toss the phone onto my bed.

If only our parents would let us have cell phones, I could text her right now and tell her how sorry I am.

If only we were sixteen, this wouldn't be a problem.

Then again, if we were sixteen, I wouldn't actually *need* to apologize because Grace and I wouldn't have been fighting in the first place. Everything would be perfect. I'd be able to wear the clothes and makeup I want to wear; the boys in my class wouldn't be such immature, smelly dorks; hostesses at restaurants wouldn't give me children's menus; I wouldn't be a flat-chested shrimp; and I'd have my driver's license and an awesome life. I'd have no reason to be mad about anything!

This whole day just stinks.

I collapse back on my bed and stare at the ceiling. When I was seven and obsessed with princesses, my dad hired a guy from his construction crew to paint a giant fairy-tale castle on my ceiling, complete with fluffy white clouds and a sparkling crescent moon. In fact, my whole room is decorated with princess stuff, down to my glittery pink walls, pink chiffon curtains, and matching ruffled comforter. I remember how much I used to love this room. How excited I was to show all the girls at school. Now it makes me want to cry.

As I lie here, stewing in my bad mood, I think about everything that's happened today and everything that's gone wrong. My obnoxious starfish dress and Grace's slime-covered sweater. Jacob Tucker and his exploding grape soda. JoJo's Pizza and their stupid kids' menu. Fighting with Grace. So far, turning twelve has been such an incredible letdown. I think about the next four years and how agonizingly slowly time goes.

And then, to my surprise, somewhere in the darkness, I hear a distant voice.

Like a ghost whispering through the walls.

"It grants wishes."

I sit up and flip the switch on my bedside lamp. The room comes into focus. There's no one there. Yet I still can't bring myself to shut off the light.

"It grants wishes."

Mrs. Toodles?

My gaze sweeps to the corner of the room, as if something is actually *pulling* my eyes in that direction. Something that's making my heart race with anxiety. Curiously, I stand up, creep over to the white dresser with the silver knobs, and kneel down in front of the bottom drawer. I ease it open and pull out the jewelry box.

La Boîte aux Rêves Cachés.

I carry the box to my desk and set it down, studying it from all sides. Then, ever so carefully, I lift the lid. That strange, eerie voice I heard at Mrs. Toodles's house is back. It sounds like a woman singing. But very far away.

I run my fingertip along the cracked velvet lining. The inside smells musty and kind of fruity, just like everything in Mrs. Toodles's house. It immediately makes me smile.

"All you have to do is write your birthday wish on a piece of paper and lock it inside with the key. The Box of Hidden Dreams will do the rest."

I bite my lip, feeling my hands tingle in anticipation.

It doesn't really work, I tell myself repeatedly. Jewelry boxes don't grant wishes. Magic isn't real.

I hastily close the lid and hurry back to my bed. I scramble under the covers and switch off the light, feeling the box watching me in the darkness.

Then a peculiar thought comes to me.

If it's not real, then it doesn't hurt to try.

It's this very thought that eventually motivates me to flip the light on again, creep back to my desk, tear a piece of paper from my notebook, scrawl out a message, and slip it inside the box. Then I close the lid and turn the key in the lock.

As soon as I'm done, I feel the tightness in my chest ease, like someone has loosened a firm grasp on my heart.

I breathe out a heavy sigh and pad back to my bed, yawning as I curl up under the covers. Just as I'm about to fall asleep, I remember something else Mrs. Toodles said.

"Whatever you choose to wish for, be sure to hide the key in the safest place you can think of. If you lose it, your wish will be locked inside the box forever."

I peel open my eyes and glance at the jewelry box sitting on my desk. I can see the brass key with the starburst top still poking out of the lock. I should probably get up and hide it somewhere safe, like Mrs. Toodles said, but my eyes are growing heavy and I'm too tired to move.

I'll find a safe place for it tomorrow.

Then, surprisingly, I fall asleep fast.

The very last thought in my mind, as I drift into dreams, is the memory of my own handwriting scribbled on the piece of paper that's now locked safely in Mrs. Toodles's jewelry box.

I wish I was sixteen.

MIRROR, MIRROR ON THE WALL

I dream I'm being attacked by a giant slippery eel. It slithers under my chin, leaving behind a trail of wet sludge. I bat at it with my hands until it finally squirms away. But when I wake up to the sound of my mother's voice yelling at me from downstairs, it's like I can still feel the slimy residue on my skin.

Shivering, I rub at my neck. My fingertips come back damp.

That's freaky.

"Adeline!" my mother calls. "Are you up yet?"

Adeline?

My mother never calls me Adeline. Does this have something to do with our conversation outside JoJo's Pizza last night? Is she taking pity on me because I complained that the nickname Addie was babyish? Or am I in trouble?

Uh-oh.

51

She must have talked to Grace's mother. She must know what happened last night. I'm about to get the lecture of the century. That does not motivate me to get out of bed. I close my eyes and roll onto my other side to try to go back to sleep, but my face smashes against something hard and . . . *furry?*

I blink open my eyes. I can't see anything, though, because there's a wall of golden-yellow hair in my face. I blow out a breath and the hair moves. Then the whole wall starts to move. It stands up and hovers over me, wiggling its entire body in some kind of excited shimmy.

Is that a . . . ?

"And don't let Buttercup on the bed!" Mom calls from outside my door. "You know she's not allowed on the furniture!"

"Buttercup," I repeat curiously.

The furry creature lets out a yelp of excitement.

It is! It's a dog! My parents finally got me a dog! This must have been my big birthday surprise! Well, they sure did an awesome job keeping it a secret. Waiting until the day *after* my birthday to give it to me. Mom even pretended to get all flustered when I brought it up yesterday. That was a nice touch.

I squeal and leap up to pet the dog. She seems to feed off my energy and starts bouncing around on the bed. "Aren't you the cutest thing ever?" I coo in an obnoxious baby voice. "Well, hello there! Hello! Yes, you're so cute! Yes, you are!"

A giant tongue protrudes and licks my face. I giggle.

I have to go downstairs and thank Mom and Dad. Eagerly, I jump out of bed and run toward the hallway, smashing right into my dresser.

OUCH!

What is that doing there?

My dresser is supposed to be in the corner. And that doesn't even look like my dresser. It's black. Mine is white. I slowly glance around the room, wondering if I'm still stuck in that creepy eel dream, because this is definitely *not* my bedroom. This is way too cool to be my bedroom.

The walls are painted a dark fuchsia pink. The dresser, nightstand, and desk are all a slick, shiny black. The bedspread is a stylish white-and-black floral design with fuchsia throw pillows. The lamps have a cool silver base with a white-and-black striped shade. And the walls are covered with framed black-and-white photographs of beautiful women I don't even know.

Where am I?

I look at the door to the hallway. At least *that* seems to be in the right place. And that was definitely my mom's voice yelling at me.

The dog yelps and paws at the closed door, wanting to be let out. I take a hesitant step toward her, but freeze when I catch sight of something else strange about the dresser. It has a mirror.

Or rather, it has what *looks* like a mirror. But obviously

it can't be a mirror because that's not *my* reflection in it. I stare openmouthed and wide-eyed at the glass. The stranger stares openmouthed and wide-eyed back at me. I reach up to touch my chin. The stranger reaches up to touch *her* chin.

I shriek and leap back.

The stranger does the same.

But . . .

How . . . ?

What . . . ?

That can't be me! That girl is tall and lean and has beautiful long, silky, *straight* hair. I mean, she does *kind of* look like me. Her eyes are the same color and her chin is the same shape, but her face is thinner, her nose is smaller, and she has only a faint sprinkling of freckles. I take a wary step back toward the dresser, pulling at my cheeks and hair and watching in bewilderment as the girl in the mirror does the same.

I tear my gaze away from the alien reflection and brave a glance down at my body, letting out another shriek.

I have *boobs*!

I mean, they're not like comically huge or anything but they're . . . *there*. Boobs where there were no boobs before.

With shaky hands, I reach toward my chest and grab on to them.

Whoa. They're real! And they feel so *weird*.

Of course, just as I'm standing there, holding the mystery boobs, is when my mother decides to barge into the room without knocking.

"Adeline. Oh, good. You're up. It's a miracle."

I drop my boobs and make a weird gesture with my hands, like I was just dusting invisible crumbs off my nightshirt.

The dog takes advantage of the open door and bolts into the hallway.

I have a million questions buzzing through my head right now—Where did the dog come from? Where did all my furniture go? Why do I suddenly have breasts?—but the one that comes bumbling out of my mouth at that very instant is "Why are you calling me Adeline?"

Mom gives me a funny look. "Because you told us to."

"I did?"

"Yes." She sighs and sticks an earring into her left ear. "How could I possibly forget the Great Name Change Charter you made us all sign?"

Great Name Change Charter?

What's a charter?

I'm about to ask this very question when Mom says, "You better hurry up. I'm not writing you another note."

"Hurry up for what?"

Mom looks like I've just told the worst joke in the world. "For school."

School?

But it's Saturday.

Isn't it?

Yesterday was my birthday and that was definitely Friday because my mom drove the carpool. And that means today is my birthday *party,* which, according to all the invitations we sent out, is on Saturday.

"Why do I have to go to school today?" I ask, confused.

Is there some kind of special weekend event happening that I totally forgot about?

Mom rolls her eyes. "Don't even try it. You're not getting out of going to school."

"But what day is it?"

Mom sighs. "Last I checked it was Friday."

Friday?

But it was Friday yesterday. Wasn't it?

"By the way," Mom says, putting in her second earring. "Do you know where my red lipstick is?"

I stare at her in disbelief. "Why would I know where your lipstick is?"

"Uh, probably because you borrowed it without asking and didn't put it back." There's a strange sarcastic quality to her voice that I've never heard before. Not to mention she's making absolutely no sense. What is she talking about? Why would I borrow her lipstick? She knows I'm not allowed to wear makeup. It's *her* stupid rule! Is this her idea of a mean joke?

"Ha ha, Mom," I say in a snarky tone. "I took your lipstick. Very funny."

She huffs impatiently. "I don't understand why you need to borrow my makeup when you have a drawer *full* of makeup."

I squint at her like she's out of focus. And to be honest, she kind of is.

"Look," she goes on. "I have to leave for work. Just put it back when you're done, okay?" Then she walks away without another word.

I stand in the doorway feeling stunned and disoriented.

Work?

But she's a stay-at-home mom. Did she get a job overnight? Come to think of it, she did look really dressed up. Normally in the morning, she wears yoga pants and a sweatshirt, but I'm pretty sure she was wearing a suit.

Mom has suits?

And what's this nonsense about having a drawer full of makeup?

I walk back to the unfamiliar dresser and yank open the highest drawer, determined to prove once and for all that my mom has clearly gone crazy. But I cover my mouth and let out a huge gasp when I see what's inside.

It's not just *full* of makeup; it's practically *overflowing* with it!

And not like the cheap drugstore kind. I'm talking

good stuff. All the brands Rory wears, plus a few I've never even heard of. I carefully riffle through the containers, growing more and more stunned by the second. There are at least five different eye shadow palettes, countless tubes of mascara and eyeliner, a handful of bronzers and blushes, and like a dozen shades of lip gloss!

What else is in this dresser?

I yank open the next drawer and let out another strangled sound. This one is completely dedicated to nail polish. There's a bottle of every color known to man.

What is going on?

Whose room is this?

It can't possibly be mine.

Do I even dare look in the closet? I'm not sure my heart can take it.

I ease open the door and am immediately knocked on my butt by the piles and piles of clothes that fall on top of me. It's like someone was in such a hurry to clean that they just shoved everything they own inside and slammed the door shut.

I know this tactic well because I use it all the time.

I swim through the heaps of clothes—which are all way too cool and trendy to be mine—until I can finally see the closet behind them. My gaze lands on something on the top shelf and my whole body freezes.

I stand up and gently pull down the blue-and-gold antique jewelry box.

It's about the only familiar thing in this entire bedroom.

La Boîte aux Rêves Cachés.

A memory flashes in my mind. It's faint and cloudy, faded with sleep, but it feels like it happened just last night. Or was it longer than that?

I remember writing words on a piece of paper. I remember placing the words in the box. I remember turning the key.

I peer down at the jewelry box in my hands. The keyhole is empty. I try to lift the lid, but it's locked.

The words on the page come flooding back to me.

I wish I was sixteen.

My chest rises and falls in heavy breaths as I stare numbly at the box. I think about everything that's happened this morning—the strange bedroom, the strange reflection in the mirror, the strange dog in my bed—and suddenly my brain starts to empty, until I'm left with only one single, mind-blowing thought.

It worked.

KUNG FU
WAKE-UP CALL

No. Of course it didn't work. That's crazy talk. The jewelry box isn't magic. It doesn't really grant wishes.

Except . . . what if it does?

I push the thought aside as I return the jewelry box to the top shelf of the closet.

There has to be another explanation for this. A *logical* one.

I just can't quite figure out what that is right now.

Maybe I have amnesia. Maybe I hit my head on something last night and I don't remember my own life. I don't remember redecorating my room or picking out all these clothes or buying all that makeup, which would be a huge shame because it's so cool!

Or maybe, I'm dreaming.

I jump on my bed and do a series of kickboxing moves to wake myself up—*pow! bam! hi-ya!*—but nothing changes.

I turn and stare into my closet at the jewelry box on

the top shelf, thinking about the story Mrs. Toodles told me. Maybe she would know what's happening.

I need to go over there. I need to talk to her.

"Have a good day! Bye!" Mom shouts from somewhere downstairs. Then, a few seconds later, I hear the sound of high-heeled shoes clacking on the wood floors and the door to the garage slams shut.

Did she really just leave? How am I supposed to get to school? If today really is Friday, then it would be our day to drive. Mondays, Thursdays, and Fridays we drive. Tuesdays and Wednesdays, Mrs. Harrington drives. Did she trade days with Grace's mom? She must have. She wouldn't just leave me without a ride to school.

Speaking of which—I check the clock on the nightstand—I'm totally late!

I start grabbing random items of clothes from the piles on the ground and throw them on, barely even noticing what I'm wearing.

I hurry back to the makeup drawer, greedily feasting my eyes on all my options. If I *am* dreaming, then I might as well make the most of it, right?

I dive in, sorting through all the palettes and shades. Except I soon realize that I have no idea what I'm doing. I'm going to just have to go with my instincts.

I choose a vibrant shade of blue shadow for my eyes, layering it on thick with a stubby brush I find in the drawer. Next, I draw along the bottom of my lids with a rich purple eyeliner and dust my cheeks with a rosy pink rouge. Finally, I top the whole thing off with a red lip-stick, wondering if this is the one Mom was asking about.

Next, I find a brush and run it through my awesomely straight hair, loving how easily the bristles glide through the silky strands. Normally, combing my hair every day is like trudging through a muddy, overgrown field, but this is like swimming through a placid lake.

I find what looks like a schoolbag hanging from the desk chair. It's much cooler than my polka-dotted back-pack. In fact, it reminds me more of an oversized designer purse than a book bag. It's hot-pink leather with black piping and a single gold snap on the front.

I grab it and head downstairs to find something to eat.

I'm relieved to find that the first floor of the house looks exactly the same. At least *something* is the same around here. Well, apart from the dog, anyway, who's sit-ting on the tile floor of the kitchen, staring intently at a silver dog dish.

At least, I *assume* it's a dog dish. It looks nothing like any dog dish I've ever seen. It's round with a white plate thing on the top and a small opening shaped like a piece of pie. The opening is empty. I assume that's where the food goes. But why is the whole contraption so huge if the food space is so tiny? Maybe it's some kind of warmer to keep the dog food from getting cold.

Is dog food supposed to be served warm?

Anyway, the whole thing looks like it's from the future. That's all I can say. And Buttercup is watching it obsessively, like it might come to life at any moment and attack her.

"All right, all right," I say, patting her soft head. "I'll feed you."

The only problem is, I'm not really sure what I'm supposed to feed her. I can't find anything in the pantry or cupboards that resembles dog food. So I pour us both cereal and milk, emptying the last of the Cheerios into the triangle-shaped hole in Buttercup's dish and throwing away the box. Buttercup attacks her breakfast like she hasn't eaten in weeks.

It's not until I'm setting my bowl in the sink a few minutes later that I realize how empty the house feels. Dad must have left for work already—confirming that it really is a weekday and I really *am* losing track of the days and, quite possibly, my mind—but where's Rory? She's usually running even later than I am. Did she have some kind of appointment before school?

I fling my bag over my shoulder and check the clock on the microwave. It's already a quarter past eight. School starts in ten minutes. It's really not like Mrs. Harrington to be this late. She's as punctual as her daughter. What if Mom forgot to tell her that she wanted to switch days? What if Grace is standing in *her* kitchen right now waiting for *us*?

I'm about to grab the phone from the counter and call Grace's house, when I hear a strange beeping sound. I spin around, looking for the source. After a second or two, I realize that the sound seems to be coming from *me*. Or rather, from my bag.

I open up the flap and root around inside until my fingers touch something cold and metal.

SHUT THE FREEZER DOOR!

IT'S A PHONE!

I close my fingers around the device and pull out the most amazing cell phone in the history of cell phones. It's like some kind of advanced model I've never even seen before.

I nearly drop the phone when I look at the screen and find three text messages waiting for me.

All of them from Clementine Dumont.

The Clementine Dumont?

But she never speaks to me. Why is she texting me on a mystery phone I didn't even know I had?

I scroll through the messages, trying to make sense of them one by one.

Clementine: Where are you? 😠

Clementine: 🐌 💅 ⏳

Clementine: Did you forget it's your day to drive?

Drive? Clementine and I carpool? But what about Grace? Does she carpool with us?

I quickly send a text back.

Me: I'm so sorry! My mom must have forgotten. She already
left!

There's a long pause before Clementine writes back.

Clementine: Your mom? 😵 😵 😵
Clementine: OMG! Did something happen to your 🚙 ?

My head is suddenly spinning. I can't keep the room
in focus.

Is that a picture of a CAR?

I reach back into my pink-and-black schoolbag and
pull out a matching wallet. With shaking, fumbling
hands, I unsnap the clasp and open it. My mouth drops
to the floor.

Inside the wallet, behind a clear plastic pocket, is a
driver's license.

With *my* name and *my* picture on it.

I dive my hands back into the bag and rummage
around until I feel it. The one thing that would make this
day even more unbelievable than it already is. My heart
starts to gallop in my chest. I hold my breath as I ever so
slightly pull my hand out of the bag that could easily kick
Mary Poppins's bag's butt.

And there it is.

Dangling from the tip of my index finger is a set of
car keys.

CUPCAKE NAILS
AND EMOJIS

A driver's license. A car. A cell phone. A dog. A new room. A new wardrobe. A new body. Makeup!

WHAT IS GOING ON?

Last night when I went to sleep, I was twelve years old. This morning, I woke up and I was this.

I'm finding it hard to catch my breath. I'm finding it even harder to rein in my rambling thoughts. Could crazy, power-smoothie-blender-brain Mrs. Toodles have been telling the truth? Does the Box of Hidden Dreams really grant wishes? Is she really a descendent of an eighteenth-century witch?

"You are a believer. You have magic in the heart."

But I can't. I can't believe. Not when it's this crazy. Jewelry boxes don't just grant wishes! People don't just wake up to find that they're four years older. That doesn't just happen!

I really need to talk to Mrs. Toodles. I'm going over there right now and getting to the bottom of this.

But just then the phone in my hand chimes again and I stare down at the new incoming message.

Clementine: If you don't get your butt over here in 2 minutes . . .

Uh-oh. She sounds really mad. I quickly type out a reply.

Me: I'm on my way. What's your address?

A few seconds later, Clementine sends me a response that's just a long string of question marks and some emoji I can't understand, but that's okay. I'm pretty sure I know where she lives. Her house is just a few streets down from Grace's.

Grace.

What about Grace? Why am I not picking *her* up? What happened to our carpool? She must have an activity before school or something.

I shout a goodbye to Buttercup, who has disappeared out a doggie door carved into the back door, and race out of the house, my heart doing a little leap in my chest when I see what's waiting for me in the driveway. Up until this point, I could almost convince myself that this was all some big practical joke. But *this*. This is real.

The car is magnificent. It's small and green and adorable. It looks like something you'd see in a chase scene through Europe. My whole body is humming as I unlock the front door and collapse into the driver's seat. I still can't believe this is really happening. I can't believe I'm about to *drive* for the first time ever. I try to remember all the things Rory does when she leaves the house. She turns the key in the ignition—which I do. She checks her mirrors for stuff behind her. I do that, too. Then she puts the car in reverse and backs out of the driveway.

I pull down on the shifter until the little red *R* lights up. The car immediately starts going backward. I let out a yelp and slam both feet against the pedals. The engine revs and the car jolts backward before slamming to a stop. I nearly smash my face against the steering wheel.

Seat belt!

That's what I'm forgetting. And judging from what just happened, I'm going to need it.

I pull on the strap and jam the buckle into the latch. Then I take a deep breath.

Okay, let's try this again.

This should be easy. It's just like driving bumper cars.

I gently test both pedals. The left is definitely the brake. I ease down on the gas. The car glides slowly backward. Much better. I keep backing up until I'm off the driveway and in the middle of the street. I should probably turn at some point. I yank the steering wheel to the left, but for some reason the car goes right, the *opposite* of the direction I need to be facing.

Why is it doing that?

I put the car in drive and inch forward, spinning the wheel the other way. Then I try again. Reverse. Turn wheel to the left. But the car still backs up to the right.

That's weird.

I inch forward once more and put the car back into reverse, this time turning the wheel to the *right*. The car goes left.

I have no idea what that's about but at least now I'm facing the right way on the street!

I press on the gas pedal again, a little too hard this time, and the car lurches forward. I panic and yank the wheel to the left, crashing into a neighbor's trash can.

Yikes.

A car horn honks behind me and I yelp and leap in my seat. That's when I realize I'm just stopped here in the middle of Sherwood Drive next to the fallen trash bin and there's a car trying to get through. I turn the wheel the other direction and tap lightly on the gas pedal. The car leaps forward again. When I finally get to the side of the road, I put the car in park, jump out to pick up the trash can, and then hop back in.

Okay, let's try to get off the street.

I anxiously put the car back into drive, making sure the wheel is straight.

This is *nothing* like driving bumper cars. The pedals are so sensitive. One little tap on the gas and the car goes zooming, while one little tap on the brake and it feels like I've hit a brick wall.

By the time I reach Clementine's house seven minutes later, I've nearly smashed into three more trash cans, a mailbox, a tree, and a kid on a bike, who I think is still crying from the close encounter. I pull up to the curb and kill the engine. My hands are trembling so hard I have to grip the steering wheel to make them stop.

Clementine yanks the passenger door open and collapses inside in a storm cloud of beachy perfume, spearmint gum, and impatience. She's even more beautiful than the last time I saw her. If she looked sixteen in middle school, then now she looks almost twenty.

"What the heck?" she practically screams. "You're like fifteen minutes late. And——" She looks at me and freezes, the words falling right off her perfectly glossed lips. "O.M. Lady Gaga. What is on your face? And what are you *wearing*?" Her hand juts out and grabs mine, ripping it from the steering wheel. "Your nails!" she shrieks, and I glance down, noticing them for the first time.

I don't know what she's getting so upset about. They're really cute! They're painted to look like tiny cupcakes with white frosting and sprinkles. *Did I do that?* If so, I have some serious skills!

"You were supposed to film the butterfly nails this

morning so we could upload it this afternoon. Did you forget that, too? What is going *on* with you? We have a reputation to uphold. And followers who count on us to upload daily."

"I—" I hesitate, not sure what to say since I have absolutely no idea what she's talking about. And I'm still shaken up about nearly crashing my adorable little car. Not to mention, I'm kind of mesmerized by Clementine's hair. It's simply gorgeous. Her golden-blond locks have been styled into perfect windswept waves that practically glisten in the sunlight. How does she do that?

Clementine snaps her fingers in front of my face. "Adeline! Focus! Talk to me. What's happening?" Her expression softens. "Oh, no. Did your mom ground you again? Is she mad that you got home late last night? You told her you were with me, right? And that it was totally my fault?"

Then Clementine lets out a gasp, which she quickly stifles with her hand. "Did he not text you back yesterday?" Her arm is suddenly reaching into my bag and pulling out my phone. I watch speechlessly as she flips through my messages. She lets out a sigh. "Oh, thank goodness." She wilts against her seat like she's just stopped World War III from happening. "He texted back." She slaps me on the shoulder. "Don't scare me like that!"

Hold up. What is going on here? Who texted me?

I grab the phone from her and see a message from someone named Connor.

Me: Hey, I heard you aced our last math test. I totally bombed mine. 😔 💔 🌠 wondering if you might be able to help me study for the next one? 📕 👍 🍉

Connor: That would be fun. How about Monday night?

Me: Perfect! See you then! 😊 💄 💋

Wow, I wrote that? I'm really obsessed with emojis, aren't I? I scan back over the messages again, suddenly catching something I didn't notice the first time. My head snaps up.

"I bombed my math test?" I ask incredulously, already cringing at the look on Dad's face when I'm forced to tell him.

Clementine bats my comment away with her hand. "No. You got an A. You just said you bombed it."

"Why would I do that?"

"So you could study with Connor."

"Who's Connor?"

She shoots me a weird look and then breaks into laughter. "Nice. That's good. Keep that up. It'll drive him crazy."

Now I'm more confused than ever.

"So, are we like going to school or are we just going to sit here?" Clementine asks.

I look down at the gearshift resting safely in park. The thought of moving that thing into drive again is making me break out in a cold sweat. "Um . . . ," I falter. "I'm feeling a little queasy this morning. Can you drive?"

She cocks a curious eyebrow. "You want me to drive your car?"

"Uh-huh."

I'm afraid she's going to start yelling at me again, telling me I'm crazy and that we never do this kind of thing. But instead, she just shrugs, unbuckles her seat belt, and says, "Okay. Sure. Whatevs."

BYE-BYE, ADDIE

On the ride to school, I sit in silence, trying to collect my thoughts while Clementine prattles on about every topic under the sun. Fortunately, though, thanks to her chaotic rambling, I'm able to figure out the following about my life:

- Clementine and I run a very successful YouTube channel, called Shimmer and Shine, where we post makeup, hair, and nail-art tutorials. (UM, COOL!)

- We are juniors in high school.
  (HIGH SCHOOL!)

- Connor McKinley is one of the cutest, most crush-worthy boys in school, and Clementine believes he may be interested in me. (ME!)

- Clementine and I are best friends. (WHAT?)

She hasn't once mentioned Grace but I'm far too wrapped up in trying to make sense of everything to ask about it. She also hasn't given me any indication of how we became best friends, a point I'm particularly interested in since she barely said two words to me in middle school. But I don't bring that up either because I'm afraid it might make me look crazy, which, trust me, I already believe I am. I don't need anyone else thinking that, too.

Clementine pulls my car into the parking lot of the high school and parks in a spot right in front. I find it strange that the spot was even open, since the rest of the parking lot is full. But Clementine didn't bother exploring any of the other aisles. She just drove straight here, like she already knew this spot would be available.

I step out of the passenger side and stare in awe at the tall brick building in front of me.

Thunder Creek High School.

I've dreamed about this moment for I don't know how long. Every time I've passed this building, I've fantasized about the day I would finally walk through those doors and strut down those hallways, and now it's finally happening!

A little faster than I anticipated, but what does that matter?

With my stomach in knots, I take a step toward the legendary blue doors, but I don't get very far. "Oh, no you don't," Clementine warns, tugging on my shirtsleeve.

"I'm sorry. I love you. But I'm too good a friend to let you walk through the front doors looking like *that*."

She then proceeds to drag me around the *side* of the building to a hidden door next to the gym. We duck into the girls' locker room and Clementine positions me in front of the mirror. I flinch at the sight of my own reflection. I almost forgot what I look like now. It's still so shocking.

I try to move away from the mirror, but Clementine holds me in place. "What did you *do* to yourself this morning?"

I cringe. "I've just been feeling a little out of it."

Clementine sighs. "You can say that again."

She digs into her own chic designer schoolbag and pulls out a packet of baby wipes and a bunch of makeup, spreading it all over the counter. Then she goes to work on my face, wiping off everything I did this morning and starting over.

I try to pay close attention to what she's doing, but she works way too fast. She's like Monet with that eye shadow palette, mixing pigments and changing brushes in a blur of movement. When she's done, I brave another glance in the mirror and nearly wilt in relief.

Clementine is a genius. She's replaced my harsh blues and dark purples with softer (and admittedly *better*) browns and shimmery golds, and my orange-red lipstick with a faint pink gloss. She's made my eyes look bigger and my nose look smaller, and she's covered all my remaining freckles with some kind of translucent powder. I mean, I always knew makeup could work wonders, but this is pure magic. I look . . .

I look . . .

I suck in a breath.

Like I'm sixteen.

Like I have everything I've always wanted.

I stand in awe, staring at my reflection, no longer afraid of it. No longer in denial.

I really *am* sixteen.

I just can't get over how much I've changed in only four years. How is that even possible? I gently graze my fingers over my pronounced cheekbones. I purse my glossy lips. I run my fingers through my silky, straight hair.

"I know, I know," Clementine says, stuffing all her magic tools back into her bag. "Your hair still needs work. We'll go get a touch-up on your Brazilian Blowout this weekend."

"I get my hair straightened?" I blurt out without thinking.

Clementine shakes her head. "You're acting so weird today."

I'm sorry. I can't help it. This is all way too exciting. I don't know how many times I begged Mom to let me get my hair chemically straightened but she's always refused.

"People would *kill* to have beautiful curls like yours; why would you ever pay to get rid of them?" was her typical response. To which I always rolled my eyes, sighed, and readjusted my tight bun.

But that was then. That was the pathetic, overly protected, caged life of twelve-year-old Addie.

This is now.

This is the glamorous, uninhibited, greatly improved life of sixteen-year-old *Adeline*.

It's like someone has unlocked the door and let me out of my prison cell. Someone has finally set me free.

And I have a feeling it's going to be amazing.

VERY LOST
AND KIND OF FOUND

In our county, there are three middle schools that all feed into Thunder Creek High School: Cheyenne, Diamond Ridge, and Sky View (mine). So needless to say, there are a *ton* of people in this building who I don't have any hope of recognizing. Not that I would even recognize the people that I actually went to school with because they've all aged four years and look shockingly different.

As we walk down the main hallway, it's hard not to stare at all the faces passing by. With each stranger I see, I try desperately to figure out if I know them. If they look even somewhat familiar. I try to focus on people's distinguishing features like big noses, close-together eyes and long necks, but it does no good. After all, most of *my* distinguishing features from middle school have been practically erased.

Meanwhile, Clementine is chattering about our vlog

again. "We really need to make a decision about our next makeup tutorial. I was thinking we could do a fun theme. Like Flower Pixie or Galactic Princess!"

"Great," I say absentmindedly. She loops her arm through mine and I suddenly get this bubbly, excited feeling in my stomach. I'm here! In high school! Walking arm in arm with Clementine Dumont! And people are smiling at us.

But the bubbly, excited feeling instantly turns flat as soon as Clementine unhooks her arm from mine and says, "So, I'll meet you after first period and we can brainstorm, yeah?"

Wait, she's not going to just leave me here, is she?

It's only right then that I realize I actually have no idea where I'm supposed to go. I obviously have a locker somewhere, but where? And how will I even know the combination to open it?

I eye the long, daunting corridor in front of us, filled with rows upon rows of red metal lockers. There have to be over a thousand of them!

"I have a better idea!" I say brightly. "Why don't you walk me to my locker right now and we'll start the brainstorming early."

Clementine frowns and looks at her phone. "Don't be ridiculous. You don't have time to go to your locker. The first-period bell is going to ring in less than two minutes."

"Oh, right," I say, feeling stupid.

"Just go to trig and I'll meet you after."

"Trig," I repeat. "Got it. What is that?"

Clementine gives me a blank stare. "What is with you today? Did you get enough sleep last night?"

If anything I got too much *sleep,* I immediately think. *Four years' worth.*

"I guess not," I say with a breezy laugh.

"Trigonometry," she says slowly, like she's afraid I might not understand her . . . which I don't.

"Oh, right." I bump my palm against my forehead. "Duh. I knew that. Trigmonogetry."

Clementine just shakes her head and then walks away and I'm left alone in the middle of the hall.

I bite my lip and glance around me, wondering what I should do next. Wander around until I find a room marked "Trig"? Ask someone for directions? My mom always gets mad at my dad for refusing to ask for directions but this is different. If I ask someone where my classroom is they'll definitely think I'm crazy.

"Hey, Adeline," a girl says, sidling up to me.

I blink and look up, squinting to see if I recognize her, but I don't. She stares at me with a confused expression, probably because I'm staring at *her* the exact same way.

"Hi," I finally remember to reply.

"You ready for tonight?"

I cringe. What is tonight? And how am I supposed to know if I'm ready for it?

"Uh, sure," I mumble.

"Great! See ya!" She beams at me and then hurries away just as another girl calls, "Adeline!" from farther down the hall.

I turn to see a petite brunette waving eagerly in my direction. "Did you get my text? Do you want to go shopping this weekend?"

Who are all these people and how do they know me?

"Um," I say uneasily, wishing that Clementine were still here to guide me through this. "I don't know." The girl's face falls in disappointment and I immediately feel guilty. "I mean, I have to check my calendar," I add hurriedly, and this seems to cheer her up.

"Okay! Text me!" She waves again and disappears down the hallway.

In the course of the next minute, three more people say hi to me from three different directions and I'm starting to feel dizzy from all the spinning I'm doing. This is so weird. It's like everyone in the school knows who I am and wants to say hi. Is this because of the YouTube channel? Clementine seemed to imply that it was really popular. I make a note to look it up later. In fact, there are a *lot* of things I need to look up once I get a free second. And the list is growing by the minute.

My phone lets out a soft chime, and thankful for a break, I pull it out of my bag. There's a reminder flashing on my screen that says:

My costume? What on earth is that about? But I don't have time to think about it now. I have to find my classroom before the bell rings. I don't want to get a tardy on my very first day of high school. I swipe off the reminder and tuck the phone back into my bag.

Okay, if I were a trig classroom, where would I be?

I turn in a slow circle before finally deciding to go left down a smaller hallway that veers off from the main one. But I'm barely able to take a step before someone calls out, "Hey! What's shakin'?"

I look up and nearly faint.

It's Berrin Mack! The lead singer (and hands-down *cutest* member) of Summer Crush! He's here! In *this* hallway. In *this* town. And he's walking toward *me*.

Okay, just act natural.

Be cool.

Just. Be. Cool.

"Hey," I say, trying to sound casual, like I totally talk to the most popular celebrity on the face of the planet every morning.

He takes a few more steps down the hallway and I can finally see his face clearly.

Okay, so it's *not* Berrin Mack. But I swear he could be his twin! Or long-lost cousin or something. He looks *so much* like him. He's tall with wavy blond hair that falls perfectly down the sides of his long, slender face, framing his dark green eyes. I mean, he should seriously enter a Berrin-Mack-lookalike contest. He would definitely win.

I put my hand to my lips to make sure my mouth isn't hanging open.

"Sorry to hear about your trig test," Berrin-Mack-Doppelganger says. "But I have to admit, I'm selfishly a little happy that you failed."

"You are?" I manage to utter, surprising myself by my ability to form a coherent sentence in the presence of such an incredibly hot guy, even if it was just two words long.

He bumps my shoulder, making my entire face flush with heat. "Yeah. 'Cause now I get to tutor you."

"Oh! You're Connor!" I say aloud before I can stop myself, and then immediately feel stupid. Especially when I see the strange look on his face.

But then he laughs like this is all a big game. "And you're Adeline!" he says with the same inflection.

This must be the guy who sent me that text. The one who's supposed to be helping me study for math next week. Is that what trig is? Some kind of math?

Just then the bell rings and Connor gives my sleeve a quick tug. "C'mon. We better run if we want to make it on time." He takes off down the hallway and for a second I stand speechless and dumbfounded before he stops and turns around. "Are you coming?"

I feel a wave of relief wash over me as I start running after him. It looks like I just found my much-needed map to Trigmotology.

Trigonopoly?

Oh, whatever. The point is, I find the classroom.

TRIGO . . . WHO?

Connor and I slip through the door of the classroom and take seats in the back. I keep my head down, fully expecting the teacher to yell at us for being late, but when I glance up a second later, she just gives me a kind smile.

If this were Mr. Bastion's math class back at Sky View, we would be getting serious sour grape face right now, not to mention those abominable yellow tardy slips. But this teacher—an older, rounder woman in a maxi dress— just merrily starts in on her lesson like nothing even happened.

So far, high school is turning out to be pretty freaking awesome.

But as soon as the teacher starts writing on the whiteboard, I realize that I can't understand a single thing. What on earth does "$y = \sin(x - \pi)$" mean? That can't possibly be math, can it? Where are all the numbers? It looks more like some top-secret spy code.

I glance around the room to see if anyone else is as lost as I am but everyone's head is down, furiously scribbling notes in their notebooks. Everyone except Cute Connor, who's looking at me.

He flashes me a smile and gestures toward my notebook. I guess I should be writing stuff down, too.

"So what would the function of tan *A* be?" the teacher asks the class, drawing another mess of inscrutable symbols on the board.

I bend my head and scribble.

The function of tan?

I read back over what I wrote and quickly add the answer.

To look better in a swimsuit?

It turns out I might actually need that study session with Mr. Cute Brains after all.

When the bell mercifully rings forty-five minutes later, I stand up, gather my things, and wait by the door for the rest of the class to get out of their seats and join me.

"What are you doing?" Connor asks.

"Lining up," I say as though it's obvious.

"Lining up?" he echoes curiously. "For what?"

I'm about to remind him that we always line up before we leave the classroom. It's school policy. But then I notice the bemused expression on his face and my confidence wavers.

Do we not have to line up anymore?

That's the best thing I've heard all day! I nearly let out

a whoop before I wisely stop myself. I've always *hated* lining up in the classroom.

Cute Connor is still staring at me, waiting for an answer to his question.

"Um." I search for something clever and witty to say. "Lining up to wait for you!"

Was that witty?

Or was that just plain lame?

Judging from the curious tilt of his head in response, I'm going with lame.

Thankfully, Clementine intercepts us a moment later, finding me inside the classroom and ushering me away, but not before saying, "Hi, Connor," in the strangest voice I've ever heard. It sounds like a two-year-old who just ran a marathon and is now totally out of breath.

Connor seems to like it, though, because his grin widens and he says, "Hi, Clementine," back to her as we leave the room.

Clementine guides me down the hallway toward what I'm praying is my locker, since I still have no idea where it is. But before we get to our mysterious destination, I hear my phone chiming wildly in my bag and Clementine screeches to a halt, her eyes popping wide open.

"You forgot to silence your phone in class? Do you like *want* to go to detention or something?"

I pull it out of my bag and look at the screen. I have ten new text messages. Who are all these people texting me?

I didn't realize I had so many friends. Twenty-four hours ago, the only friend I really had was Grace, and now . . .

Where is she, anyway? I haven't seen her all day. We must have totally different schedules this year. Knowing her, she's probably taking all the advanced classes.

A second later, that bizarre reminder appears on my screen again.

Don't forget your costume!

I quickly swipe past it to see what all these text messages are, hoping that one of them might be from Grace. But I don't recognize any of the names.

I click on the first one—from someone named Annabelle—and read it. Or at least, I *try* to read it. But it's more confusing than Trigolosophy.

Annabelle: 👗🥿🌙👫⛩️🔍✨💜💜💜

Clementine rips the phone from my hand and gasps. "Ugh, she is *such* a kiss-up."

I lean over her shoulder, trying to see what she sees, but the text is still just a gibberish of pictures.

"What did she say?" I ask, trying to sound casual. "I didn't get a chance to read it."

"She wants to hang out with us tonight. She's totally sucking up to you to try to get to me."

I squint at the screen. She got all *that* from that big mess?

"Really?" I ask, grabbing the phone back and staring at the text in amazement, trying to match what I see with Clementine's translation. Is this how people text? All those years without a cell phone have really set me back.

"Don't you dare invite her to come with us." Clementine snatches the phone back. "Here, let me respond."

"Yeah," I agree gratefully. "It's probably better if you do." I wouldn't even know what to say if I *could* speak the language. Clementine obviously has some kind of issue with this Annabelle girl. Maybe she did something horrible to her. Maybe she stole Clementine's boyfriend and is trying to pretend it never happened. Whatever it is, it must be bad to warrant the scowl on Clementine's face as she quickly taps out a single-key reply and hands the phone back to me.

I stare in bewilderment at the screen.

Me: 🐙

Huh?

"Hi, guys!" someone says, and I glance up to see a girl I faintly recognize as Emma Sandoval. She always hung out with Clementine in middle school but never said much to me. "*Loved* your last upload!"

"Thanks," Clementine says with a sigh of relief. "It

was such a nightmare of an episode to film. First we couldn't decide on which nail art to do. I wanted to do butterflies and Adeline wanted to do galaxy nails. But I said *everyone* is doing galaxy nails."

Emma nods knowingly. "Everyone *is* doing galaxy nails."

Clementine nudges me with her elbow. "I know. See? So we compromised on the cupcake nails. Then there was the whole fiasco with the hair. . . ."

As Clementine continues to tell Emma the tragic saga about my roots not cooperating with the straightening iron, something catches my eye across the hallway.

It's a girl.

She's standing in front of an open locker, surrounded by a group of people so I can't really see her entire face. But as they all talk and move animatedly, I catch glimpses of her over their shoulders and between their heads.

Is that . . . ?

I take a step to the left and stand on my tiptoes, trying to see over the crowd of heads.

It isn't until someone walks away and I get a clear view through the pack that I know for *sure* that it's her.

I cover my mouth to stifle the small shriek that escapes. She's changed so much! She's way taller now—she must have grown like six inches—and her hair isn't braided anymore. It hangs long and loose down her back. Also it's darker. Almost a light brown, instead of the sandy blond it used to be. Her cheekbones are more pronounced and her eyebrows are thinner, but it's definitely still her. It's still my best friend.

"Grace!" I call out excitedly and sprint across the hallway, nudging my way through all the bodies to reach her.

I can't believe how happy I am to see her. It feels like forever, even though I know it's only been a day. Well, for me, anyway. But so much has happened! I can't wait to tell her about the magic jewelry box and Mrs. Toodles's story and the crazy morning I've had. And the dog! Oh my gosh! Wait until she hears about Buttercup! She's going to freak out.

But I never get to talk about any of those things. Because I never actually *get* to her. Right before I reach the locker, a rough hand suddenly pulls me back and starts jostling me down the hallway. "What are you doing?" Clementine hisses, looping her arm through mine again. "We're going to be late for second period."

As we turn the corner, I glance back at the locker where Grace is standing. I try to meet her eye, to silently tell her that I'm sorry for rushing off like that and that I'll definitely find her later, but the group of people has re-formed their little bubble and I can't even find her in the crowd.

EXSQUEEZAY-MOI

The whole walk to class, Clementine prattles on about more ideas for themes for our next episode of the Shimmer and Shine vlog, but I'm barely listening because I can't stop thinking about Grace and how different she looked. In only four years. I have so many questions. Like what classes is she taking now? When did she stop braiding her hair? Does she have a boyfriend?

The thought of Grace kissing a boy makes me nearly giggle aloud. She was always squeamish about that kind of stuff. Although she used to kiss the poster of Cole from Summer Crush all the time.

I hope we have lunch together. Or maybe even a class together. I'm dying to talk to her.

Clementine leads me up the stairs and into room 202, which from the decorations on the wall—a picture of the Eiffel Tower, a French flag, and a movie poster for *The*

Hunger Games in French—I'm guessing must be a French classroom.

Gosh, if it's really been four years, then I must be fluent by now!

The French teacher claps twice. *"Votre attention, tout le monde. On commence! Asseyez-vous, s'il vous plaît, et sortez vos cahiers de vocabulaire."*

Okay, maybe not.

I have *no* idea what that woman just said. There was nothing about a ham sandwich in there. But everyone else—Clementine included—is digging through their bags, taking out notebooks and pens, so clearly *they* all speak much better French than I do.

Between the math class and the cryptic text messages, this whole morning has been a nonstop barrage of foreign languages. I'm starting to feel like high school isn't just another building, but a whole other planet.

"Psst," Clementine whispers to me. I look over at the next desk, where she's pointing adamantly at a notebook with the word *vocabulaire* written on the front.

Vocabulaire. That looks a lot like vocabulary.

"Pourquoi n'avez-vous pas votre cahier? L'avez-vous encore oublié?"

Why is everyone suddenly looking at me? And why is the teacher practically *glaring* at me?

"Mademoiselle Adeline," she says pointedly.

Uh-oh, that's me.

Clementine lets out a heavy sigh and reaches into my schoolbag by my feet, pulling out a blue notebook and slapping it on my desk.

Has that always been in there?

"Excusez-moi, Madame," Clementine says in an impressive accent. *"Adeline ne sent pas bien aujourd'hui."*

I blankly stare down at the notebook on my desk. The word *vocabulaire* stares back at me. Dazedly, I flip through it, my mouth hanging open as I watch page after page of my own handwriting whiz by.

And it's *all* in French.

I wrote this?

How could I have possibly written all that if I can't understand a single word the teacher is saying? Apart from my own name, anyway, which is technically cheating, because my name *is* French.

And yet I'm clearly *in* this class. I have the notebook. The teacher knows who I am.

Except I can't remember any of it.

It's like my body has fast-forwarded to age sixteen but my mind is still stuck at twelve. There's a huge four-year gap in my memory.

I think back to all the confusing things that have happened today: my mom going to work, a dog in my bed, an entirely new bedroom complete with an entirely new wardrobe, driving to school with Clementine Dumont. Then, at the same time, people I've never spoken to in my entire life are sending me text messages and waving and wanting to hang out with me after school.

As the teacher continues to talk nonsensically in French, I pretend to be paying attention, when actually my head is spinning with questions.

What exactly happened in the last four years?

Why can't I remember any of it?

And, most important, what else is hiding in that four-year memory gap?

BEWARE OF LOCKER 702

The day is half over and I still haven't seen the inside of my locker. I don't even know where it is. When lunch period rolls around, I get the genius idea to go to the head office and tell them I forgot my locker combination. I almost expect the receptionist lady to give me a dirty look like Mrs. Mansfield always does at the middle school office whenever I ask for things, but she just smiles sympathetically. "Oh, sweetie. Has it been one of those days?"

I nod and sigh. "Yes."

She reaches out to pat my hand and then turns toward her computer, tapping away at the keys. "I keep telling the administration they work you kids too hard these days. With all of those honors classes and homework and testing, it's too much!" The printer next to her hums to life and she grabs a piece of paper as it appears on the tray.

"Here you go, my dear." She slides the page across the

97

desk to me. "You take it easy. Sixteen is way too early to burn out."

I'm not sure what she means by all that but I smile and thank her as I walk away, glancing down at the piece of paper in my hand and nearly sinking to the ground in relief. There, printed across the top, is not only my locker combination, but also my locker number.

I fight the urge to run back to the reception desk and kiss the lady on the cheek.

I'm about to go and seek out locker 702, when Clementine finds me and drags me to the cafeteria, sitting us both down at a table with a group of girls *and* boys.

Boys!

I haven't eaten lunch with a boy since the third grade. Yesterday, I wouldn't have been caught dead sitting with any of the boys in my class! But that's probably because they were all stupid and immature like Jacob Tucker, the boy who gave me the exploding grape soda yesterday. . . .

Or four years ago.

But it quickly becomes apparent that these boys are totally different. They're all super grown-up and actually interesting. And they don't have to tell disgusting dirty jokes or make fart noises to get us to laugh. They just say funny things.

I search the cafeteria for Grace, but I can't find her. I recognize some of the people she was hanging out with in the hallway earlier. They're sitting three tables away, but she doesn't appear to be with them. I wonder if she has a different lunch period than I do. Or maybe she had to go off to study somewhere.

Clementine notices me glancing around the room. She leans in and whispers, "He told me he had a doctor's appointment."

He? Does she think I'm looking for Cute Connor? She must.

Then she adds, "Don't worry, though. He'll be there tonight."

A bolt of electricity instantly shoots through me at the thought of seeing him again. I want to ask Clementine what's happening tonight—that's now the third time that someone has mentioned something going on—but I'm afraid it will make her even more suspicious of my strange behavior than she already is. So I drop it.

※

I try twice more to find my locker throughout the day but I keep getting intercepted by Clementine. Although it's not like I can complain. She always ends up leading me to all my classes. Without her, I'd probably still be wandering the halls like a nomad, wondering where I'm supposed to be.

But now it's the last period of the day and I can't wait any longer. I know I'm supposed to be in English because that's what Clementine said right before she scurried off for her chemistry class.

I pull the paper from the receptionist out of my pocket and follow the numbers etched into each locker until I find the one I'm looking for.

702.

I'm really hoping the contents of this locker will give me some much-needed clues about my new life. I carefully dial in the combination and pull up on the lever, yanking the door open. I let out a gasp and leap back as an avalanche of stuff comes tumbling out, threatening to bury me alive, just like the clothes in my closet this morning.

Maybe coming here wasn't such a good idea. Do I even use this locker? Or do I just cram it full of junk and shut the door?

As I bend down to start scooping up things, my head knocks against something hard and I fall back onto my butt.

"Ow!" I cry, rubbing my forehead.

"Oh, gosh! I'm so sorry!" says a deep male voice.

I look up to see what I've bumped into. Or rather, *who*. It's a boy with dark brown hair—almost black—a round face, pale skin, and large, expressive brown eyes. Also, he smells kind of amazing. Like minty soap. But that's not the first thing I notice. The first thing I notice is how cute he is. (There appears to be no shortage of cute boys in this school!) Then I notice how familiar he looks. Except I can't figure out why.

He rubs at his forehead, too. "I saw you open the locker. Murphy's law, right?"

I blink in confusion. "Who?"

He chuckles. "Murphy. You know the old saying, 'Anything that can go wrong, will.'" He quickly swats his hand in the air. "Never mind. Here, let me help you."

I watch in stunned silence as he gathers up the various papers, pens, and trash items from the floor and starts organizing them into piles. I feel my face prickle with shame. Even though I don't remember collecting all this junk, it doesn't mean I'm not totally embarrassed that this *super*cute guy is picking it up for me.

"That's okay," I say quickly, taking the random items from his hands. "You don't have to do that. I'll just stuff it all back in."

He stands up and for the first time I notice how incredibly tall he is. He must be over six feet! He laughs. "That might be how you got into this mess to begin with, Addie."

Addie.

He knows my name. My *nickname.* Come to think of it, I haven't heard that nickname all day. Everyone has been calling me Adeline. My mom, my teachers, Clementine. Even Cute Connor.

So why is this boy calling me Addie? It must mean we

know each other well enough—or long enough—for him to use my old nickname. He *does* look really familiar, but I can't for the life of me figure out who he is.

And it's not like I can just come right out and ask him.

"Are you going to English?" he asks as I shove the last of the debris into my locker and slam the door, vowing never to open that thing again.

"Oh, yeah. I am!" I say with way too much enthusiasm. I'm just excited that he's in my class, which means he can show me where it is. And I might be able to learn his name.

"So, how's your sister doing?" he asks as we walk down the hallway.

"She's good," I say. "She's . . ." But my voice trails off. I was going to tell him that she has yet another Boyfriend of the Week or that she spends most of her time hanging out at the Human Bean with her friends, but then I realize, with a surprise flicker of sadness, that all that was four years ago. I actually don't know anything about my sister's life now.

"Is she liking Rice?" he asks.

I squint at him. "You mean like fried rice?"

He chuckles. "You're hilarious, Addie. No, I mean, Rice University. The college. It's her third year there, right?"

College?!

My sister's in college?

I suppose that makes sense. Four years ago she was sixteen, which means now she's . . .

Oh my gosh! She's twenty!

My sister is not even a teenager anymore. She's, like, a grown-up.

I feel a small twinge of disappointment when I realize that I completely missed out on her last years of high school. Graduation, applying for colleges, watching her dress up for prom. I wonder who she went with. Henry? No, she couldn't have still been together with Henry. She used to switch boyfriends every week.

I have so much to ask her. So much to catch up on. Where is Rice University, anyway? Is it far? Could I go visit her this weekend? Maybe I can spend the night in her dorm room! How cool would that be?

It's right then I realize that we've stopped walking and are standing in front of a door with a name plaque that reads "Mr. Heath." I assume this must be our English class. Minty-Soap Boy is just staring at me, waiting for an answer to his last question.

"Oh!" I say, shaking my head. "Yes. She's liking it."

I guess, I add silently in my head.

He smiles. "That's good. My mom was asking about her the other day."

His mom?

Is he an old family friend? Do his parents hang out with my parents?

103

How on earth do I know this person?

It suddenly occurs to me how odd it is that this boy seems to know more about my life than I do. I'm about to prod him for more information, but the train of thought instantly derails as soon as we step inside our English classroom and I see who's sitting in the very front row. My stomach does an eager flip.

This is it. This is my chance to talk to her and *finally* get some answers!

"See you later!" I say to Mystery Boy. Then I sprint to the second row and seat myself right behind Grace Harrington.

ADDIE VAN WINKLE

Grace doesn't even acknowledge me. She's too busy reading the book in her hands, which is typical Grace. She *loves* reading. Sometimes I joke that when she's absorbed in a book, the apocalypse could be going on outside her window and she'd just continue flipping pages like nothing was happening.

I lean forward to tap her on the shoulder but before I can make contact the bell rings, startling me, and the teacher starts his lesson. Frustrated, I slump back into my seat.

I guess I'll have to talk to her *after* class—I glance at the clock—fifty minutes from now.

But I don't think I can wait that long. I'm *dying* to ask her how she's been and what she's been doing the past four years. I'm so buzzing with the anticipation of getting some answers, I can barely sit still.

I have to talk to her now. Which means I have no choice but to write her a note.

Grace usually hates when I try to pass notes to her in class. She's such a stickler for the rules and she's always so afraid of getting caught by the teacher. But when you're the only two people in your *entire* seventh grade without cell phones, you kind of have to get creative. Especially if there's something you need to say that absolutely can't wait until the end of the class period. Like right now.

I quietly rip a page from my notebook and start scribbling.

OMG! We need to talk. Something CRAZY has happened to me and you're the only person I can tell!

"Washington Irving's short story 'Rip van Winkle,' which you all should have read last night, is *full* of themes," the teacher, Mr. Heath, is saying passionately, swinging his arms around like a crazed circus performer. "Who can tell us one of them?"

I fold up the note and subtly lean forward, dropping it over Grace's shoulder at the exact moment that her hand shoots into the air to answer the teacher's question. The note ricochets off her elbow and flies back to hit me in the face before dropping into my lap.

Panicked, I look to the teacher. Thankfully, he doesn't seem to notice what happened.

"Yes, Grace?" he says.

"Nostalgia," Grace replies knowingly, lowering her hand.

"Go on," the teacher prompts.

"Washington Irving is clearly a nostalgic man who's very sentimental about the past," Grace continues. "Rip van Winkle falls asleep for twenty years and returns to his town to discover everything has changed and his wife is dead. This mirrors Washington Irving's own struggles with being away from home for long stretches of time. It's simply an exaggerated reflection of his own subconscious and maybe even a projection of his guilt."

My mouth falls open. This is the first time I've actually heard Grace speak since I woke up in this strange new world. She doesn't even sound like herself. She sounds so . . . so . . .

Smart!

I mean, sure, Grace has always been really smart. She gets good grades and studies extremely hard, but she's never seemed so grown-up before. I actually feel this small twinge of pride for her.

"Great!" Mr. Heath commends. "Excellent observations, Grace. Who else spotted a theme? J.T.?"

I turn to see the dark-haired boy who walked me to class lower his hand as he starts talking about the character's wife.

Aha! J.T.! His name is J.T.!

Except that doesn't help me in the slightest because I

don't know any J.T.s. At least, I don't think I do. But then why does he look so familiar? Like a memory that's just out of reach?

While the teacher's attention is occupied by J.T.'s answer, I attempt to deliver my note to Grace a second time. I slyly lean over my desk, pretend to yawn so I can extend my hands out, and then drop the folded-up paper over Grace's left shoulder.

It lands right in her lap.

Success!

She glances down and I feel my stomach coil with excitement as I picture her reading it and writing back, gushing about how she can't wait to talk to me and let's meet after class. Or better yet, let's go to the Human Bean and catch up over lattes!

But all my coffee-filled fantasies instantly crash to the ground as I watch Grace stuff the note into her backpack on the floor without even reading it. Without even *opening* it.

I can't help feeling a little annoyed. What if I had written something super-important? What if it had been a life-threatening emergency? How could she not even look at it?

I roll my eyes. Apparently, even at sixteen, Grace is still playing by the rules, afraid of getting caught by the teacher. At least *some* things haven't changed much.

"Adeline?" I nearly jump when I hear my name.

Uh-oh. I've been caught.

I brave a glance at Mr. Heath, who's staring expectantly at me.

"Yes?" I ask, trying to sound innocent.

"What themes did you notice in 'Rip van Winkle'?"

I stare numbly back at him, then at my desk. I don't even *have* the story in front of me. It's probably in my bag, but it's not like I can start looking for it *now,* while he's waiting for me to respond.

"Um . . ." I fumble, trying to buy time. I think back to what Grace just said. Something about a guy who fell asleep and woke up twenty years later. Well, I can certainly relate to that! I basically *am* Rip van Winkle. "Confusion?" I finally say.

Somewhere in front of me, I hear a mocking snort.

Was that Grace?

No. Grace wouldn't do that. She's my friend. Why would she mock my answer in front of the whole class? She wouldn't. Because it most definitely wasn't her.

"Interesting," Mr. Heath says. "What do you mean by that?"

"Um," I say again, feeling less and less intelligent by the second. Compared with Grace's smarty-pants answer, I'm starting to sound like a babbling buffoon. "I just think if someone woke up to find everything in their life changed, they'd be, like, superconfused."

Mr. Heath nods, rubbing his chin thoughtfully.

I go on. "A lot can change in four—um, *twenty* years. And if you weren't there to see it happen, you'd wonder what you missed out on. Like when everyone you know has watched the season finale of a TV show and is talking about it the next day, but you had to go to dinner with your parents and missed it."

"Tremendous," Mr. Heath praises, to my relief. "What Adeline has just done is taken the theme of displacement and made it relevant to herself and her peers by comparing it to a modern-day medium like television. Absolutely tremendous."

I can't help but beam. Ha ha! Maybe I'm not so bad at this high school stuff after all.

Grace's hand rockets into the air again.

"Yes, Grace," the teacher prompts.

"I disagree. I think she's completely missed the point."

What?

"How so?" the teacher asks, looking intrigued.

Without turning around, Grace says, "It sounds to me like Adeline"—she pronounces my name with an unmistakable disgust—"didn't actually read the story and is just piggybacking off of *my* answer, adding some vague fluff about television in order to impress everyone."

I let out a tiny gasp. What is she doing? Why is she totally putting me down in front of the teacher? In front of the *whole class*? That's *so* un-Grace-like.

"*Did* you read the story, Adeline?" Mr. Heath asks, and now everyone is staring at me.

I'm caught between a hundred different conflicting emotions right now. I can't decide whether to be angry at Grace for making me look bad or panicked that I actually *didn't* read the story and now the teacher will find out.

I finally just resort to honesty. "No. I'm sorry. I didn't."

The teacher nods. "Well, thank you for your candidness, Adeline. But make sure you have it read for tomorrow so you can participate fully in the discussion. Okay, let's talk next about Rip van Winkle's hometown."

As he launches into a new discussion topic, I glare at the back of Grace's head. I can't believe what she just did. Is she mad at me about something? She can't still be upset about the slumber party. For her that was four years ago, right? Maybe she's mad about something else. Maybe we got into a fight recently and I can't remember it because it's lost in this annoying memory gap in my mind.

Whatever it is, I'm going to figure it out.

When the bell finally rings, signaling the end of what has felt like the longest school day of my life, Grace jumps from her seat and darts out of the classroom like she's running from a zombie invasion. By the time I stuff my notebook and everything else back into my schoolbag and follow her, she's halfway down the hallway and I have to sprint to catch up.

"Hey! Grace! Wait up!" I call, but she doesn't turn around.

I run faster so I can jump in front of her, forcing her to stop.

"What?" she snaps.

I fight to catch my breath. "What was all that about? Are you mad at me or something?"

She scoffs at this, like it's the most absurd idea she's ever heard. "No, I'm not *mad* at you."

Except the way she says it, she sounds mad.

"Then why did you say those things in class?"

"It was an analytical discussion of Irving's story. I was simply offering a differing point of view."

I frown. "Huh?"

She lets out an impatient sigh. "I have to get to marching-band practice." Then she tries to step around me, like the conversation is already over.

But it's not over for me. I still have so much to talk to her about.

"Marching band!" I exclaim, my eyes lighting up. "Of course! The trumpet. We play the trumpet. I almost forgot about that!"

She gives me a baffled look. Like I'm the Loch Ness Monster, finally coming out of the swamp.

"I'll walk there with you!" I say, certain that if Grace is in marching band, I must be, too. After all, we started trumpet lessons together when we were seven. And yes, she was always more advanced than me, but I can't imagine her deciding to join the marching band alone. It sounds like just the kind of thing we would discuss at great length together in the Hideaway—making lists of the pros and cons until the wee hours of the morning as we brainstorm all the possible high school activities to join.

Grace shakes her head as she lets out a dark laugh that doesn't sound at *all* like Grace's usual high-pitched, cheerful one. "You? In marching band? Now, that would be uproarious."

Then she walks off without another word, and I'm left alone in the hallway, wondering what happened to my best friend.

And wondering what *uproarious* means.

HOME (ALMOST) ALONE

I tell Clementine I'm still not feeling that great and ask if she'll drive my car home. She parks it at the curb in front of her house and waves goodbye, telling me to get some rest so I'll be ready for tonight.

Even though I pretend I'm going to drive home from there—getting behind the wheel, buckling my seat belt, and all that—I'm actually still too terrified to try driving again. The most I can bring myself to do is turn the key in the ignition and tap on the gas pedal ever so slightly, moving an inch at a time, until I'm three houses away. So Clementine can't see my car from her window.

Then I drop the key in my bag and walk home instead.

The whole way, I can't stop thinking about this crazy day and everything that's happened. It's the first time I've actually had a moment to myself to contemplate it all.

But no matter how many times I replay the events in

my head, one thought always seems to push its way to the front.

And that's Grace.

Why was she so rude to me in class and in the hall-way? Why wouldn't I be in marching band with her? From the day we were born we did practically everything together. Why would high school be any different?

When I get home, I bound up the front steps and yank on the door handle, but it's locked. I find this pretty strange because it's almost never locked. Except at night when we go to sleep.

I scrounge around in my schoolbag until I find my keys again. Sure enough, there's another key attached to the chain that I didn't notice before. I stick it in the lock and turn. The door pops open.

"Mom!" I call out, slamming the door behind me and dropping my bag on the kitchen table. "I'm home! Mom? Where are you?"

But only silence follows. Then I remember with a slump that she's not here. She works now, and I actually have no idea when she'll be home.

I almost call out Rory's name next, until I remember what that J.T. guy told me. Rory is gone, too.

And suddenly, for some reason, I feel tears welling up in my eyes, threatening to spill over. That is until Butter-cup the dog comes barreling down the stairs, jumping up to try to lick my face.

Well, at least *someone* is here to greet me when I get home.

I take the dog into the backyard and run around with her for a few minutes until we're both tired and winded. Buttercup gulps down half the water in her bowl and I fill a glass from the sink and chug it in a similar fashion. Then Buttercup stares at her futuristic food dish again, like she's waiting for it to magically fill all by itself.

"Hungry again?" I ask incredulously.

How many times a day does a dog eat? As many times as humans?

I still can't seem to locate the dog food, so I fill her bowl with cheese puffs and she gobbles them up with the same ferociousness as she showed this morning.

Gosh, this dog is *really* passionate about food.

After she's finished her snack—which honestly takes about five seconds—I trudge up the stairs to my room. Buttercup follows obediently behind, like a panting shadow.

Taking a deep breath, I decide to brave my closet again. Fortunately, most of the clothes are already on the floor from when they jumped out and attacked me this morning. With the persistence of a TV crime detective, I start pulling everything down from the shelves, searching for clues. Something that will help me make sense of this insane day.

Apart from a few knickknacks and old school notebooks, nothing in my entire closet is familiar. The clothes are way cooler, the shoes are three sizes bigger and most of them have heels on the bottom, but most of my stuff is gone. My collection of glass princess figurines is nowhere to be found. My stuffed animals are no longer lining the bottom shelf. And all my board games are missing.

In fact, there doesn't seem to be a single trace of my old self left in here.

Buttercup pushes her way into the closet, nosing through a pile of winter clothes that I haphazardly dumped out in my search.

"I know," I tell her, petting her head. "It's a mess."

She sniffs at a pair of polka-dotted fuzzy socks before scooping them into her mouth and happily trotting out of the room.

"Hey! Bring those back!" I call, but she's already gone and I'm too tired and defeated to chase after her.

I drag myself to my desk and open the laptop that's sitting there. It's nicer and fancier than the one I used to have. Probably a newer model. It takes me a moment, but I finally locate the Internet browser and open a search page.

Except I don't know what to search for.

It's not like I can put in, "What happened between me and my best friend?"

Instead, I search for Rice University, discovering with an acidy taste in my mouth that it's located in Texas. Two thousand miles away.

Texas?

Why would my sister decide to go all the way to Texas?

And then, for some reason, completely out of nowhere, I get a hopeful suspicion that this entire day has been one big joke. Some kind of prank. My sister isn't really gone. She's right there, in the next room, painting her toenails a bright turquoise color or picking out clothes for some big date with Boyfriend of the Week. If I knock on her door, she'll yell at me and tell me to go away and stop being pervy, just like normal.

I scoot my chair back and venture down the hallway, tiptoeing as if someone else in the house might hear me. Sneaking into my sister's room has always required the stealth and dexterity of a first-class spy. But it isn't until I gently twist the handle and push the door open to find it immaculately clean and depressingly barren that it finally hits me.

This is real.

This is my life.

Rory would *never* keep her room this clean.

Shoulders slouched, I step inside, taking this rare opportunity to peek around. She almost never let me in her room before.

I look under her bed and through her closet and open every drawer, waiting for that feeling of victory to come over me. Waiting for that satisfaction of knowing that I'm *finally* able to snoop through Rory's stuff. But it never comes. Because there's not much left to find anymore. Most of the drawers are empty, apart from a few discarded T-shirts or pajama bottoms that she left behind.

She's really gone.

Even her bulletin board—where she used to hang pictures she took with her friends or boyfriends, or funny comic strips that my dad found for her in the newspaper, or makeup tutorials that she ripped from a magazine—is mostly empty. All that's left is one lonely picture of her at the Human Bean, posing in a booth with Camilla, one of her best friends.

And then suddenly, an idea hits me. Honestly, I'm not sure why I didn't think of it earlier.

All those pictures that Rory used to pin up were originally taken with her phone. . . .

I race back down the stairs, Buttercup barking and running after me, thinking I've restarted our backyard chase game. I find my schoolbag on the kitchen table and dump out the entire contents until I locate my phone.

How could I not realize it?

How could I have been so blind?

This phone is a time capsule. The answers have been right here the entire time.

And now, more than ever, I'm determined to find them.

GRACE-LESS

When I swipe my phone on, I'm bombarded by another attack of texts and alerts. I have twenty new messages in my inbox. Half are from Clementine and the other half are from even more people whose names I don't recognize.

Am I really friends with all these people?

There's also another reminder not to forget my costume—whatever that means—but I ignore everything, vowing to deal with it later. I have more important things to do right now.

When my screen is finally clear of notifications, I start exploring the phone. This day has been so crazy and confusing I haven't even had a chance to look closely at it until now.

I swipe through page after page of apps. There are so many, I start to get dizzy.

Do I actually use all these?

I can't even figure out what most of them are.

After searching for what feels like hours, I finally locate my photos folder. I click on it and start scrolling through countless rows of pictures.

This is what I should have been doing from the very beginning! This has all the answers! My sixteen-year-old self takes at least ten pictures a day. It's like my entire life is documented right here. Everything I've missed.

Most of the pictures are selfies of Clementine and me. Making bored faces in the hallway at school, laughing in the cafeteria, hanging out at the mall, drinking coffee at the Human Bean (I knew it! I *do* hang out there!), filming our beauty tutorials. Some pictures have other people in them, too. People I sort of recognize from today.

As I scroll through the photos, I get that same pang of sadness that hit me earlier today when I thought about missing my sister's graduation. It's obvious from these pictures that I have a pretty amazing life at age sixteen. I wear cute clothes, my makeup always looks good, I'm constantly smiling or laughing, and it appears I have tons of friends. But as hard as I try, and for as long as I stare at the pictures, I still can't remember any of these moments. It's like they all happened without me. Even though I'm *in* all of them.

It's like I just skipped over everything.

A shortcut right through my life.

But the most disheartening part is I can't find one picture with Grace in it.

I scroll and scroll and scroll, all the way back to the

very beginning. To the first photo I took, which is dated around the time I would have started high school. When my parents finally bought me a cell phone. There are thousands of pictures. Of me, of Clementine, of Rory, of Buttercup as an adorable, fluffy little puppy.

But Grace isn't in any of them.

It doesn't make sense! Grace and I are best friends. At least, we *were*. When we were twelve.

Discouraged, I toss the phone aside. As enlightening as it was, I still have so many questions.

Like *why* don't Grace and I hang out anymore? And how did I become friends with Clementine? From the looks of those photos, we've been friends since at least freshman year.

Which means something happened between the end of middle school and the beginning of high school. Something that flipped my entire life upside down and turned my best friend into my enemy.

Something I can't, for the life of me, remember.

PROVOKING LOUD LAUGHTER

My mom doesn't get home from work until after seven o'clock. I was too hungry to wait for her to make dinner—does she even still *make* dinner anymore?—and I don't know how to cook, so I just ate peanut butter off a spoon because I couldn't find any bread or jelly to make sandwiches.

When she walks through the garage door, I'm so happy to see a friendly, *familiar* face that I jump out of my chair at the kitchen table, letting my peanut butter spoon clank to the floor, and throw my arms around her.

She startles but eventually hugs me back.

"Adeline?" she says cautiously. "Are you okay?"

I sniffle, feeling tears start to form in my eyes. "I had a weird day," I say, knowing that I can't tell her what really happened. I'm not sure I can tell anyone. Not without risking being thrown into a mental institution.

But then I realize, with another punch of sorrow, that there is one person I could have told.

Grace.

She might not have believed me right away—she's way too logical and scientific for that—but maybe she would have believed me eventually. At the very least, she would have listened. And she would have tried to help.

That is, if we were still friends.

And that's when I start crying. Like uncontrollable, messy sobs, complete with rivers of snot and floods of tears. Right into my mother's crisp black suit, which unfortunately looks pretty expensive.

"Hey, hey," she coos. "What happened? Do you want to talk about it? Did you and Clementine get into a fight?"

I shake my head. "No. It's just . . ." I pause to sniffle. "High school isn't exactly what I thought it would be."

I exhale a raspy breath. It's the truth. And it feels so good to say aloud.

My mom chuckles knowingly and pulls back to kiss my forehead. "Nothing ever is."

It's right then, being so close to her and looking into her eyes, that I notice how much older she looks. There are lines on her face that weren't there before, and new streaks of gray in her hair.

"Mom?" I ask, stepping back and rubbing my nose with the palm of my hand.

She smiles and sets her stuff down on the table. "Yeah?"

There's so much I want to ask her. Why did she go back to work? Why did Rory choose a college halfway across the country? What happened between Grace and me? But I know all those questions will just make me sound crazy. So I stick to something safe and normal. "How was work?"

She breathes out a heavy sigh as she walks into the kitchen and opens the fridge. "Oh, you know, the usual. Same thing, different day."

I bite my lip in frustration and try again. "Do you like your job?"

She peers at me from around the side of the refrigerator door, her eyebrows pinched together, and I fear that I might have asked the wrong question. But then she simply smiles and says, "It's a whole lot better than sitting around here all day doing nothing."

For some reason her answer makes me feel defensive. "But you didn't sit around here all day doing nothing. You were a mom. You did things around the house. You took care of us."

Mom gives me another bewildered look and then chuckles softly. "Sure, when you were younger there was more to do. But now with Rory off at school and you with your own car and all of your friends, it doesn't make a lot of sense for me to stay home. It's not like you need me here anymore."

My fists clench at my sides. I'm not sure why this

makes me so angry. I want to argue that it *does* make sense. That I *do* still need her here. But I quickly realize that it may not be the truth.

I'm still figuring out this new life of mine. I'm still putting all the pieces together. Maybe she's right. Maybe now that I'm sixteen, I *don't* need her anymore.

I admit the idea makes me feel strangely excited and completely alone at the same time.

She goes back to searching through the fridge. I think about offering her my peanut butter, but then I remember I dropped my spoon, and when I bend down to look for it, I see Buttercup pushing it around the kitchen floor with her nose, trying to lick off the last bits of food.

"Mom?" I ask.

"Hmm?"

"Do you know what happened to my trumpet?"

She closes the fridge and places an armful of ingredients for what looks like an omelet on the counter. "I'm pretty sure it's in the basement."

"What's it doing in the basement?" I ask, confused. That seems like a pretty inconvenient place to keep it.

Mom retrieves a small frying pan from a cabinet and places it on the stove. "We put it there after you quit."

"I quit?" I screech without thinking. Mom shoots me a weird look. I try to erase the shock from my face and remind myself to play it cool. Act natural. "Oh, yeah. That's right." I pause, chewing pensively on my bottom lip. "So, um, I'm totally blanking, but *when* did I quit, again?"

Mom turns on the burner. "What is this about?"

"Nothing. I was just, you know, thinking about life and the choices we make."

Mom laughs like this is the funniest thing she's heard in years. "You were just thinking about life?" she mocks.

I cross my arms, slightly offended. *"Yes."*

She throws a slab of butter into the pan and tilts it, coating the bottom. "Okay. Well, I'm pretty sure it was seventh grade. Shortly after your twelfth birthday. Do you want an omelet?"

I dig my nails into my palms, trying to hide the frustration in my voice. "No thanks. I already ate. I'm just going to go upstairs and . . ." But then suddenly my mind goes blank. Truthfully, I have no idea what I'm going to do next. I want answers and I still don't know where to find them. "Get a head start on my homework, I guess."

Mom raises her eyebrows skeptically. "Don't you have plans tonight?"

"Probably," I mumble as I head up the stairs. Then, under my breath, I add, "Not that I'd remember if I did."

❋

I pace anxiously around my room, trying to sort through these jumbled pieces of information in my head. But they still don't seem to want to fit together in any way that makes sense. There are far too many holes.

Grace hates me.

Clementine is my best friend.

I pretended to bomb a math test to impress Cute Connor.

My sister goes to a school named after a side dish.

I run a beauty vlog.

I quit playing the trumpet.

I can't believe I quit! I mean, sure, I was never really that good at it, but it was one of our things. Grace's and mine. We started lessons together when we were seven. My mom would drop me off at Grace's house every Wednesday and the teacher would come over and we'd play together. We used to drive Grace's little sister, Lily, crazy with all our loud honking and off-key scales. She would walk around the house in noise-canceling head-phones that were way too big for her tiny head.

I think back to the hallway after English class today. When Grace laughed in my face and said, *"You? In march-ing band? Now, that would be uproarious."*

I grab my phone and type *uproarious* into a search.

The definition doesn't make me feel any better.

up-**roar**-i-ous: provoking loud laughter, hysterical.

Well, that's pretty rude. She thinks the very idea of me in the marching band is funny? I could be in marching band. I can walk and play an instrument at the same time. What does *she* know?

Obviously a lot more than I do. I didn't even know that I'd quit.

My phone vibrates in my hand. It's another one of those stupid reminders.

Don't forget your costume!

"What does that mean?" I yell at the phone.

"What?" I hear my mom call from downstairs.

"Nothing!" I call back and throw the phone onto my bed. Then I collapse next to it, burying my face in the chic fuchsia throw pillows.

I wanted to be sixteen so badly, but so far, it's nothing like I thought. None of it makes any sense. I don't understand how one life can change so much in only four short years. I just wanted to be older so I could have a cell phone and wear makeup and not shop in the kids' department.

I didn't think I'd have to trade in my best friend to get those things.

My phone vibrates again. I sigh and swipe at the screen to find another text message from Clementine. This one says:

Clementine: Pick you up for the dance at 9? 🎸 💃 🎭 💋

WHAT????

I grip the phone tightly in my hand, staring at the

screen with my mouth hanging open and my heart banging against my rib cage. Is this what everyone was referring to when they were talking about something happening tonight?

"There's a dance?" I shriek, leaping to my feet. I start jumping up and down on my bed, all my anger and worries and unanswered questions instantly forgotten.

My mom, having evidently heard all the commotion, comes running into my room a moment later, still gripping her spatula. She stops short in the doorway when she sees me bouncing like I'm on a trampoline. "Are you okay?" she asks warily.

"There's a dance tonight!" I shout back.

"I guess that means you're feeling better?" Mom confirms.

"There's a dance toniiiiight!!!!" I sing at the top of my lungs, laughing giddily before doing a seat drop and landing on my feet.

Mom shakes her head and laughs. Then, right before turning around to go back to the kitchen, I hear her mutter to herself, "Oh, to be a teenager again."

SHIMMER AND SHINE

My first high school dance! My first high school dance! All those years watching Rory get ready for dances— dresses, shoes, makeup, jewelry, perfume!—and now it's finally, *finally* my turn!

I spend the next five minutes buzzing around my room like a bee on a sugar high, until I finally catch a glimpse of my clock.

Clementine said she'd pick me up at nine and it's already quarter after eight! I have less than an hour to get ready. Okay, time to focus.

First, I need to find something to wear. Which shouldn't be hard, given that my closet is full of awesome clothes that most definitely did *not* come from the kids' department.

Except it *is* hard. Because all those awesome clothes are either still in a heap on my floor or messily hung up in my closet in no particular order. Why is my sixteen-year-old self such a slob? Why doesn't she take better care of her stuff? It's like she doesn't appreciate it at all.

After ransacking the piles and piles of fabric on the floor, I finally find something I love. It's a strapless knee-length dress with a silver sequin top and flowy turquoise skirt that's short in front and long in the back. It looks like something a Greek goddess would wear. You know, if a Greek goddess were going to an awesome high school dance!

I find a stunning pair of sparkly silver high heels in the back of my closet. They're a little hard to walk in because they're so high, but I'm a quick learner. I'm sure I'll get the hang of it by the time Clementine arrives. Besides, they're too gorgeous *not* to wear. And when I slip them on, it's like I've magically grown three inches.

How tall am I now, anyway?

I slide out of the heels, grab a pencil, and run over to the doorframe. With my back pressed firmly against the wood, I run the pencil back and forth across the top of my head. Then I turn around and nearly faint.

I've grown almost a foot!

I'm five foot four inches tall now!

I'm practically a supermodel!

I guess Mom was right. My preteen growth spurt came after all.

After finding a beautiful matching silver necklace,

bracelet, earrings, and a sequined clutch to top it all off, I take a deep breath and pull open the magic makeup drawer. A huge grin spreads across my face. I'd almost forgotten how incredible it is. Lip glosses in every shade. Eye shadow palettes lined up like books on a shelf. More eyeliner pens and pencils than I have regular pens and pencils in my desk!

I reach for a pressed-powder compact and pop it open, ready to cover my face in the silky cream-colored pigment. But suddenly I flash back on Clementine's expression this morning when she witnessed my last makeup attempt, and my smile collapses.

Because of that four-year memory gap, I really have no idea what I'm doing with this makeup business. My sixteen-year-old self may be a professional beauty vlogger with tons of eager followers, but *I'm* completely clueless.

And then it hits me.

I'm a professional beauty vlogger! Clementine and I have a successful beauty vlog on YouTube! My skills are all documented!

I grab my phone, open up the YouTube app, and type "Shimmer and Shine" into the search box. The results come back instantly, with hundreds of videos each with tons of views and comments. I scroll through them in complete awe.

We're practically celebrities!

I click on one called "Date Night Prep" and prop the

phone up against the mirror of my dresser. A few seconds later, my own face comes onto the screen.

It's obviously the sixteen-year-old face I have now (which I still haven't completely gotten used to) and my makeup looks incredible.

"Hi! It's Adeline here for Shimmer and Shine," YouTube Me says gleefully to the camera. "Today I'm going to show you how to get this smoking-hot date night look."

Whoa. I sound so mature and sophisticated.

The scene changes and suddenly I'm looking at a close-up shot of my own face. The camera pans from my eyes—which are expertly painted with shimmery golds and browns—across my highlighted cheekbones, and down to my lips, which look full and sparkly.

"Isn't this look divine?" YouTube Me says. "It's super-easy, you guys. Here's how I did it."

The scene changes again and now I'm looking at myself with a clean face. I'm standing in front of a bathroom mirror with a bunch of makeup and brushes spread out on the counter in front of me.

"I'm going to start with my cream foundation in the shade of Tauptastic and my number-seventeen concealer brush," YouTube Me explains.

I watch in awe as the girl in the video skillfully brushes foundation onto her face in quick circular strokes, smoothing out her skin and covering the scattering of freckles on her cheeks. I locate the exact same foundation she's using and the matching brush, and attempt to copy the technique. It's a lot harder than she makes it look.

Following the rest of the tutorial, I apply bronzer, eye shadows, eyeliner, mascara, lip liner, lip gloss, and blush. There are a *lot* of steps involved, and so many tools. More than I ever imagined. It takes me three times as long as it does on the video because I have to keep pausing and rewinding to figure out what the heck she's doing. Plus, I still can't get over how weird it is to be watching myself do all these things I don't remember doing and then attempting to do the exact same thing on the exact same face . . . with much-less-impressive results.

When I'm finished, it certainly doesn't look as good as it does on YouTube Me's face, but I can already see a vast improvement from this morning. I suppose the rest of it will just take practice. YouTube Me has had a lot more experience than I have.

It takes me a few minutes to navigate the stairs in these heels—and I nearly bite the dust twice—but I finally get downstairs a little after nine, my heels making loud *clopping* noises on each step. My parents are watching television in the family room. I stop in the doorway and stare at my dad. It's the first time I've seen him since I woke up in this new life. It's so weird! He's literally aged four years overnight. He looks mostly the same, but the hair around his temples is grayer and he has a few more wrinkles around his eyes.

My parents both leap up from the couch when they notice me standing there.

"You look wonderful!" Mom gushes.

"Pretty snazzy," Dad agrees.

My face grows hot with embarrassment. "Mom. Dad. Stop!" I whine.

"Just let me take one photo!" Mom pleads.

"Fine," I allow. "One."

She snaps a shot on her phone and smiles at it. "Is Clementine picking you up?"

"Yes."

"I like that you two decided to go without dates," Mom says.

Dad guffaws. "Yeah, me too."

So we chose to go together? Does that mean we had the option to go with boys?

I feel my heart start to race at the thought of seeing Cute Connor tonight. Is he going to want to dance with me? Maybe I should change my shoes. I can barely walk in these things, let alone tear up a dance floor.

"Remember," Mom warns. "Home by midnight."

I look at her, totally confused. "What? Why?"

She narrows her eyes in my direction and then looks to my dad.

"Don't start with that again, Adeline," Dad says sternly. "A curfew is a curfew and we're not changing it."

"I have a curfew?" I blurt out excitedly. Rory was always the one with the curfew. I was always the one staying at home playing Monopoly with my parents while she was out having a wildly good time.

Mom and Dad exchange a puzzled look. "Yes, you have a curfew," Mom replies.

"That's so cool!" I gush, shuffling toward them as fast as I can move in these shoes and giving them both hugs.

"Okay," Mom says suspiciously. "What do you want?"

"Nothing!" I swear, pulling back. "Nothing at all. I'll be home by midnight. I promise!"

"Good," she says, but she still sounds hesitant. "And maybe tomorrow you can finally clean out the playhouse."

"The playhouse?" I repeat as I teeter awkwardly to the window. I let out a tiny gasp when I see the small yellow-and-white Victorian house in the backyard. It's still there! After four years.

Our Hideaway.

A sour feeling starts to prickle my stomach when I think about all the photos I found on my phone today and Grace's obvious absence from them.

"Yes, the playhouse," Mom replies as Dad goes to the pantry to grab a snack. "Remember, I put it up for sale online? It needs to be cleaned out in case anyone calls to come look at it."

Suddenly, the room starts to spin. "You put it up for sale?" I practically shout.

Mom blinks in surprise. "We talked about this last

week. You told me you didn't care because you never use it anymore."

"I said that?" I ask, shocked.

She laughs. "Your exact words were 'Mom, I'm way too old for that stupid thing.'"

I cringe at the impression my mother does of me . . . or of sixteen-year-old me. She sounds so rude and stuck-up. Surely, she's exaggerating. I can't possibly sound like that.

"Anyway," she goes on, "I'm sure it'll make another little girl very happy. So will you clean it out this weekend?"

"I . . . ," I begin, but I can't even finish. The thought of clearing out Grace's and my Hideaway and watching it get taken apart so someone can haul it away in pieces is too much to think about right now. It's making my throat sting and my eyes water. And I can't risk ruining my makeup. It took way too long to finish the first time.

Fortunately, I'm saved by the sound of a car honking in the driveway. I take a deep breath and straighten my dress. This is my first high school dance, and I refuse to let anything get me down.

"Teeth check?" Mom asks.

I open my mouth wide like I'm in the dentist chair and mom laughs. "No. I mean, do you want me to check your teeth for food before you go?"

"Oh. Right." I show her my teeth and she gives me a thumbs-up.

"You're good."

"Breath check?" Dad asks, walking out of the pantry with his hand in a bag of potato chips. "I learned on the podcast today that it can take days for malodorous foods like onion and garlic to work their way through your system."

"Dad," I complain. "Gross." Although I'm secretly happy that he hasn't changed too much in the past four years. He's still listening to that stupid podcast.

Mom draws me into another hug, and when she pulls back, I swear I see mist in her eyes. "You look so beautiful. I just can't believe how grown-up you are."

There's another honk outside and I stick my clutch under my arm and totter unsteadily toward the door. "Yeah," I say with a smile. "That makes two of us."

SEVEN BOYS

It's official. I heart high school. This dance is ah-mazing. They've completely transformed the gym into a sparkly kaleidoscope of stars and spotlights and red carpets. The main lights have been dimmed so that the thousand small twinkly lights hanging from the ceiling can be seen. There's a canopy of gold star-shaped balloons hovering just above the dance floor, and someone has painted a huge mural of the Hollywood sign on the wall, with a brilliant full moon shining over it.

The theme is "Hot Hollywood Nights," and it's clearly working, because I feel like a celebrity who's just arrived at the Golden Globes.

Middle school dances are *nothing* like this. First of all, they keep all the lights on so the chaperones can keep an eye on everyone at all times. And second, we never get cool decorations like this. If there's any theme at all, it's usually something lame and childish like a carnival or a "party under the sea."

This is seriously legit.

Clementine and I pose for a picture on the red carpet, in front of a large banner with our school mascot on it. A professional photographer snaps the picture and we immediately run to the little screen and gush over it.

"See," Clementine says as she types her email address onto the screen so the computer can send the photo to her. "I told you turning down all those boys and going as BFFs was the best option. Look how totally stellar we look. We'll be the most talked-about couple at this dance." She presses Send and taps my nose affectionately. "And you wanted to go with dates. Silly Adeline."

I let out a nervous laugh. "I forgot. Was it two or three boys that asked me?"

Clementine scrunches up her face like she just smelled a fart. "Two or three? Try seven."

"*Seven?*" I shout.

Seven boys asked me to the dance? And I turned down all of them?

Clementine's face twists even more, like she's suddenly confused. "I'm pretty sure it was seven." She starts listing them out on her fingers. "Nick, Asher, Isaac, Liam, Reid, Harrison, and that one guy, I always forget his name. R.D.? L.J.?"

"But not Connor?" I confirm.

Clementine purses her lips. "C'mon. You know Connor is way too cool to ask a girl to a dance. He'll be here stag just like us. And when the time is right, I'll make *sure* you dance with him."

My heart starts to gallop in my chest. "Really?"

"J.T.!" she blurts out. "That's his name. I knew it was some kind of initials."

"J.T.?" I echo curiously. "He asked me?"

"Yeah." Clementine barks out a laugh. "But it's not like you were going to say yes to *him*."

I remember the supertall dark-haired boy who tried to help me clean up all the junk that fell out of my locker. He was so nice. And really cute.

"Why not?"

"Because he's lame. He's been lame since middle school."

Middle school. Is that where I know him from? Did he go to Sky View Middle School with us?

"Besides, this is so much better. Now we can dance with anyone we want." She winks at me. "Instead of being tied down to just one date. Variety is the spice of life, you know."

A hip-hop song comes on and Clementine lets out the loudest squeal I've ever heard. "Yes!" she screams as she grabs my arm and pulls me onto the dance floor. "This is SO my jam."

She starts moving flawlessly to the hard, edgy beat and

I struggle to keep up. It's difficult because (a) these high heels are nearly impossible to dance in (I really should have changed shoes), and (b) I don't know the song. I'm used to dancing to much more upbeat pop stuff like Summer Crush.

Clementine flips her hair and bumps her hip against mine. I try to match her movements, bending my knees and rocking side to side with my butt out.

I look ridiculous.

"What song is this?" I yell to Clementine over the music.

She just laughs in response, which I take to mean I should know what song it is. I wonder if it's one of our favorites. Except it doesn't sound at all familiar.

It probably came out sometime in the past four years. That's why I don't recognize it. Not only have I missed out on four years of my life, apparently I've also missed out on four years of music.

Oh my gosh! That means there's probably like four new Summer Crush albums out by now! I feel a flutter of giddiness explode in my chest. It's the same sensation I always got when Grace and I listened to a new album for the very first time. We *always* listened to them together. We would have album release parties in the Hideaway.

I wonder what the new albums are called. And what songs are on them. I bet they're even more amazing than the last four. I get this sudden urge to find Grace so I can ask her which tracks are her favorite. But then I remember the way she looked at me in the hallway today. Like I was infected with an incurable disease. And my throat starts to get tight again.

That is, until Clementine grabs my arm and pulls me close so she can whisper, "Look who just walked in."

I lift my head and my eyes land right on Cute Connor. He's standing near the dance floor, scanning the crowd. He looks incredible in dark jeans, a white button-up shirt, a black jacket, and a skinny tie. His hair is still a little bit wet, as though he just hopped out of the shower, and in this dark room, his blue eyes seem to shine almost as brightly as the roving spotlights scattered throughout the gym.

His gaze travels across the room before finally landing on me. Then his lips curl into a smile that nearly makes me topple over. And not just because I'm still trying to balance on these three-inch heels.

He starts to make his way over, his eyes never leaving mine.

"*This* is why you turned down seven guys," Clementine whispers silkily into my ear. "It's time to make your move."

THE FIVE RULES
OF FLIRTING

Make my move? I don't have a move. I don't know *any* moves! I'm only twelve! Are twelve-year-olds supposed to have moves?

No, but sixteen-year-olds are, a voice inside my head responds.

I think I'm going to throw up.

"You're not going to throw up," Clementine says.

Did I say that out loud?

"Relax," she whispers in my ear as Connor continues to make his slow, catlike approach across the dance floor. He looks like he's in one of those slo-mo walking scenes from a movie. All he needs is a wind machine blowing his hair around. "I'm going to walk you through this."

"Hi, Adeline. Hi, Clementine," Connor says, nodding at both of us.

"Hi, Connor," we reply in unison, which I admit

sounds totally cheesy. Clementine shoots me a death look out of the corner of her eye, which I'm guessing means she's going to do the rest of the talking. That's totally fine by me since my tongue has suddenly grown to the size of a cantaloupe.

"What's up?" Clementine asks, giving her hair a playful toss.

It looks so supercool, I decide I *must* give it a try. I lean slightly forward to gather all my hair over my left shoulder, then whip my body back. But I must do it too hard because I lose my balance on these humongo shoes and start to topple backward.

Thankfully, Connor reaches out to catch me just before I fall.

"Easy there," he says with a chuckle. "Don't hurt yourself."

My face flares with heat. I try to laugh it off.

"This dance is pretty lame, isn't it?" Connor asks, curling his upper lip.

Clementine makes a *psh* sound and then says, "Yeah, totally."

And I repeat, "Yeah, totally," even though it's a complete lie. I think this dance is the coolest thing *ever*.

"But, you know," Connor goes on, "we should probably make the most of it. Don't you think?"

It's then that I notice he's staring right at me, as if he's expecting me to say something. Or do something. Except I have no idea what that is. So I just mumble, "Y-y-yeah-zuh."

Yeahzuh?

That's not even a word.

Embarrassment warms my cheeks again and I remind myself to take deep breaths and stop acting like a crazy person.

"So?" Connor asks, still staring at me with that expectant look.

Clementine bumps me with her hip and I nearly lose my balance all over again.

"So," I repeat, unsure why everyone in this conversation seems to know what's going on except me.

Connor lets out a throaty laugh. "Do. You. Want. To. Dance. With. Me?" He enunciates every word, ending the question with a wink.

A lightning bolt of electricity travels through my body.

"Me?" I confirm doubtfully.

Connor laughs again. "Yes. You."

My heart leaps into my throat. My fingers search for something to grab on to. They find the hem of Clementine's dress and squeeze.

"Hold on," she says to Connor. "Just give us a second."

Connor cocks a curious eyebrow but then holds his hands up in surrender. "Sure. Take your time."

Clementine grabs my arm and pulls me right off the dance floor. She keeps dragging until we're clear out of the gym. The quiet hallway is a welcome reprieve from all that noise. Although the screaming in my head seems to follow me.

"Okay," Clementine says in a brusque tone. "What has gotten into you?"

"I'm scared," I tell her, and it's the honest truth.

"You're scared," she repeats in disbelief. "Of Connor?"

"Of everything! I've never danced . . ." My voice trails off.

I want to tell her that I've never danced with a boy before, because it's true. But I'm willing to bet that if sixteen-year-old Adeline is the kind of girl who turns down *seven* boys, then *she* has probably danced with plenty.

I've seen Rory dance with a few of her boyfriends. And I've seen couples dance a million times in movies. Also, one time Grace and I pretended to dance like boy and girl to our favorite Summer Crush ballad in the Hideaway but we couldn't keep a straight face for more than twenty seconds and we ended up collapsed on our sleeping bags in a fit of giggles.

"You've never danced . . . ?" Clementine prompts me to finish the sentence.

"I've never danced . . ." I begin to panic. What am I supposed to say now?

I stare down at my feet.

"In these shoes before!" I finish with relief. "I'm afraid I'm going to fall over. I think they're too high."

Clementine sighs and sticks out her hand, palm-side up. "Give me the shoes. I'll hold them. You can dance barefoot."

"Is that allowed?"

Clementine doesn't answer this. She just shakes her head and points at my shoes. I quickly slide out of the heels, my feet screaming in relief as I wiggle my toes. I had no idea how uncomfortable those diabolical things were until my feet were liberated from them.

"You can do this," she tells me. "Just remember our five rules of flirting and you'll be fine."

Five rules of flirting?

"Uh," I fumble. "Remind me again."

Clementine looks like she wants to scream, but she starts listing out the rules on the fingers of her left hand. "Tease him. Flirt with your eyes. Say his name a lot. Find excuses to touch him. Don't smile with your teeth."

She says all this so fast, I barely even catch two words of it. And now my pulse is racing. I need to lie down. "Wait, what was the first one again?" I ask.

Clementine sighs impatiently and pushes me back into the gym. "Just go."

I walk anxiously toward the dance floor, trying to remember the five things that Clementine just told me, but they're all swirling around in my head like a tornado.

Something about flirting with your eyes? What does that even mean? How do you flirt with your eyes?

I think about running. I think about just taking off in my bare feet and sprinting all the way home. It's not that far. It'll only take me about ten minutes if I go really fast . . . and I don't step on anything sharp. I could duck out the back door of the gym and—

"There you are," a voice says.

I look up to see Connor walking over to me, that adorable grin on his face. He bows like he's in an old movie and extends his hand. "May I have this dance now, Miss Adeline?"

My knees practically give out.

I still can't get over how much he looks like Berrin Mack. And *I'm* going to be dancing with him!

Okay, deep breaths. You can do this.

A slow song comes on—another melody I don't recognize—and Connor wiggles the fingers on his outstretched hand. "Are you ready?"

I want to tell him that no, I'm not ready. That I won't be ready for four more years. But then my mind flashes back to last night in the Hideaway with Grace. Before we got into that huge fight and she called her mom to go home. Before I made the wish on Mrs. Toodles's magic jewelry box. Before I woke up in this life.

"Aren't you curious what a high school dance is like?"

That was the question I asked Grace. Because I *was*

curious. I still am. That's why I made the wish. Because I wanted to know what it would be like to be here. To get all dressed up. To dance with a cute boy.

Now here I am. All dressed up. And boys don't get much cuter than Connor.

"Yes," I tell him, sliding my hand into his. "I'm ready."

SMILING LIKE A
DUCK-BILLED PLATYPUS

I'm dancing! With a boy! Who looks just like Berrin from Summer Crush!

This is exciting. And scary. And nerve-racking. And I think I might vomit.

No, I silently scold myself. *You'll be fine. Remember what Clementine told you.*

Right. The five rules of flirting.

I just have to remember what they are.

Connor's arms are wrapped around me and we're swaying gently to the music. Every once in a while, he looks down at me with those gorgeous blue eyes and I feel like my face is going to melt right off.

Flirt with your eyes! I remember that one. But how does one flirt with their eyes? It must be similar to batting your eyes, like I've seen people do in movies. Mostly animated ones, but still.

As Connor smiles down at me, I focus superhard on fluttering my eyelashes. *Open. Closed. Open. Closed. Quick. Quick. Quick.* To be honest, it doesn't feel like flirting. It feels like I'm having some kind of eyelash spasm.

"Do you have something in your eye?" Connor asks.

I stop fluttering.

"No. I mean, yes. But I got it."

"Good." I feel his arms get a little bit tighter around me.

Huh. Maybe it worked after all.

Okay, on to the next rule. I think it was something about teasing him and saying his name a lot.

I'm not sure how teasing someone is supposed to make them like you more, but Clementine seems to know what she's talking about so I guess I'm just going to have to trust her.

"Hey, Connor," I say.

He smirks. "Yes, Adeline?"

"Connor," I repeat his name, feeling stupid already.

"Adeline," he echoes back, his eyebrow cocking.

"Your nose is like really big."

He stops swaying and his arms drop to his sides. He gives me a strange look that I can't interpret. Is it working? Is he *swooned* by my teasing?

"And your ears kind of stick out like a monkey's."

"What?" he asks, tilting his head.

I giggle, pointing at him. "Now you really look like a monkey!"

He laughs too, but it sounds much more forced. "Is this a game I don't know about?"

Actually, he sounds kind of annoyed. I really don't think I'm doing this right. Was I supposed to tease him about something else?

"And your breath smells like farts." I try a different approach.

He takes a step back. A *really* big step. Uh-oh. That can't be good.

"My breath . . . Wh-what are you talking about?" he stammers, looking extremely confused, and definitely not swooned. He blows into his hand and sniffs it.

"That's okay, though!" I rush to say. "I heard that it can take up to a few days for malodorous foods to make their way through your system."

He stares at me for a moment, like he's trying to solve one of those Trigoniatry problems. Then he shakes his head and moves back toward me, wrapping his arms around my waist again. But I definitely feel the change. His grip is much looser and I can see hesitation covering his face.

This is not going well. I have to figure out how to fix the situation.

What were the other flirting rules? Something about smiling? But did Clementine say you were supposed to smile *with* your teeth or *without* your teeth?

It must be *with* your teeth. Why would you smile without your teeth? You'd look like a duck-billed platypus or something. And I'm pretty sure duck-billed platy-puses aren't known for their flirting.

I pull my mouth into a wide grin, making sure to reveal as many teeth as I can. It feels a bit uncomfortable. Like my mouth is being stretched too far and my cheeks are going to pop right off, but I must be doing it right, because Connor smiles back at me. I admit, it doesn't look like his usual carefree, friendly smile. It looks kind of strained. In fact, it *almost* looks like a grimace.

I have to come up with another rule fast.

How many have I done already? There was the eye flirting, the teasing, saying his name, the teeth smiling. That's four. There's just one left. What was it?

Find an excuse to touch him?

Yes! That's it!

Touch him? But where? We're already touching. My hands are on his shoulders and his hands are around my waist.

"I really like . . . ," I start to say, cringing at how squeaky and panicky my voice sounds. I search his face, before finally coming up with ". . . your chin!" I reach up and pinch his chin with my thumb and forefinger.

I can't help but notice Connor leaning back a little. "Um, thanks." His voice sounds uneasy.

"I also really like your earlobe," I say, moving my hand to his ear, but he ducks away just as I'm reaching toward it and my finger jams right into his ear canal.

"Ow!" he cries out, pulling away from me and holding

his hand to the side of his head. "What are you doing? Why are you sticking your finger in my ear?"

Now he sounds pretty angry. I *know* that was not the goal of the five rules of flirting. Which means I did them wrong. Just like I do everything wrong.

"I'm sorry," I say hurriedly. "I'm really sorry." And before he can say another word, or I can screw anything else up, I take off. I push through the other couples on the dance floor, searching the gym for Clementine.

Instead I find someone else.

Actually, *find* is the wrong word. I smack right into him, my nose bashing into his chest because he's about a foot taller than me.

After the dizziness fades and I check my nose for blood, I lift my head to see J.T. standing there, his dark eyes narrowed in concern.

"Whoa," he says, placing his hands on my shoulders to steady me. "Are you okay?"

"Yeah," I mumble, glancing around for Clementine. This dance is *not* turning out how I'd hoped and I kind of just want to leave.

"Are you looking for your date?" J.T. asks.

"I didn't come with a date," I say automatically, still scouring the crowded gym for any sign of my friend.

"Oh," J.T. says before falling very quiet. It's only now that I focus my attention on him. His head is bowed and he's looking at the ground with a solemn expression.

Great. I've said another wrong thing. I've screwed up again. I've upset yet *another* cute boy.

"When you said you couldn't go to the dance with me, I just assumed it meant you already had a date," J.T. says. He sounds so sad. Like I've just told him his dog died. "But I get it," he goes on, still looking at the floor. "You just didn't want to go with *me*."

He starts to walk away and I'm so confused by the whole exchange it takes me a moment to come out of my trance and catch up with him. "Wait. J.T. No. That wasn't it at all."

"It's okay," he says glumly. "You and Clementine have this little popular-duo thing going and I don't fit into that. It's fine. I get it."

Once again, it takes me a second to respond because I'm so mystified by his words. "What? No. It's not like that."

At least, I don't think *it's like that.*

But then I flash back on what Clementine said earlier in the night about J.T. being lame. Is that really why I turned him down? Because I'm too popular to be seen with him?

That can't be true. I wouldn't think like that.

"Clementine thought it would be a better idea if we came to the dance alone," I explain. "Then we could dance with anyone we want."

I say the words but there's no emotion in them. I'm

just parroting what Clementine told me earlier. The truth is, I'm starting to wonder what kind of person sixteen-year-old Adeline really is.

I know she's the kind of person who has a lot of friends. Or at least a lot of people who text her and talk to her in the hallway. She's the kind of person who gets asked to the dance by seven different guys and turns them all down. She's also the kind of person who hangs out with Clementine Dumont instead of Grace Harrington.

But what else? What am I missing?

"Oh?" J.T. asks, looking uplifted by my explanation. "So that means I could still ask you to dance?"

I feel my chest tighten again at the thought of going back out on that dance floor. Of trying to follow Clementine's stupid five rules of flirting and most definitely failing all over again. But then I look into J.T.'s hopeful eyes, and I feel a twinge of something I can't identify.

I can't turn him down now. Plus, he kind of intrigues me. I want to know more about him. I want to figure out why he seems so familiar.

I smile. "I guess it *does* mean that you can ask me to dance."

He grins back and I love the way it crinkles his eyes. Like the smile is spreading all the way across his face. "Addie, would you like to dance with me?"

I pretend to think long and hard about it. Just to make

him laugh. It works. He chuckles as he waits for my answer.

I may not fully know what kind of girl I've become. But I know what kind of girl I was. And what kind I want to be.

It's the kind of girl who says yes.

And that's good enough for now.

DANCING WITH THE STARS?

Dancing with J.T. is *nothing* like dancing with Connor. He's not suave and formal. He's silly and clumsy and he makes me laugh. For the first half of the next song, he pretends like he's on some ballroom competition show, straightening his neck like a pretentious ostrich and guiding me all around the dance floor, using our arms to cut through the sea of slow dancers. Then he spins me in a million circles until I'm dizzy and dips me so far down, my hair brushes the floor.

We get several dirty looks from other people but J.T. doesn't seem to care. He just continues his uncoordinated routine in which we constantly bump into each other and step on each other's toes.

I giggle as he twirls me out and back in, catching me ungracefully in his arms as my head gets caught in his armpit. "Ready for my signature death-defying aerial spin move?"

"Probably not."

He cocks an eyebrow. "Are you sure?"

"I really don't want to come to school on Monday on crutches," I joke back.

He shrugs. "Fair enough." Then he pulls me close and I catch a whiff of that delicious minty scent again. I wonder if he uses spearmint soap.

We dance normally for a little while, swaying gently to the beat while J.T. hums along to another ballad I don't recognize.

I'm having such a good time, I almost manage to forget that catastrophe of a dance I had with Connor. Who is this J.T. guy? And why didn't I just say yes to him in the first place? He's so much fun to hang out with.

"I'm sorry I turned you down," I say quietly, ducking my head a little so I don't have to look him in the eye. "It would have been fun to come to the dance with you."

J.T. stops humming. "That's okay. I suppose I deserved it. Karmic payback and all."

"Payback?" I repeat curiously.

"Yeah, for what I did to you in the seventh grade."

I peer up at him in confusion.

"Don't tell me you don't remember," J.T. says. "The exploding grape soda? I've felt bad about that for years! But if you don't even remember then I've wasted all that energy!"

Grape soda.

Jacob Tucker.

J.T.

Oh my gosh! How could I not figure it out? How could I not recognize him?

Probably because he's completely transformed in the past four years. He got so tall and his voice got so deep. He lost all his baby fat. And he smells *way* better.

But now that I really look at him, his eyes are the same. That must be why he seemed so familiar.

"You're Jacob Tucker!" I exclaim before throwing my hand over my mouth. I can't believe I just said that aloud. He's going to think I'm so crazy. And who knows? Maybe I am. Maybe this whole day has been one crazy delusion and I'm still lying in my bed at age twelve making it all up in my head.

"I mean, you're Jacob Tucker," I say, trying to recover. "Of course I remember. How could I forget? I had to walk around with a purple stain on my clothes the whole day."

He frowns, looking guilty. "Sorry. I was such a doofus back then. I only did it because I had this huge crush on you."

WHAT?

Jacob Tucker had a crush on me? But I always thought he hated me! Why would you shake up a soda can and then give it to someone you *liked*?

"Are you serious?" I ask.

He laughs. "Oh yeah. Big-time. You couldn't tell?"

"No!" I practically yell. "How was I supposed to know that? All your friends laughed at me!"

Now he looks mortified, dropping his gaze to the floor and shaking his head slowly. "I know. I was an idiot. I assumed because I picked grape soda you would get it. You told me it was your favorite in like the second grade and I remembered. But I was worried if I just gave it to you, my friends would make fun of me. So I shook it up first." He laughs. "You would think I'd have grown up a little bit in four years, but unfortunately I don't think I'm much better now at telling girls how I feel."

I swallow hard. He lifts his head and stares at me so intensely that I have to look away. Is he trying to tell me that he *still* has a crush on me?

Did Clementine know? Did my sixteen-year-old self know?

J.T.—I mean, *Jacob*—clears his throat. "So, shall I show you some more of my killer dance moves?"

I smile, happy for the change of subject. It was starting to get really warm inside this gym.

"Bring it," I tell him.

He grips my hand tighter and I brace myself for whatever ridiculous, over-the-top move he's going to attempt next, but he never gets the chance. The song comes to an end and the DJ's voice booms over the speaker system.

"How are you doing, Thunder Creek High Spartans?"

The audience lets out a whoop and I feel a shiver of excitement ripple through me. Thunder Creek High Spartans! That's me! I'm one of them. I'm a Spartan!

Wait, what is a Spartan?

Some kind of bear?

"Are you ready for some all-star talent?" the DJ asks, and the crowd goes crazy again.

"Oh," Jacob says with disappointment. "It looks like they're starting the talent show already."

Wait, what talent show?

"There you are." Clementine appears in front of us and I immediately feel Jacob's hand slip from mine. "I've been looking *everywhere* for you."

Her gaze flicks suspiciously from me to Jacob. Is it just my imagination or did she just give him an evil sneer?

"C'mon," she urges, taking my hand. "Let's go. It's time to get ready."

Get ready for what?

The DJ's voice returns. "Contestants, please make your way backstage for Thunder Creek's Got Talent."

"Did you remember your costume?" Clementine asks.

And that's when all the pieces click together in my brain and my knees turn to mush as a million reminders flash through my mind at once.

Don't forget your costume!

Don't forget your costume!

Don't forget your costume!

Uh-oh.

ADELINE
DON'T GOT TALENT

Oh, no. This is not happening. I am *not* going up on that stage in front of all these people.

Clementine grips my hand and leads me into the hallway. My mind is spinning, while my lungs are fighting for air.

"I don't think I can do this. I'm really not feeling up to it," I tell her.

She swats this away with her hand. "Don't be ridiculous. Of course you can do it. We've been practicing for weeks."

I want to scream at her that *I* haven't been practicing for weeks! I haven't practiced at all. I don't even know what I'm supposed to do up there, let alone how to physically do it. For all I know, sixteen-year-old Adeline could have been spending the past four years learning to play the banjo or juggle knives or contort her body like a human pretzel.

Oh, gosh, I'm going to faint.

I'm seriously going to pass out.

I eye the front door of the school. My escape. I need to find a way out of this.

"I . . ." I struggle for an excuse. "I didn't bring my costume!" I finally blurt out, hoping it will do the trick.

Clementine sighs impatiently. "How could you forget? I only set like twenty reminders on your phone!"

I start for the front door. "Well, I did. So let's just go home."

Clementine grabs my hand again and pulls me back with a groan. "No way. We've been preparing for this for weeks. You are *not* bailing on me." She puts her hands on her hips and thinks for a moment. "We'll just have to do the dance routine in our dresses."

Dance routine?

There's a dance routine?

I was kind of hoping our talent would be something I could just wing like . . . I don't know, standing on one foot. I can totally do that. I can't wing a choreographed dance routine!

"I don't think that's a very good idea," I tell her. "This dress is kind of short in the front and—"

"We're doing it," Clementine says bluntly. "It'll be cute. Just be careful on some of those split moves."

Split moves????

I feel sweat forming on the back of my neck. Is it hot

in here? I suddenly can't breathe. Where is all the oxygen in this place? Who stole all the oxygen?

"I'm sick!" I exclaim, pulling Clementine to a stop and rooting my feet to the floor. "I can't do it. I have a headache."

Clementine groans again and keeps pulling. She's surprisingly strong. "I don't care."

"I get terrible stage fright."

"No, you don't."

"I think I came down with Ebola!"

Clementine stops and turns around, giving me the same evil look I swore I saw her give Jacob Tucker just a second ago. "You're acting kind of cray-cray. Why are you getting so freaked out? *You* choreographed the dance!"

That doesn't do me any good if I can't actually *remember* choreographing the dance!

"Now stop being a baby and let's do this thing," Clementine commands.

I look up to see that we've reached the back entrance to the stage. I close my eyes and make a wish.

I wish I was at home playing board games with my parents.

I wish I was anywhere else but here.

I wish I was twelve again!

But when I open my eyes, I'm still standing in front of that stage door and Clementine is still glowering at me with her arms crossed. She pulls open the door and waits for me to enter first. Probably to make sure I don't try to run the other way, which, believe me, I've definitely considered.

This is my life now. And it's quite clear that Clementine isn't going to let me run away from it. So I let out a long, surrendering sigh and walk through the stage door.

COUNTING DOWN TO DISASTER

When I was seven years old and Rory was eleven, our family went camping in Rocky Mountain National Park. Rory and I decided we wanted to go off on an adventure together, even though our parents warned us to stay close to the cabin. But we didn't listen. We wandered too far and eventually got lost and couldn't find our way back. We traveled in circles for what felt like hours, and it was getting darker. I kept whining to Rory that I was scared and she grabbed my hand and told me it would be okay and to stop being such a baby.

Then we saw the mountain lion.

It was standing on the path directly in front of us, legs crouched, body bent toward us like it was getting ready to pounce.

For a second, both of us went very still and quiet. Rory squeezed my hand so tight, I was afraid she was going to break it. The mountain lion roared at us, baring sharp, jagged teeth that can only accurately be described as fangs.

We both screamed.

The mountain lion responded by hissing back at us.

We screamed louder.

Eventually, our screams frightened the animal away and our parents, who had been looking for us for the last hour, followed the sounds until they found us.

The whole thing lasted about thirty seconds. But in those thirty seconds, I honestly thought I was going to die.

That was the most scared I've ever been in my entire life.

Until right this second.

The curtain rises and I'm standing on the stage of the Thunder Creek gymnasium as one thousand students stare back at me and a song I've never heard in my life starts piping through the speakers.

Clementine quietly counts us off. "One, two, three, four . . ."

The only problem is, I have absolutely no idea what she's counting us off to. I don't know the routine. I don't remember choreographing it. Or practicing it. Or even signing up for this stupid talent show. I don't remember anything from the past four years and now I'm going to die from public humiliation. This entire gym full of people is going to laugh at me and I'll be exposed as the phony that I am.

I don't know what I was thinking. I don't belong here. I'm not ready to be sixteen. I don't want to be in high school anymore. I just want to go back to middle school, where it's safe and I know what I'm doing and math still has numbers in it and Grace and I still hang out and Rory still lives in the house and my mom doesn't work.

It's too much. Too many things have changed. I don't like it.

I want out!

"Five, six, seven, eight . . ." Clementine finishes the count and she's off, leaping into the first steps of the routine choreographed by cool and popular sixteen-year-old Adeline. A girl who films YouTube tutorials and has a dog named Buttercup and a drawer full of makeup and drives a cute green car and puts framed black-and-white photographs of strangers on her walls.

A girl I barely recognize.

Clementine shoots me a dirty look as I watch her finish the first eight-count. Walk one, two, three, out four, head roll, ball change, and kick.

Wait a minute.

I know those steps. I choreographed those steps. But not with Clementine. With Grace. Back in the Hideaway when we were twelve.

Which, for me, was just yesterday.

Is this the same routine I used to do with Grace? The one we choreographed after binge-watching three entire seasons of *Dance for Your Life*?

As Clementine breaks into the second eight-count, still waiting for me to join in, with an angry scowl on her face, I watch her carefully, making double sure that this *is* the same dance and not just the same opening.

The next eight-count is exactly as I remember it. Grace and I borrowed most of the steps right from our favorite *Dance for Your Life* routine.

Down one, hair flip, shoulder, shoulder, step, pause, and turn.

Thank the heavens! I'm saved! I know this dance! I can do this dance! Grace and I practiced it a million times in the Hideaway!

I join in on the third eight-count, much to Clementine's obvious relief. I may not recognize the song, but the dance is exactly the same.

Well, the steps are the same, anyway. Clementine has added some really impressive flair to the whole thing. The way she does the hip, hip, look in the third eight-count almost makes me blush.

By the time we reach the grand finale—body roll, kick, turn, slide down, splits!—I'm breathless but totally pumped. We hold our final positions as the music fades out and the gym explodes in cheers and catcalls and clapping.

Adrenaline buzzes through me and I feel like I'm flying.

They loved it!

Clementine and I bow five times and I beam at the audience, feeling like a rock star.

That is, until my gaze lands on the girl in the front row.

She's staring up at me with her mouth hanging open and tears brimming in her eyes.

It's Grace.

Even though she's four years older, and her hair is no longer braided, and her face has changed so much, I recognize that look. It's the same look she gave me that night in the Hideaway—*last* night—when I accused her of being immature and babyish. And the same look she had when her grandpa died.

It's her heartbroken look.

Suddenly, I get it. I understand. My stomach fills with butterflies. Not the good kind. The sick, yucky, guilty kind.

This was *our* dance. We choreographed it. And I stole it.

Our eyes meet and for a long moment we just stare at each other as the proud, beaming smile slowly falls from my face. Then Grace turns and pushes her way out of the gym, holding her hand over her mouth like she's trying to keep her sobs locked inside.

SORRYS AND PLEASES

I run from the stage.

I can hear Clementine calling my name somewhere behind me, but I don't stop. I have to find her. I have to make this right.

When I tumble out the stage door, I see Grace scurrying down the hallway, her hand still cupped over her mouth. I dash to catch up to her, pulling on her arm to make her stop.

"Grace," I say breathlessly. "Wait. Please, let me explain."

Grace appears surprised to see me but quickly washes the emotion from her face, replacing it with a blank neutral expression. "Explain what?" she asks and I can tell she's trying to sound indifferent, like she doesn't care. But I know her. I've known Grace since before we were born. I can tell when she's faking it.

"About the dance," I say breathlessly. "I didn't know

that's what we were doing. I didn't know that we were going to steal our dance. I mean obviously I *knew*. On some level. But it wasn't *me* who did it."

Grace's eyebrows knit together and I can tell she's trying to follow what I'm saying but failing miserably. That makes two of us.

I sigh and start again. "Something happened last night, Grace. Something crazy. Do you remember our fight in the Hideaway? On the night of my twelfth birthday?"

Grace rolls her eyes. "I don't have time for this." She tries to step around me, but I jump in front of her.

"Please," I beg. "Just let me explain. I *need* to explain. I have to tell someone or I'll burst. And you're the only one I can tell. Maybe you won't believe me, but I *have* to at least try."

She crosses her arms and glares at me. I take this as a sign that I'm allowed to continue. I clench my fists at my sides, trying to form my thoughts into comprehensible sentences, but no matter how I rearrange the words, nothing sounds right in my head. Nothing seems to make sense of this totally nonsensical situation.

Grace lets out an impatient groan, tossing a lock of hair over her shoulder.

"Your hair got so long," I say wistfully, reaching out to touch it.

Grace leans back, out of my reach. "Get on with it," she snaps.

Oh, right. We probably don't play with each other's hair like we used to.

"Okay," I say, steeling myself with courage. "There's really no right way to do this so I'm just going to come out and say it. Last night, I was still twelve years old."

Grace narrows her eyes. I can tell she's confused but she's also not trying to run away again so I take that as a good sign. "Remember Mrs. Toodles?" I ask. "My crazy neighbor?"

Grace nods.

"Well, she gave me this really old jewelry box for my birthday—my *twelfth* birthday. And she told me it had magical powers. It used to belong to some old witch. She told me if I wrote down a wish and locked it inside, my wish would come true. I didn't believe her. Because c'mon, seriously? A magic jewelry box that grants wishes, right? But after we had our big fight in the Hideaway, I decided to try it. I made a wish to be sixteen, thinking if I was sixteen, everything would be okay. We wouldn't fight anymore. We'd be all mature and grown-up."

Grace rolls her eyes again but, still, she stays put.

"I locked the wish inside the jewelry box," I continue. "I never in a million years thought it would work. But it did work. I woke up here. In this life. When everyone is older. And so much has changed. I can't figure anything out. I don't understand why you're not in any of the photos on my phone. Or why we don't seem to hang out anymore. Or why I quit playing the trumpet! I just wanted

176

to be older so I could wear makeup and have a cell phone and go to high school dances like Rory did, but it seems like everything is different. *Too much* is different."

I can feel the tears welling up and I wipe them away with the heels of my hands. Grace is just staring at me with this kind of slack-jawed empty expression. I'm dying to know what she's thinking. Does she believe me? Will she take pity on me? Will we run home together and grab our sleeping bags and hang out in the Hideaway all night talking about everything that's happened in the last four years?

Will things go back to the way they were?

"Adeline," Grace says in a measured tone. I nearly collapse in disappointment when I hear those three syllables. It's so strange hearing her use my full name. I know it's not a good sign.

"Grace," I argue before she can go on, but the tears are really starting to flow now and it's hard for me to speak. My nose is running and I have no more dry hand heels to wipe everything away. "Please don't walk away again. Please just tell me you believe me. *Please!*" My voice is wobbly and broken. "Let's go back to the dance and tell the DJ to play Summer Crush and dance around like crazy people. Just like we used to do. Let's go back to the way it was, okay?"

I don't know why—maybe it's my tears or the number of times I said please—but Grace's expression seems to soften as she looks at me. I feel my hopes rise. For a moment, I actually think she might say, "Okay, Addie. Let's do that."

But she doesn't.

That moment quickly passes, her face hardens again, and I see the girl from the hallway today. The one with the tough exterior and cold, unforgiving eyes.

"Adeline," she says again. This time it doesn't just disappoint me. It stabs me in the chest. "We can't just go back to the way things were. Things haven't been that way for almost four years. I don't know what's gotten into you. Maybe you're having some major life crisis or something, but I honestly don't know why you're coming to me with it. It's not like we're friends anymore."

She turns away from me. This time, I don't have the willpower to try and stop her and soon I'm left alone in the hallway, listening to the distant sound of yet another unfamiliar song playing in the gym.

For a long time, I just stare at the space where Grace once stood. Like I truly believe she might poof out of thin air. I stand there until I hear the music die down and the DJ's voice announce, "The judges' votes have been tallied, and we now have the winners of our Thunder Creek's Got Talent competition. The first-place winners are . . . Clementine Dumont and Adeline Bell!"

That's when I can't take it anymore.

That's when I sprint out of the building, still barefoot, and run all the way home.

THE GREAT QUEST

My feet are grimy and sore from running down the sidewalk without shoes, and I've sweat through my gorgeous dress, but I'm grateful to be home. It feels safe. And comfortable. And familiar.

The house is eerily quiet. My parents must already be asleep. I climb the stairs to my bedroom, my body feeling heavier and heavier with each step. Buttercup is sprawled out across my comforter with her butt on my pillow. Her tail is the only thing that moves when I walk in. It wags eagerly, smacking the pillow with a series of loud *thwaps*.

The sight brings a smile to my face, but it's a weak one at best.

I drop my clutch on the nightstand and collapse onto the bed next to her, stroking her soft fur. I'm so exhausted. I feel like I've lived in this sixteen-year-old body for ten years rather than just a single day.

"What happened to my life?" I ask Buttercup.

Her tail smacks the pillows harder in response.

"When did everything fall apart?"

Thwap. Thwap. Thwap.

I hear my phone vibrating inside my clutch. It's probably Clementine wondering where I am. But I don't care. So I don't even look.

I curl onto my side and press my face against Buttercup's back. I let the tears fall freely, crying until my eyes are red and Buttercup's fur is wet and I fall asleep.

❋

In the morning, I wake up feeling determined.

It's Saturday, which means I don't have anything to do or anywhere to go until Monday morning, and I'm going to use that time to fill in the four-year gap in my memory. I'm going to figure out what happened.

I get out of bed and scramble through my desk drawers until I find a notebook and a pen. I sit on my bed, flip to a blank page, and scribble out two questions.

Why aren't Grace and I friends anymore?
How did I become friends with Clementine?

I bite the tip of my pen as I stare down at the paper and reflect on the last twenty-four hours. I think about yesterday at school, all those text messages I got, the conversations I had with Connor and Jacob Tucker, my YouTube makeup tutorials, the look on Grace's face when Clementine and I finished our dance routine for the talent show. And then I write down a third question.

What kind of person is sixteen-year-old Adeline Bell?

I underline that one twice and close the notebook.

The reality of the situation is, I need answers. I need to talk to someone who has been around for the past four years and might know things.

I call my sister, Rory, but it rings and rings and then goes to voice mail. "Hi! It's Rory. I'm off being awesome. Leave a message if you want to be awesome, too."

I hang up without leaving a message. She wouldn't have any answers, anyway. She left for school two years ago and it's not like she paid a lot of attention to me when she *was* around. Besides, if I really want to ask her the right questions, I'd have to tell her the truth about what happened to me, and I doubt she would believe it.

I doubt anyone would believe it.

You'd have to be crazy to believe a story like that.

You'd have to be . . .

"You are a believer. You have magic in the heart."

Mrs. Toodles!

I was planning on going over there yesterday, but

somehow I never found the time. She'll believe me for sure. She's the one who gave me the magic jewelry box in the first place.

I'm not sure how much she'll actually *remember* about the last four years, given her power-smoothie blender brain and all, but at the very least she might be able to help. She might have some advice or ideas.

I scoot off my bed, throw on some clothes and shoes, and bound down the stairs, surprised to find the kitchen totally empty. It's Saturday. My dad doesn't work on Saturdays, which means normally Mom is cooking breakfast and Dad is doing the dishes, rambling on about some interesting fact he learned from his podcast that day.

But the house is quiet.

I find a note on the refrigerator door that says, "Went to brunch."

My parents went out to eat without me?

That's kind of rude.

But I don't really have time to be offended right now. I have to get to Mrs. Toodles's house so I can finally get some answers.

I hurry out the front door, checking to make sure it's not locked behind me, and run the entire half block until I reach the small one-story cottage-style house on the corner. I race up to the front door and knock. Then I step back and wait.

It always takes Mrs. Toodles a while to answer the

door. Sometimes she doesn't hear the knock the first time and sometimes she's back in her bedroom and has to waddle her way to the foyer.

But today, it's taking an unusually long time.

I try to peer through the windows, but the blinds are closed.

I don't remember Mrs. Toodles having blinds. I'm pretty sure she had curtains in the windows. Really old, tacky ones with porcupines on them. Maybe she finally got sick of them.

I knock again but there's still no answer. It's been almost five minutes. She definitely should be here by now. Is she sleeping? Did she go out?

Never, in my years of living on this block and visiting Mrs. Toodles, have I ever seen her leave this house. She gets everything delivered. Her groceries, her laundry, Chinese food every Sunday night. But maybe she's changed in the past four years, like everyone else. Maybe she joined an old-lady cards club. Or plays bingo on Saturdays.

I knock a third time, waiting another few minutes before finally giving up and walking back to my house.

When I get there, I open the fridge and root around for something to eat, but there's not much. I search the pantry for cereal but then remember I fed the rest of the box to Buttercup yesterday. Not that *she* seems to remember that. She's back at her dog dish, staring unblinkingly at the wedge-shaped hole.

"Have you eaten this morning?" I ask, giving her head a pat.

She seems to understand the question, because she lets out a yelp and wags her tail, still keeping her eyes trained on the dish.

I laugh. "I guess not."

I try once again to find the dog food, but come up short. Maybe she doesn't eat dog food. Maybe she eats people food. I find a box of frosted strawberry Pop-Tarts, break one into small pieces, and put it in her dish. She devours it before I realize that was the last one.

And I'm really hungry.

Great.

My only other option is a bag of onion bagels I discover in the freezer. Mom is *still* buying these disgusting things? I toast it, slather it with cream cheese (to mask the onion flavor), and go upstairs to grab my laptop. My plan is to start with my computer files. There has to be something in there that will serve as a clue to unraveling the past four years.

The first thing I find is a folder called "Shimmer and Shine." It contains video files from the vlog. As I eat my bagel, I watch a few of the episodes. Clementine and I are really good at this beauty vlogging stuff. Our videos cover everything from makeup to nail art to hair braiding, and even a few tutorials on how to properly wash your face—as if people don't already know this.

Even though the subject matter is pretty cool, I can't help but notice my face in all the videos. I'm smiling at the camera but it doesn't look like I'm actually having any fun. As soon as each tutorial is over—before Clementine stops the recording—my smile always seems to drastically fall, like someone ripped it clear off my face.

Like I was only smiling for the camera.

After closing the Shimmer and Shine folder, I find a file called "Great Name Change Charter" and curiously open it.

It's a scan of a document that reads:

WE, THE UNDERSIGNED
(FRANK RICHARD BELL, MARJORIE ELLEN
BELL, AND AURORA LEIGH BELL), DO SOLEMNLY
SWEAR TO TERMINATE THE USE OF THE CHILDISH
AND BELITTLING NICKNAME OF "ADDIE" WHEN
REFERRING TO OR ADDRESSING OUR DAUGHTER/
SISTER, ADELINE RACHEL BELL. FROM THIS
DAY FORTH, ADELINE RACHEL BELL SHALL BE
REFERRED TO AND ADDRESSED EXCLUSIVELY BY
HER FULL LEGAL NAME OF ADELINE.

This must be that charter my mother was talking about yesterday. I actually made my whole family sign it. All their signatures are on the bottom next to a date that tells me I wrote this right before I started high school.

I shake my head and close the document.

It seems like a lot of effort to go through just for something as silly as a name. I mean, really, what's so bad about "Addie," anyway?

After about twenty more minutes of searching, I've uncovered little more than a few extra pictures of me and Clementine, and a bunch of school assignments from the past few years—including an impressively long book report on *The Little Prince* that I wrote entirely in French. None of these things are extremely helpful in solving the mystery of my life.

I'm about to call off the search entirely when a folder catches my eye. It's nested deep inside a bunch of other folders and it's labeled "Graddie."

Graddie.

The combination of the names Grace and Addie.

Excitedly, I brush bagel crumbs from my hands and click it open. Inside are over a dozen movie files. I let out a giddy *yip* only to groan a moment later when I see that they're all dated *over* four years ago.

Before I made the wish.

I sulk as I open a random file and watch Grace and me, at age eleven, performing one of our choreographed routines for the camera we set up on a tripod in the Hideaway. We keep having to start over because every time we look at each other we start giggling.

Frustrated, I slam my laptop closed and carry my crumb-filled plate to the kitchen.

I don't need to be reminded of how *amazing* my friendship with Grace was. I need to figure out *why* it ended! I need to . . .

The idea hits me the moment I drop my plate into the sink.

I need to search by date.

If I made the wish the night of my twelfth birthday, then I should look for files that exist *after* that night.

I run back to my laptop, open it up, and sort every file on the hard drive by date, starting with the most recent and ending with the oldest. I scroll all the way back to the day of my twelfth birthday and that's when my eye snags on something.

It's another video file.

It's dated the week *after* I made the wish and it's called "Seventh-Grade English Project—*Romeo and Juliet* Retelling."

That's right! We were assigned in English class to do a story retelling. Grace and I were working on it together. It's one of the things we talked about before we got into that huge fight. We couldn't agree on which story to retell. Grace wanted to do a fairy tale and I wanted to do . . .

Curiously, I glance at the file name again.

"Seventh Grade English Project—*Romeo and Juliet* Retelling"

Huh. I remember the disgusted look on Grace's face when I suggested *Romeo and Juliet* that night in the Hideaway. I wonder how I finally convinced her to do it.

I click Play and lean forward.

Music comes in over a black screen. I immediately recognize the song. It's one of my favorite Summer Crush ballads. It's called "Not for All the Money in the World." It starts out really soft, just an acoustic guitar and Berrin's husky voice singing, "He promised you diamonds. I promise to give you the world."

Then an image fades in. It's a girl walking in tall grass. It takes me a moment but I soon recognize the field as the one right behind our house. And the girl is . . . Oh my gosh, it's Rory! What is she doing in our English project?

A moment later, a guy walks up to her and swings her around, kissing her. When he sets her back down I see that it's Henry. Rory's boyfriend! Or at least, he was *that* week.

The song continues and the next scene is Rory and Henry sending text messages to each other. She's in a beautiful living room—*our* living room!—and he's working in a dusty workshop, which I recognize as one of my dad's construction sites.

It takes me a few more scenes before I finally realize what this is. It's the exact idea I told Grace about in the Hideaway that night. It's a modern-day retelling of *Romeo and Juliet* in a music video! In this version of the story, Rory is Juliet, a rich girl, who's fallen in love with Romeo, who comes from a poor part of town. But her father—

played by my dad—doesn't want them to be together. He tries to keep them apart.

I chew on my nail as I watch the story unfold. I know how *Romeo and Juliet* ends in Shakespeare's version—both of them die!—and I hope that Grace and I chose to alter the ending in our retelling.

The song reaches its big crescendo at the bridge, where Berrin sings, "And I'd never hurt you. And I'd never deceive you. And they can take everything that I am, but I would never leave you . . . not for all the money in the world."

At that moment, Rory (Juliet) is now at college, living her new life without Henry (Romeo), just like her father wanted. She talks to people and laughs at jokes, but you can see in her eyes that her heart is empty.

But by the time Berrin gets to the final chorus and the rest of the Summer Crush boys join in, Henry (Romeo) suddenly appears from behind a parked car. He's driven all the way up to the campus to see her! I let out a sigh of relief as they kiss and the song fades out and the screen goes black again.

Wow! That was so good! I'm all emotional now. I almost cried when I thought she was going to go off to college without ever seeing him again.

I'm so happy Grace finally went along with my idea, because that was amazing. We *had* to have gotten an A on this.

The credits start to roll across the screen. I'm about to shut off the video when the last line freezes me in place.

Written, Directed, and Produced by Adeline Bell

Then it's over. The video file just ends.

I stare at the screen in shock. Where is Grace's name? What did *she* do on the film? She had to have done something!

I let out a tiny gasp and cover my mouth as a realization hits me.

Did I do the project *alone*? But that was a whole week after our fight. We had to have made up by then. I mean, Grace and I have gotten in our fair share of squabbles over the years, but we *always* make up. Usually the very next day.

So what happened?

I'm about to go back to my search to see what other files are dated around the same time when the doorbell rings, making me jump and Buttercup bark. I walk to the front door and peer through the peephole to find Clementine standing outside looking annoyed. I let out a sigh. I really don't want to deal with her right now. I know she's mad that I left her at the dance right after we won first place and she's going to want an explanation. But I just don't have one to give. At least not one she'll believe, anyway.

Maybe if I just wait long enough, she'll go away.

"I know you're in there!" Clementine calls from the other side of the door. "I can hear you sighing. Open up!"

With another sigh, I do as I'm told and swing the door open, trying to paint on a smile. "Hi, Clementine. What's up?"

"Don't you *Hi, Clementine* me," she replies brusquely. "What on earth happened to you last night? You totally ditched me! I had to get up on that stage and accept our award all by myself. Do you know how embarrassing that was? And why haven't you been answering any of my texts?"

I open my mouth, hoping something clever and brilliant will come out, but before I can utter a single sound, Clementine says, "You know what? Save it for the car. We're beyond late."

I cringe. What are we late for? Where is she going to drag me to next? What grand plans does Clementine have for us today?

I grab my bag and follow Clementine out the door. "Where are we going?"

She huffs so loudly it sounds like a tornado. I have a feeling she's really starting to lose patience with me. I don't blame her. I'm losing patience with me, too.

"The salon!" she says agitatedly. "You said you needed a touch-up for your straightening, so I made us appointments."

I really don't want to go anywhere. I don't want to

do anything except continue searching for clues until my mystery is solved. But I admit the idea of going to get my hair straightened does cheer me up a little bit. And really, how long could it take? Thirty minutes? An hour? I'll be home and back on the hunt in no time.

TOUCH-UPS AND BREAKDOWNS

I've never been so bored in my entire life. We've already been here for *three* whole hours and I don't think my hair is even close to being done. How does it take this long to straighten hair? Are they straightening every single strand individually?

Clementine has been chatting away nonstop about our vlog. She's decided on a theme of Flower Power! And she wants to do daisy manicures, rose-tinted makeup, and hippie braids. But all I can think about is how I'd rather be doing this stuff with Grace. Why don't Grace and I have a YouTube vlog together? Why don't Grace and I hang out at the salon together? Why wasn't it Grace and me up on that stage last night for the talent show? It should have been us.

What went wrong?

And why do I have the unsettling feeling that it's my fault?

"By the way, what happened with Connor last night?" Clementine asks, bringing me back into the moment. "I saw him leaving right before the talent show."

My stomach clenches.

He left?

That's how horrible our dance was. It made him not even want to be there anymore.

"Yeah," I say awkwardly. "That didn't go so well."

"What happened?"

I sigh. I don't really feel like getting into it. Especially not with Clementine, who will probably just end up lecturing me about not flirting correctly. "Let's just say I don't think Connor will be my first kiss."

Clementine tips her head back and laughs, causing the woman working on her hair to jump out of the way. "Your first kiss? Yeah, right."

What?

Did I already have my first kiss? Did I miss it? Who was it with? Was it amazing? Was it beautiful and romantic and swoon-worthy? Was it under the stars with a half-moon and Summer Crush's "Midnight Without You" playing in the background just like I always pictured it?

"I'm not letting you do that one over," Clementine goes on, still cackling. "You're stuck with Gavin Palmer's sloppy wet lips in the closet for the rest of your life."

Sloppy wet lips in the closet?

That doesn't sound romantic at all!

And I don't even know anyone named Gavin Palmer.

I slouch in my salon chair. This is the worst. I skipped right over my first kiss. I'll never be able to get that back.

"Oh, and before I forget," Clementine says, completely oblivious to my desolate mood. "If Annabelle asks to hang with you this week, you need to say no. We're boycotting her."

"We are?" I ask, thinking back to that text message I got yesterday from someone named Annabelle. I remember how it sent Clementine into a tailspin.

"Yes," Clementine replies passionately.

I blink and look up at her. I'm sitting in the salon chair, waiting for yet *another* product to "process" in my hair. According to Jeff, the guy who has apparently been straightening my hair for the past two years, we're nearly finished. But he's been saying that for an hour and I'm starting to lose faith in his promises. Clementine is in the next chair getting a retouch on her hair coloring, which I've recently learned is not naturally blond.

"Why is that again?"

Clementine flips a page in the magazine she's been reading. "She parked in our spot last week."

"I didn't realize we had assigned spots in the school parking lot."

Clementine gives me another one of her now-familiar have-you-lost-your-mind? looks. "We don't. But everyone knows the spot in the front row next to the handicap is ours."

I'm so confused. "So," I begin, trying to get this

straight in my head. "We're not hanging out with Anna-belle because she parked in a spot that's not *technically* ours?"

"No," Clementine says, and I feel somewhat relieved. Because that did seem ludicrous. "We're not *only* not hanging out with her. We're also not *talking* to her."

"What?" I blurt out. "But that makes no sense."

Clementine huffs like she really doesn't have time for this. And apparently she doesn't because instead of re-sponding to me, she flips another page in the magazine and changes the subject back to the vlog. "So, you'll come by tomorrow and we can film it?"

"Uh," I stall, feeling kind of antsy at the thought of spending another few hours with Clementine. She's kind of a lot to take. "I don't know. I might have plans to-morrow."

Clementine closes the magazine with a *slap*. "What plans? You don't have plans."

Sheesh, is she always this bossy?

"I could have plans," I argue, getting defensive.

"I would know if you had plans."

"Maybe I made plans without you," I say, instantly regretting it because Clementine looks like she just swal-lowed a bug.

"What's gotten into you?" she asks, glaring at me in the mirror.

I look down at my lap and mumble, "Nothing."

"Something," she challenges. "Because you've been acting totally freak-o since yesterday. First there was that horrific makeup job and then you totally wigged out at the dance. And what about you talking to that loser Grace after the talent show? I saw you, you know."

"Grace isn't a loser," I snap.

Clementine narrows her eyes at me. "She's in marching band."

"So? What's wrong with being in marching band?"

"I don't even know where to begin explaining to you what's wrong with that. And I shouldn't have to. You said it yourself just last week. Marching band is for loners who can't get a date."

My eyes widen in shock. "I didn't say that," I insist, but my voice is lacking conviction, because the truth is, I have no idea what I've said. I have no idea about anything that's happened in the past four years. And I'm starting to feel like I don't *want* to know.

Clementine opens her magazine again. "You said it. So I don't know why you were even talking to her."

"She used to be my friend," I say quietly, feeling the weight of my words crush down on me.

"Yeah," Clementine agrees, flipping the page. "*Used* to be."

Just then a small timer dings and Jeff comes over to lead me to the sink so he can rinse my hair. When I get back to the chair and he faces me toward the mirror, I nearly flinch at the sight of my unfamiliar reflection. I still haven't gotten used to the way I look. But now, as Jeff combs and blow-dries my hair, and I watch the silky, straight strands tumble around my shoulders, I've never felt less like myself.

And I wonder if I ever will again.

THE WALLOWING
WILL HAVE TO WAIT

The entire drive home, Clementine hounds me about coming over tomorrow to film the vlog. I finally agree just to get her to stop bugging me about it. By the time she drops me off at my house, I just want to sulk alone in my room.

Buttercup immediately jumps onto the bed. I slide out of my shoes and sit down next to her, stroking her fur. "You know you're not allowed on the furniture, right?"

She collapses onto her side with a dramatic sigh.

Somehow I don't think it's a rule either of us abides by.

I pull out my phone and try calling Rory again, but just like last time, it rings and rings and goes to voice mail. "Hi! It's Rory. I'm off being awesome! Leave a message if you want to be awesome, too!"

I don't leave a message.

A few minutes later, there's a knock on my door and Buttercup and I both turn our heads toward the sound.

"Who is it?" I call out.

"Mom."

Buttercup automatically jumps down from the bed and curls up on the floor. I stifle a giggle and tell her to come in.

"There's someone at the front door for you," Mom says, poking her head in.

I groan and fall back, pulling a pillow over my head. "I don't want to see her," I grumble, assuming it's Clementine back to tell me about yet another idea for the Flower Power vlog. If I have to hear her debate pink or green daisies one more time, I'll stick my head in the oven.

"It's not a *her*," my mom says, cocking a playful eyebrow.

I turn and look at her. Is it Cute Connor? Why would he come looking for me after the total idiot I made of myself last night?

"Who is it?" I ask, momentarily forgetting about my misery.

"Jacob Tucker."

I immediately sit up. "Jacob Tucker?"

My mind flashes back to last night and how much fun we had on the dance floor. Then I feel a stab of guilt when I remember how I just left him there once they announced the talent show.

Maybe he's here to yell at me.

Maybe *he* hates me now, too.

I certainly wouldn't blame him.

"Yeah," Mom says with a shake of her head. "I swear, every time I see that kid he looks different. I don't think he's stopped growing since the seventh grade!"

I giggle. "I know, right? He's as tall as a tree!"

Mom chuckles too and it feels good to at least share this part of my life with her, even if I can't tell her *everything* that's been going on. "It's amazing how fast you all have grown up. It feels like only yesterday you were in middle school."

I nod, staring down at my chic black-and-white comforter, tracing the floral pattern with my index finger. "You have no idea," I mutter under my breath.

Mom sits down on the bed next to me and lifts my chin up with her finger. "Hey. Is everything okay? You've been acting a little . . . *off* lately."

I bite my lip to hold back the flood of tears that threatens to spill out. "Yeah. No. I don't know. Sometimes I feel like time is moving *too* fast and I wish it would slow down so I could figure things out."

My mom lets out a jovial laugh. "You? The Queen of Shortcuts wants time to slow down?"

I laugh too, because she's right. I do love my shortcuts. I always have. "I know," I say. "I guess it just feels like *too* many things are changing."

Her face turns serious. "Like what?"

I shrug. "Like you working and Rory two thousand

miles away at school and you and Dad going out to brunch without me."

"Oh, sweetie. If I had known you wanted to go to brunch, I would have woken you, but you always like to sleep in on Saturdays."

"It's fine," I tell her. The last thing I want to do is make my mom feel bad. "I just . . ." I let my voice trail off. I can't think of anything else to say. I'm not sure there's much else *to* say.

Mom grabs my hand. "I know Rory leaving for school was hard on you."

I shrug. Maybe it was. Maybe it wasn't. How am I supposed to remember?

"That's why we got you a puppy," Mom goes on. "To help you with the change."

That's why I finally got a dog?

Not because I begged and pleaded and my parents finally gave in? But to replace my sister?

I glance down at Buttercup coiled into a ball on the floor and suddenly feel a wave of sadness wash over me. I never got to see her as a puppy. I saw some pictures on my phone but it's not the same.

Mom must read the sorrow on my face because she begins to rub the top of my hand with her thumb. "But not everything changes," she tells me. "Despite what it looks like, some things *do* stay the same."

"Like what?"

"Like your dad and I will always love you."

I roll my eyes. "I know *that*."

"Trust me," she says. "There are some things that will never change. You just have to look a little harder to find them."

I nod. I'm not sure I believe her but, admittedly, I feel better.

Mom stands up. "Anyway. You should probably go downstairs and rescue Jacob before Dad starts talking about the history of earwax or something and bores the poor kid to death. It's just so weird to see him here. I don't think he's been to the house since your twelfth birthday party."

I lift my head in surprise. "Jacob was at that party?"

"Yeah," Mom says. "Remember? But he was so sweet and brought you those cans of Grape Crush soda."

My eyes go wide. "Did he shake those up, too?"

Mom clearly has no idea what I'm talking about. "Huh?"

"Never mind," I mutter.

He must have brought them as an apology for the exploding one he gave me at school. He said at the dance yesterday that he felt really bad about that.

"I only did it because I had this huge crush on you."

I feel my face get hot at the memory. I still can't believe Jacob Tucker had a crush on me. He was always so annoying!

"Unless" Mom goes on. "Would you prefer *not* to see him? I can tell him to leave. Or who knows, maybe he *wants* to hear about the history of earwax. Maybe that's why he came over in the first place." She winks at me.

I let out a weak laugh. I remember when Dad used to make all of Rory's boyfriends listen to his random ramblings. She was always so mortified.

Not that Jacob is my boyfriend or anything.

Obviously.

I'm about to tell my mom yes, I'd prefer not to see him. Because honestly, I'm not sure I want to see anyone right now. I just want to lie here and wallow in my misery. But the idea that Jacob Tucker was at my twelfth birthday party, the day after Grace and I had our big fight in the Hideaway—that he might *know* something about the collapse of our friendship—keeps niggling at me.

After all, I've been looking for someone who might have the answers. And he *has* been around the past four years.

Maybe he can help me solve this seemingly unsolvable puzzle.

I stand up and slide my feet back into my shoes. "Tell him I'll be right down."

MINT-CHIP FINGERS

Jacob suggests that we go get ice cream. It's honestly the best idea I've heard in a long time. We walk to Happy Cones down the street and we both order a double scoop of mint chip. Jacob even pays for mine, which is kind of sweet.

We find a table outside. The weather is perfect. The sky is blue. The sun is shining. It's not too hot or too cold. I barely even noticed it when I was out with Clementine earlier. It's almost like she comes with her very own rain cloud.

As we eat our ice cream, I still can't get over how different Jacob Tucker—*J.T.*—looks. He's changed so much. I know I have too but it almost seems like he's an entirely different person.

"When did you start going by J.T.?" I ask, praying it's not one of those things that I should already know and he's not going to give me that look that everyone's been giving me for the past two days.

But he barely blinks at the question. "Freshman year. When I joined the swim team. The coach started calling me J.T., then the other guys on the team joined in, and within a few weeks, everyone was calling me that. Even my parents." He licks at his top scoop. "What about you? When did you switch to Adeline?"

I think back to the Great Name Change Charter that I found this morning. It was dated the summer before I started high school. "Around the same time."

He nods. "I guess high school is the start of new things for a lot of people."

I bite my lip, pondering his words. They're more right than he knows. "Yeah. I guess so."

Jacob leans back in his chair. "This is nice."

"I know," I agree. "It's such a beautiful day."

He shakes his head. "No, I mean, you and me, hanging out. It's nice."

He smiles at me and I feel my cheeks warm.

"I was honestly surprised when you agreed to dance with me yesterday," he admits.

"Why?"

He shrugs and takes another lick of his mint chip, avoiding my gaze. "I don't know. It just seems like you and Clementine kind of . . ." His voice trails off and I wait anxiously for him to finish the sentence, but instead, he shrugs again and catches a runaway stream of mint chip that is dripping down his cone.

I'm instantly reminded of what he told me last night at the dance.

"You and Clementine have this little popular-duo thing going and I don't fit into that."

I feel a cramp in my stomach and suddenly my ice cream no longer looks as delicious as it did five minutes ago.

How many people have I managed to isolate since I started hanging out with Clementine Dumont?

"Jacob?" I ask, and quickly correct myself. "Sorry, I mean, J.T."

He laughs. "It's okay. You can call me Jacob. I kind of like it."

"Okay, *Jacob*," I repeat with a grin. "How much do you remember from my twelfth birthday party?"

He looks surprised by my change of topic. I agree it kind of came out of nowhere. "Wow," he says. "That was a long time ago." Then he thinks about it for a moment. "That was the party where you and Grace had that huge fight, wasn't it?"

My whole body goes numb. All I can feel is the cold stickiness of my mint-chip ice cream melting down my hand. Jacob reaches out to wipe it away with his napkin.

"Are you okay?" he asks. "You went kind of zombie eyes there for a moment."

"We had a fight?"

Another fight?

After *the one we had in the Hideaway?*

He laughs. "I can't believe you don't remember. It was pretty epic."

I shake my head dazedly. "I . . . I must have spaced it. What was it about?"

He laughs. "No clue. I just remember you two were screaming at each other. About all kinds of things and then she started crying. It was pretty dramatic. Grace stormed off and then the party just kind of fizzled out." He's staring at me now with an almost inquisitive expression. "You really don't remember this?"

I let out a long sigh. I really don't. I wish I did. I wish I had all the answers. I wish I could finish this massive puzzle that only seems to get more confusing with each piece that I find.

But obviously, I don't say any of that. I just shrug and say, "I guess I blocked it out."

Jacob nods like he understands and points toward my melting cone. "So, am I redeemed? Did I successfully make amends for the seventh grade yet?"

I laugh weakly. "Getting there. Although I still have no idea why I would invite you to my birthday party after you gave me a can of exploding soda."

Jacob takes a bite of his cone. "I'm pretty sure your mom invited me. You know, because of the whole neighbor thing. You ignored me the whole time."

I laugh. It feels good. "That sounds more like it."

My barely touched ice cream has pretty much melted in my hand. I toss it into a nearby trash can and proceed to lick mint-chip goo off each of my fingers one by one.

Jacob watches me closely before cracking up.

"What?" I ask, pausing with my pinky in my mouth.

He shakes his head. "Nothing. You're just . . . always surprising me, Addie." He stops, correcting himself. "Sorry, I mean *Adeline.*"

I smile, echoing his words from earlier. "It's okay. You can call me Addie. I kind of like it."

SWEET COFFEE
SLUDGE

The next morning, I decide to go straight to the source. Enough is enough. I get dressed and walk the five blocks to Grace's house. I know the journey well. I've only walked it a thousand times before.

Unfortunately, I have to pass by Clementine's house (and my abandoned car) to get there and I'm really worried she's going to see me and come running out to yell at me. I already texted her this morning to tell her I wasn't feeling well and ask if we could film our vlog Monday night instead.

She did *not* seem happy when she texted me back. All I got was that stupid octopus emoji, which I know, from when she texted Annabelle on Friday, is not a good sign. But I don't really feel like dealing with her or her octopuses right now. I have too many other things on my mind.

I duck my head and hurry past Clementine's driveway, holding my breath the whole time. Thankfully, her front door remains closed.

When I get to Grace's house, I've managed to completely psych myself up. This is it. No more dodging the question. No more running away. I will make her talk to me. I will make her believe me. I will make her tell me everything that happened.

And I will not leave until she does.

I jab my finger against the doorbell with persistence. I keep ringing and ringing until the door finally opens.

But it's not Grace standing there. To my surprise, it's her little sister, Lily. Except she's not little anymore. Last time I saw her she was a tiny eight-year-old with pigtail braids and glasses. Now she's tall and willowy and obviously wears contacts. I quickly do the math and almost gasp when I realize she's now twelve. The same age as me! Or, as I *was*, up until three days ago.

"Addie?" she says, squinting at me like she doesn't recognize me. "What are *you* doing here?"

Her question is like a punch in the stomach. It confirms all the dreadful things I've learned over the past few days. That Grace and I aren't friends. That we barely speak. And that I obviously don't come around here anymore.

"I'm looking for Grace," I say, standing up straight and tall. I need to project an air of confidence. I am someone who will not accept the word *no*. I've come here for answers and I will not leave until I get them.

"She's not here."

My whole body sags in disappointment. "Oh," I mutter, turning to leave. "Okay."

But just before the door closes behind me, I'm struck with an idea and quickly spin back around. "Lily?"

She opens the door again. "Yeah?"

"What are you doing right now?"

She looks completely astonished. "Me?"

I nod. "Yeah, *you*."

She glances around her, as though the answer were written on one of the walls of her house. "Um, nothing. Just watching some TV."

I bite my lip. "Do you wanna, I don't know, hang out?"

She stares at me openmouthed and speechless for a long moment. "You want to hang out with *me*?"

"Yeah," I confirm. "I want to hang out with you. How about we go get lattes at the Human Bean?"

Her eyes nearly pop out of her head and I have to laugh. I know exactly how she feels. It wasn't that long ago that I was her age. I remember I used to beg Rory to take me to the Human Bean to hang out with all her cool friends, but she always said no. And every time I'd pass by the coffee shop, I'd stare longingly into the window, counting the days until I was one of those cool people, sitting in a booth, sipping yummy coffee drinks, and gossiping about whatever cool people gossip about.

"The Human Bean?" she repeats, clearly in denial. "You want to go to the Human Bean with me?"

I nod. "It's been a long time since we hung out. I want to catch up."

She stands in the doorway for a few more stunned seconds until finally turning and bolting into the house, returning at lightning speed with shoes on her feet and a small purse hanging from her shoulder. She closes the door behind her. "Okay," she says, completely out of breath. "I'm ready."

I giggle, feeling a small twinge of longing for the days when something as simple as going to a coffee shop with a sixteen-year-old would have been the most exciting thing to happen to me in months.

❋

The Human Bean is packed with people. It's actually my first time in here but I'm too busy watching Lily's reaction to bother with my own. She's completely awestruck and maybe even a little *star*struck. Especially as we make our way to the counter and nearly every single person says hi to me and calls me by name. It's like an extension of the hallway at school. I still can't get used to it.

"You are like the most popular person on earth!" Lily whispers as we wait in line to place our orders.

I laugh. "Not really."

She nods vehemently. "Yes, you are. No one even knows who Grace is at school. I mean, besides her band friends."

We reach the front of the line and I order a latte. Not because I like lattes. I don't even know what a latte tastes like. I've never had one before. But that's what Rory used to drink whenever she'd come here with Boyfriend of the Week. And the only reason I know that is because I'd often find empty to-go cups in her car with her name written on the side underneath the words *nonfat latte*.

"Nonfat," I add quickly.

"Me too," Lily orders, beaming at me. "This is so exciting!"

I beam back. "I know, right?"

She gives me a strange look. "Don't you come in here like every day?"

I try to play it off. "Well, you know, not *every* day."

The barista returns with our drinks and we take them to an empty table by the window. Lily watches me, waiting for me to take the first sip, probably so she can copy me. The problem is I don't know what I'm doing either. *I* need someone to copy. I don't know how to drink a latte. Do you just drink it? Do you blow on it first? Do you swirl it around in the cup?

But I have to act cool. I have to set an example. I can't let Lily know that I'm just as clueless as she is.

I smile at her and bring the lidded paper cup to my

lips. I really hope it doesn't taste too much like coffee. I hate the taste of coffee. I tried my dad's coffee once and I gagged and had to spit it out in the sink. It was so bitter.

I take a tentative sip.

And immediately spit it out all over the table.

Oh, gosh, it's horrible!

It tastes *just* like coffee! Maybe even *worse* than coffee.

Lily flinches, backing away from my projectile latte and looking at me like I'm a total fraud. Which, of course, I am.

I can still taste the icky bitter sludge in my mouth. I grab a napkin from the dispenser and start wiping down my tongue while I make disgusting gagging noises. I sound like a cat trying to cough up a fur ball.

A few people turn to look at me and I try to play it off, flashing Lily a sweet, innocent smile. "Be careful," I warn her. "It's very hot."

"Oh," she says, her confusion fading. "Right."

I glance around the small coffee shop. I recognize most of the people here as Thunder Creek High students. They're all talking and drinking coffee like it's the most delicious thing in the world. How do they do that? How do they not vomit?

And more important, how am I supposed to finish this whole cup I just bought? I know I must *like* lattes. I've seen myself drinking them in pictures on my phone. So what's wrong with me now? Is coffee an acquired taste?

My gaze lands on someone I recognize from school. I'm pretty sure it's Annabelle, the girl Clementine is boycotting. She's standing next to a small counter by the door. I watch as she removes the lid from her cup, dumps four packets of sugar in, and stirs the coffee before replacing the lid.

Sugar!

I didn't add any sugar. No wonder this tastes like I just licked a rusty metal pole.

Lily sniffs at her cup and is about to take a sip. I reach out and smack her hand. "Sugar!" I say desperately. "I forgot the sugar. Don't drink it yet."

I walk over to the counter just as the girl is leaving. "Hi, Adeline," she says brightly.

I stand there speechless for a moment, wondering how I should respond. If I'm right, and this *is* Annabelle, didn't Clementine tell me not to speak to her?

I shake my head. That's ridiculous.

I'm done following orders from Clementine. Especially when they make no sense whatsoever. If this girl's biggest crime is parking in an unmarked parking spot, then she definitely doesn't deserve to be ignored.

"Hey, Annabelle!" I say brightly. "Nice to see you."

She glances behind me at the table where Lily is sitting. "Where's Clementine?" she asks.

I shrug. "I don't know."

She looks a little bit scandalized by my response.

Am I supposed to know where Clementine is? Am I supposed to keep tabs on her at all times? Should I have a Clementine-tracking app on my phone?

The girl glances once again in the direction of our table, then gives me a hurried fake smile, and continues out the door.

Huh. That was weird.

I grab a handful of sugar packets—as many as I can fit in two hands—and two wooden stirrers, and carry them back to the table. Lily watches as I proceed to dump packet after packet into my cup. I don't even know how many I put in there. I lose count after six.

"Why did you order nonfat if you were just going to add that much sugar?" Lily asks.

I stop stirring. "Uh . . . I just like the taste better. Otherwise it's too . . . you know . . . fatty."

She looks like she wants to question me but decides better of it and just starts emptying packets into her own cup.

I stir my drink, which now feels a little bit like sludge with all that sugar in it, and take a sip.

So much better. Now it kind of tastes like a hot milk shake.

"So," I begin, trying to sound as casual as possible. "How's Grace doing?"

Lily takes a cautious sip of her drink. "She's good." Then her eyes narrow suspiciously at me. "Why are you asking?"

"I can't ask about my best friend?" I swallow, catching myself. "I mean, my *old* best friend."

A lump suddenly forms in my throat. I take another sip of coffee milk shake to shove it down.

"She's good," Lily says again, this time with a much more guarded tone. "Are you here to get dirt on her? Are you trying to use me in some kind of prank? Is that why you're being so nice to me?"

I choke on my drink. "What? No! It's not a prank. I'm not . . ." I pause, feeling so flustered. "Is that really something you think I would do?"

Lily shrugs and leans back in her chair. "I don't know. You guys haven't talked since you ditched her on the English project back in middle school and she failed the assignment."

"What?" I screech so loudly, more than a few nosy people look over. I lower my voice and lean in so we're not overheard. "I did that?"

Lily squints at me. "You mean, you don't remember?"

I open my mouth to argue. Surely Lily got the details mixed up. Surely I wouldn't do that to my best friend. But then the memory of that music video I found comes flooding back to me. The *Romeo and Juliet* retelling starring Rory and Henry. Grace's name wasn't in the credits. I did it alone.

It suddenly feels like my chest is tightening around my heart, threatening to squeeze it to death. I can't breathe. I feel sick. The sugary sludge coffee is rising up in my throat.

I abandoned my best friend.

And she failed the assignment because of it.

Is that why she barely speaks to me? I mean, I wouldn't blame her. That's a terrible thing to do to someone.

I realize that Lily is still staring at me, waiting for an answer. "Of course I remember," I say, trying to keep my voice light. "I'm just wondering what Grace's side of the story was."

Lily crosses her arms defensively over her chest. "There's no *side* to the story, Addie. What you did sucked."

"Yeah," I say softly. "I . . . I feel really bad about that." I bow my head and stare at my lap. "Did this, by any chance, have something to do with the fight we had at my birthday party? Did Grace ever tell you about that?"

"You mean the fight about the gift?"

The gift?

What gift?

I suddenly remember Grace coming over the night of the fateful slumber party and saying something about saving my gift for the party tomorrow. She seemed so excited about it.

That's what caused our big epic fight?

Seriously, how bad could the gift have been?

Did she give me poison ivy?

I want so badly to ask Lily what the gift was but I'm afraid it will only make me look even more insensitive than I already do. So I just mumble, "Yeah. That fight."

"Why did you ask me to hang out?" Lily asks, her tone still cautious and full of suspicion.

I bite my lip. Honestly, I just wanted answers. I wanted the truth. But now I'm not sure I can handle any more of the truth. Every time I learn something about the past four years, I hate who I've become even more.

"I don't know," I whisper. "I guess I just missed Grace a little. And you remind me of her."

Lily looks surprised by my answer but I can see her softening a bit. She uncrosses her arms and gives me a sympathetic look. Then she says in a tender voice, "I doubt she'd ever admit it, but I think she might miss you, too."

ONE STEP FORWARD, ONE STEP BACK

On Monday morning, I wake up early, before the sun is even up.

After I dropped Lily off at her house last night, I walked to the park and sat on one of the swings, thinking long and hard about everything. All the things I've learned about myself over the past few days.

Then I made a decision.

I have to stop fighting reality. I have to stop trying to change the past, because the past can't be changed. Whatever I did in the last four years can't be undone.

The truth is, Grace and I aren't friends anymore. We aren't twelve years old anymore. We're new people. *Different* people, which means I have to handle things differently.

I have to *fix* things differently.

And that's exactly what I intend to do. Just because

things have changed for the worse, doesn't mean they can't be repaired.

Starting today, I will fix this friendship.

I know Grace and I got into a huge fight on my twelfth birthday and then another fight at my birthday party. I did a horrible thing by ditching her on the English project, but that was years ago. I figure the reason we've continued to drift apart since then is because we have completely different interests. And the only way we can drift back together is if we start sharing some of those interests.

I spent half the night poring over our high school yearbooks from the past two years, studying every club, activity, and honor society that Grace Harrington is a part of. If I can just join *one* of those clubs or activities, then I'll be able to show Grace that we still have loads in common. That we can still be best friends, despite the mistakes I've made in the past.

I've narrowed it down to three possible options:

1. Join the marching band.
2. Join the science club.
3. Get accepted into the Math Honor Society.

Okay, I admit that last one is pretty much a long shot, given that I can't even pronounce Trigo . . . whatever-the-heck-it-is, but that's okay. One of the other ideas will work. I'm sure of it.

I text Clementine to tell her I'll be going to school early today to work on a special project, which is not technically a lie. Saving my friendship with Grace *is* a special project. A very, very special project.

Clementine doesn't respond, which I figure means she's still sleeping. It is pretty early. But I didn't really have a choice about getting up this early. According to the Thunder Creek High School website, marching band has practice an hour before school starts today, and I want to be there at least twenty minutes before that.

Another thing I did last night was watch YouTube tutorials on how to drive, and now I'm feeling much more confident about getting behind the wheel again, even if the idea does make my palms sweat just a little bit.

When I get downstairs, the house is quiet. Everyone is still asleep. So I grab a piece of fruit, pour some cheese puffs into Buttercup's bowl, and head out the door.

I have to walk about ten minutes to get to my car because it's still parked near Clementine's house, where I left it on Friday. I unlock the doors and get behind the wheel, taking a huge breath before turning the key in the ignition and putting the gearshift in reverse. According to YouTube, the secret is to only use *one* foot for the gas pedal *and* the brake pedal. I was trying to use both pedals at the same time. Not good.

I carefully ease my foot off the brake and onto the gas pedal. The car inches backward ever so slowly.

This is good. This is very good. This is progress.

Because I'm going backward, I pull the wheel the *opposite* direction from where I want to go. This was another key lesson in those videos. Who would have thought you have to steer left to go right?

I inch backward and forward, again and again, until I'm in the middle of the street, facing the *right* way!

Success!

Now I just have to survive the next two miles until I get to school and I'll be home free. Or school free. Or school imprisoned?

Whatever.

With my foot firmly on the brake, I push the shifter into drive and once more ease onto the gas pedal. The car responds, crawling forward. I let out a giddy yelp.

I'm doing it! I'm driving! And not crashing!

Fortunately, the drive to school is pretty straight. There are only two turns and three stoplights total. It does take me about twenty minutes to go two miles because I'm driving at about half the pace of an elderly turtle, but what counts is I get there in one piece. And my hands aren't shaking like leaves in a hurricane when I arrive. I find a parking spot in the second row and hurry to the football field, where I see members of the marching band already starting to congregate with their instruments.

As I get closer, I spot Grace standing in the center of the field, playing a few scales on her trumpet to warm up. I walk right past her, causing her to lower her trumpet and stare incredulously at me, and approach the only adult on the field, Mr. Reynolds, the director of the marching band. I recognize him from his picture on the school website. He's standing off to the side of the field, flipping through a binder.

I have my speech all prepared. I practiced it multiple times in front of the mirror last night.

I stop in front of him and he looks down at me, squinting from the sun that's just rising over a nearby hill. "Can I help you?" he asks.

"Yes," I say, "I play the trumpet and I'd like to try out for the marching band."

His brow furrows. "Tryouts were two months ago, at the beginning of the semester."

I nod. I have already anticipated this response and have planned accordingly. "Yes, I realize that but I read the bylaws for the district's extracurricular activities online and it says that if a student has been absent for a large majority of the semester due to illness or transferring schools, he or she *can* audition as long as he or she is able to catch up with the rest of the team or group."

This is actually true. I really *did* look it up.

"So you've been absent?" he confirms.

"Um. Yes."

Okay, so technically I haven't been ill and I didn't transfer schools but my *memory* has been absent for the majority of the semester so I think that counts.

"And *can* you catch up with the rest of the group?"

I nod confidently. "Absolutely!"

"So I take it you've been in a marching band before?" Mr. Reynolds asks, looking unconvinced.

I swallow. "Yes. Obviously."

Okay, *this* part is a lie. I haven't been in a marching band before. But last night, my trusty new friend YouTube provided me with several videos of marching bands and it doesn't look that hard. So they walk while they play. What's so difficult about that? And yes, it's technically been four years since I played the trumpet, but *actually* for me, it's only been a few days, so I should still be able to play well enough to pass a silly little audition.

Mr. Reynolds sighs and flips to a different tab in his binder. "Well, we are actually short a few players in the brass section. Do you have your instrument?"

I hold up the dusty box with my trumpet in it. I found it in the basement last night, after I came up with my brilliant plan to resurrect my friendship with Grace.

"Fine. Why don't you jump in with them for some box drills and let's see how you do. We'll start with scales in G major and work our way up."

My stomach lurches.

Ugh. Scales.

I hate scales.

Which one is G again?

"Okay!" Mr. Reynolds calls into a megaphone. "Every-one line up!"

All the people standing around chatting are suddenly zooming across the field, getting into positions. I look to Mr. Reynolds for help. "Martinez is out sick today. Take her spot on the thirty, fourth from the left."

I give him a blank look.

He sighs. "The big gaping hole behind the tuba player."

I turn and look at the field, where a hundred people have just instantly formed a perfect rectangle. I notice a hole three rows back from the front. "Right!" I call out, pulling my trumpet from the box. "Got it!"

I run to the empty space and take my position.

"Ten-hut!" Mr. Reynolds calls.

What?

I look left and right. The trumpet players on either side of me have raised their trumpets up to their mouths in a sharp, succinct movement, their postures suddenly rigid.

Did I join the marching band or the military?

I try to match their stance.

"One, two, three, four, five, six, seven, eight!" Mr. Reynolds counts off, and before I can even get my fingers in the right spot, everyone around me is moving. Marching forward in small, even steps, while flawlessly playing the G scale.

I hurry forward, still trying to remember where my fingers are supposed to go. But by the time I start playing, I'm already two notes behind. I play the next notes quickly, trying to catch up, but I can hear the sound in my ears and it's totally off.

Was I supposed to tune this thing?

The girl to my right shoots me a glance out of the corner of her eye.

I do my best to ignore her and keep marching. When I get to the final note in the scale, I'm pleased to hear it sounds more or less on key, and I've even managed to sync up my steps with the group.

I did it!

I made it!

It's over!

I stop playing and lower my trumpet before quickly realizing that I'm the only one. Everyone else is still playing. They've started a new scale. The problem is, I have no idea which one it is. It's definitely not G major again. Is it A minor? My fingers fumble around the pistons but I can't seem to get them right with all this marching. I pause for just a second to set up my alignment and that's when the entire swarm of musicians changes direction.

Without any warning!

Just a second ago, everyone was marching straight, and now they're all marching to the left. The girl next to me—the one who gave me the stink eye for playing the wrong notes—slams into me and I go tumbling into the grass, my trumpet falling from my hands.

I expect the whole group to come to a halt, out of respect for the downed player, but they don't. They just keep marching. There's an entire parade of trumpet, trombone, and tuba players stomping toward me. I cover my head and scoot back, trying to avoid getting trampled. Some of them step on my toes. Others bang my forehead with their knees.

"Stop!" I call out, but no one can hear me above the raucous scales.

I have no choice but to try and escape. Taking advantage of the small gap between feet, I push myself up, just managing to get onto my knees, when the swarm changes direction again and now they're all marching backward. I get smacked in the face by someone's butt and tumble to the ground again.

I quickly crawl out of the way to avoid more collisions with more butts. It seems that crawling is the only way I'm going to make it out of here alive, so I scramble on all fours to the right, because that's where there appears to be the fewest bodies. But just as I'm about to escape the horde, they change direction a third time and start marching right.

"Ahh!" I scream as the throng of stomping feet comes at me again. I crawl faster. They march after me. Like a pack of zombies.

I crawl and crawl until my knees and hands ache and I'm panting. Then I hit a wall. Actually, it's not a wall. It's a pair of legs. I glance up to see Mr. Reynolds hovering over me with his megaphone.

He gives me a disapproving look. "Halt!" he yells, and the band stops. "At ease!"

I collapse onto my back and struggle to catch my breath. That's when I hear the giggles. They start small but quickly spread through the group like a breeze blowing through a forest.

"Enough!" Mr. Reynolds calls into his megaphone. The band quiets down.

When I finally find the strength to pull myself to my feet, I spot Grace in the formation. She's covering her mouth with her hand to whisper something to her neighbor, who starts laughing all over again.

Apparently, she was right all along. That was uproarious.

A SWAP
OF HEARTS

Okay, so marching band is out. That was a stupid idea anyway. I don't even like playing the trumpet, which is probably why I quit in the first place. On to the next item on my list: join the science club. Unfortunately, though, the science club doesn't meet until after school, so I have to wait.

Before first period, I look for Clementine, but I can't find her. Not that I know where she normally hangs out or anything, and she doesn't respond to any of the texts I send. So I just head to my first period. Trig. It takes me a few minutes to find the classroom, but once I do, I remember who's *in* my trig class.

Cute Connor.

He's sitting in the back row with his head bent over his notebook. Until this very moment, I'd almost managed to forget about the whole fiasco at the dance, but now it comes rushing back in a wave of humiliation. I can't believe I told him he looked like a monkey! What was I thinking?

I slide into the seat next to him and keep my head down. When I peer up to see if he's even noticed my presence, he's looking right at me. Our eyes meet for just a second before we both look away.

After class, he stops me just outside the door. "Hey," he says, inching his bag up his shoulder. "About today. I'm not sure I can tutor you. I have this . . . thing I have to do." He looks at his feet. "It's super-important. I can't get out of it."

"That's fine," I say, knowing that he's lying. You don't have to be in high school to read *that* awkward body language.

When I get to French class, Clementine is sitting way in the corner, surrounded by a group of girls, and there are no available seats next to her. I try to catch her eye as I come in but she's staring down at something on her desk, giggling. Actually, *all* the girls around her are staring at her desk, giggling.

I inch closer to see that they're looking at Clementine's phone.

"Look!" Clementine says, covering her mouth. "Now she's actually crawling!" The girls break out in more laughter and I feel something sticky form in my gut.

What are they looking at?

Then I hear it. Mr. Reynold's voice yelling, "Halt! At ease!"

It's coming from the phone.

Oh, no.

I shuffle closer to Clementine's desk. Close enough that I can see what's on the screen. Then my whole body turns ice-cold. There I am, crawling on my hands and knees, trying to escape being trampled by a bunch of tuba players.

Someone filmed it?

Clementine sees me approach and quickly shuts off the phone. "Nice performance," she says and I don't miss the sarcasm dripping from her words.

The other girls do their best to stifle their giggles.

"If you weren't a YouTube star with our vlog, then you are now."

Someone put it on *YouTube*?

Oh, gosh, this is not happening. This is *not* happening.

Just a second ago YouTube was my best friend; now it's my mortal enemy.

And why is Clementine acting so mean? Is she mad at me because I didn't hang out with her yesterday to film our vlog? I told her we could do it tonight and she said that was fine. Are we really supposed to hang out every second of every day? Can't I have other friends, too? She clearly does.

Whatever. I find a seat on the other side of the room and listen to the teacher yammer on in French, trying to pretend like I understand a word she's saying. I'm getting really good at that.

Pretending, that is.

By the time I get to English class, I'm itching for this day to be over. Everyone has seen "Marching Band Fail" on YouTube now. The link spread fast and I'm pretty much the laughingstock of the school. Fortunately it's the last period of the day, so I only have fifty more minutes to go. Then I get to try my luck again with Grace's science club.

Jacob is already seated at a desk near the back. He gives me a friendly wave and I smile and wave back. At least someone still likes me around here. Although maybe he just hasn't seen the video yet.

I take a seat three rows behind Grace, who doesn't even acknowledge that I've entered the room. Not that I expected her to.

The bell rings and Mr. Heath gets up from his desk. "Okay, so after our class on Friday, I got to thinking a little bit more about 'Rip van Winkle.' Yes, this is what English teachers like me do on the weekend. We sit around thinking about fictional literary characters. Sad, I know."

The class snickers.

"And I thought we should explore the theme of nostalgia a little bit more, because it's definitely an important one that we'll see throughout many works of literature." He snaps his fingers. "So, I'd like you to work on a little project."

Everyone lets out a simultaneous groan.

Mr. Heath frowns. "Where's your faith? This happens to be a *fun* project."

Judging from the faces around the room, no one is convinced.

"Nostalgia is basically a longing for the past. It comes from the Greek root *nostos,* meaning 'homecoming.' Washington Irving explored this theme in his short story 'Rip van Winkle,' and now I want *you* to explore the theme in your own way. I want you to do a personal presentation about nostalgia. Something that represents the passage of time and how *you* personally feel about things that live in your past. You can get as creative as possible. There are really no guidelines. You can do a poem. You can do a painting. Whatever you want. Use your imaginations." He turns and begins to walk back to his desk before remembering a last detail. "Oh, right. And I'm going to assign you to do this project in pairs."

Pairs?

I immediately sit up straighter.

A partner project?

That's an even better idea than joining the science club! I'll be Grace's partner! We'll be forced to hang out together! She'll *have* to listen to me if she wants to get an A, and knowing Grace, she'll do *anything* to get an A, even hang out with the likes of me.

This is so perfect. This will fix everything. We'll hang out, talk about our project, and I'll show her that we still have tons of fun together and should be best friends again.

It's kind of poetic really. It was a school assignment that broke us apart, and now it will be a school assignment that brings us back together!

"You'll be picking random playing cards out of this hat." Mr. Heath holds up a ratty old fedora and gives it a shake. "There are two of every card in here. Two jacks, two kings, two fours, you get the picture. Whoever has the same card as you is your partner. No complaining, no switching, that's it. You must work with your partner on the assignment."

I blow out a breath. How am I supposed to make sure I get paired with Grace? There are over twenty people in this class!

Think, Addie. Think.

Mr. Heath starts walking around the classroom with the hat. He stops at each desk to allow the student to draw a card. When it's Grace's turn, I lean forward in my seat so that I can see what she's picked.

The six of clubs.

Six. Six. Six.

I *have* to pull out a six. My whole plan hinges on this very moment.

When the teacher gets to my desk, I close my eyes and bite my lip in concentration. Grace and I always had this weird psychic connection. It never appeared when we were trying but it always seemed to work when we needed it most.

And right now, I need it more than anything!

I reach my hand into the hat and feel around. There are at least ten cards left. I try to *sense* which one could be the other six. I wait for one to speak to me.

It does.

This one!

My hand wraps around a playing card.

This is it! This is the one! I'm sure of it.

I pull the card out and hold it to my chest as Mr. Heath moves on to the boy sitting next to me, who looks extremely uninterested in the assignment. The hood of his sweatshirt is up and I'm pretty sure he's hiding a cell phone under his desk.

I suck in a huge breath and ever so carefully peek at the card, without letting anyone else see it.

My heart plummets.

It's a seven.

A seven!

So close!

I glance over at Hoodie Boy and my eyes widen when

I see the six of hearts sitting on his desk. He's barely even looking at it. His attention is back on the phone under his desk.

"Okay, everyone!" Mr. Heath says when the hat is empty. "Stand up and find your partner."

I start to panic. I have to be paired with Grace. I can't let this opportunity pass me by! I glance around the room for help. Everyone is slowly grumbling and rising from their seats to search out the student holding the matching card. My gaze lands on my neighbor's backpack on the floor and I'm struck with an idea.

Forget psychic abilities. Forget magic. It's time to *make* something happen for myself.

With my card safely tucked between my fingers, I stand up, trying to look innocent as I begin to make my way down the aisle. But my foot accidentally gets caught in the strap of Hoodie Boy's backpack and I go tumbling across his desk. The boy catches me, looking really annoyed by the whole thing. I think he dropped his phone in the scramble.

"Oh my gosh! I'm so sorry!" I exclaim. "I must have tripped."

The whole class is now staring at us.

"Adeline, are you okay?" Mr. Heath asks.

"Yup!" I say, bouncing up. "I'm just a superklutz! Sorry!"

I admit it was a louder crash than I anticipated and

I must have hit my side on the corner of Hoodie Boy's desk because it's suddenly throbbing in pain, but it was worth it.

I furtively look down at the new card in my hand.

The six of hearts.

Mission accomplished.

I JUST WANNA KNOW YOU

Grace does *not* look happy when I show her my card. I try not to let her reaction deter me. It's all temporary. She only *thinks* she doesn't like me. But that's because she thinks I'm still the shallow, snobby popular girl who films beauty tutorials and hangs out with Clementine Dumont.

But I'm different now. I'm not that girl. Maybe I was, in another version of my life, but I've made my choice. I don't want to be her. I want to be me. And I want to be friends with Grace.

"So," I say, smiling as I take the seat next to hers. "Do you want to meet up after school today and start working on the project?"

"I have science club after school," Grace says dismissively.

"That's okay," I chirp. "We can meet after!"

Grace raises her hand and Mr. Heath promptly calls

on her. "How much of our final grade does this project count for?"

The question definitely stings. Does she really hate me *that* much?

Mr. Heath gives Grace an impatient smile. "A large chunk of it, okay?"

Grace harrumphs and turns back to me. "We can meet after my club. Where?"

"My house?"

She sighs. "Fine."

❋

I tap my feet nervously against the coffee table as I take another sip of the large, overly sugared latte that I picked up from the Human Bean on the way home. It's cold now but I don't care. It gives me something to do with my hands. Although, in hindsight, I probably should have ordered a small. This thing is huge. I'm already so caffeinated I feel like my hair is going to buzz right off my scalp.

I spent the past hour getting the family room ready for Grace's arrival. I have her favorite Summer Crush album playing. I made a bowl of her favorite mix of cheddar and caramel popcorn—Grace has always been a super-fan of sweet and salty mixed together—and placed it on the coffee table. I even bought a few issues of Grace's favorite science magazine and spread them out on the side table.

Everything is perfect.

Now I just have to wait.

Although, I admit, the waiting is making me more anxious by the second. I didn't realize how many weird noises our house makes when it's empty. I jump at every little sound, thinking it's Grace knocking or Grace ringing the doorbell or Grace climbing over the fence in the backyard—which is just ridiculous because why would she do that?

I've tried to busy my mind by making a mental list of all the most memorable moments from our friendship. My plan is to *casually* drop a few into the conversation. You know, to *subtly* remind her of how great everything was when we were friends.

By the time she arrives, I'm so jumpy and nervous I have to clasp my hands together to keep myself from fidgeting.

"Hi," she mumbles when I open the door. I can tell she's uncomfortable being here. In my house. She tries to hide it but Grace does this weird ear-tugging thing when she's nervous and she's doing it now.

Buttercup ambles out of the kitchen to see who's here and I don't miss the elated surprise on Grace's face, although she definitely tries to hide it. "You got a dog," she says blankly. Like she's just commenting on the weather.

"Yeah. This is Buttercup. We got her two years ago. Buttercup, this is my best friend."

Grace winces at the title and I clear my throat. "I mean, this is . . . um . . . Grace Harrington."

I feel ridiculous. Why am I introducing Grace to the dog like she's an ambassador?

"I thought we could work in the family room," I say quickly, changing the subject.

"Sure. Whatever." Grace shrugs and Buttercup trots happily in front of us, leading the way.

Grace sets her bag down and sits on the couch, eyeing the popcorn on the coffee table.

I lift the bowl and offer it to her. "I made cheddar-caramel popcorn."

She shakes her head. "I'm not hungry."

Okay, so this is going to be harder than I thought. I need something to break the ice. Get the conversation rolling.

"How was science club? It sounds really fun. What do you guys do?"

"Let's just work on the project," Grace says tersely, getting a notebook out of her bag and clicking her pen.

"Okay." I bite my lip, trying not to let my confidence waver. This will work. I just need to have faith. I refresh my smile and keep my voice upbeat. "Why don't we start by making a list of things that *we're* nostalgic about and then hopefully one of those will spark an idea."

This is not a random suggestion. It's all part of my plan. I think it's quite brilliant, actually. If I can get Grace to talk about things from the past that make her happy, then I can easily segue into all the funny stories I have lined up to remind her of.

But Grace quickly dismisses my idea. "Let's just write a short story. I'll start it and then I'll email it to you and you can finish."

I frown. I know exactly what she's trying to do. She's trying to avoid spending time with me. I sit in silence for a moment as Berrin Mack croons the second verse of "I Just Wanna Know You" (Grace's favorite Summer Crush song) over the speakers.

"We're supposed to work on this together," I point out, hoping my voice doesn't sound as crushed as I feel.

Grace leans over her notebook, scribbling something. "I know. And we will. Just over email."

My eyes start to burn with tears. I fight to keep them at bay. "I don't think that's what Mr. Heath had in mind."

Grace crosses her arms. "Do you have a better idea?"

I think about what Lily told me yesterday. How I left Grace to fend for herself on the last English project we did together. We were planning to make a video but I ended up doing one myself. That's where all this animosity started. So that's where I need to make amends.

"Why don't we make a video?" I suggest, trying to sound casual, like this idea has just popped into my head.

I can see Grace flinch at the suggestion. "No," she says automatically, resuming her scribbles. I'm not even sure she's writing anything in there. I think she's just trying to avoid looking at me.

"Why not?"

"Because it's a terrible idea," she says, and I instantly feel her hostility.

I close my eyes, summoning strength. "Grace," I say gently. "If this is about what happened in seventh grade, then I can promise you I won't—"

But Grace cuts me off before I can even finish the sentence. "I don't want to make a video, okay?"

I bite my lip to keep the frustration from boiling over. Why won't she just talk to me about this? "Okay," I mumble for what feels like the tenth time in the past five minutes.

She taps the pen against her teeth. "I Just Wanna Know You" continues playing in the otherwise silent family room. It's almost at the best part. The final chorus, when all the boys join in on the harmonies and the guitars pick up and the drums do this awesome bum-di-bum-BUM thing, and then—

Grace slams her notebook down on the coffee table. "Argh! I can't even think with all this noise!" She grabs the remote and turns off the song.

The silence is suffocating. Now I feel like I really might cry. I squeeze my lips together tight.

Grace goes back to tapping her pen against her teeth. Now that the music is off, the sound is starting to grate on my nerves.

"I know," she says suddenly. "How about we do a slide show of the past sixteen years. We can show pictures of us with things that made us happy at that time. Like favorite toys or stuffed animals when we were little, or eating our favorite flavor of ice cream."

"Buying new clothes!" I add, getting excited.

She nods. "Yeah. And playing in the ball pit."

Buttercup lets out a bark, obviously getting just as into it as we are.

I laugh. "Yes, and getting you, Buttercup," I assure her.

Grace's face lights up, and for a minute I can almost see my twelve-year-old best friend in there. The one who used to get excited about tea parties and sleeping bag obstacle courses. "We can use the pictures to show not only how *we* changed, but how the things that made us happy changed, too."

I jump to my feet. "My mom has a ton of pictures of the two of us together as kids!"

Grace's smile instantly falls off her face and she looks down at her notebook again to write something. "Maybe we should just stick to individual pictures. With just one person in them. You know, to keep things simple."

My heart sinks into my chest with a thud. "Oh. Right. Okay, sure."

"So," she goes on without looking up. "Why don't we both go home and gather some photos, then we'll meet again tomorrow and start putting it all together with a script. Okay?" There's something about her voice as she says this. It sounds so rigid and formal. Like a robot.

"Okay," I agree. "Good idea."

She glances around the family room, her eyes landing momentarily on the stack of science magazines I put out, before drifting to the bowl of popcorn on the coffee table, which she still hasn't touched. "And," she begins stiffly, "I think it's best if we meet in the library from now on."

My whole body sags in defeat. "But isn't it more comfortable to meet here? Or we could do it at your house?"

"No," Grace says instantly. "The library is better."

I exhale. She is *not* making this easy on me.

"Okay," I agree, resigned. "We can meet there tomorrow."

Grace closes her notebook and puts it in her backpack before zipping it up.

That's it?

She's leaving already?

But she just got here.

She stands up and starts to walk toward the kitchen. I jump to my feet and follow after her, trying to come up with something to say that will make her change her mind about leaving. But everything that floods through my head—watch a TV show, choreograph a dance, listen to music—are all outdated suggestions of things Addie and Grace *used* to do together. And I realize I have absolutely no idea what Grace likes anymore. Since it's clearly not Summer Crush.

Grace pauses momentarily by the kitchen window, her gaze drifting outside. I follow her line of sight until I understand what has caught her eye. The yellow-and-white Victorian playhouse sits in the backyard like a relic. An ancient ruin abandoned by an indigenous tribe long ago.

"You still have it," she says, and her voice sounds funny. Almost scratchy.

"Yes!" I say, my spirits suddenly lifting. Maybe she'll want to go inside. Maybe she'll want to have a tea party for old times' sake. "My mom was talking about selling it, but I'm not sure that's such a good idea. It has so many memories, you know? It's . . ." I search for the right word. "Nostalgic!"

Grace is quiet for a really long time as she stares outside at our Hideaway. I don't say anything because I don't want to interrupt whatever thought process she's having. Maybe she's feeling sentimental about the past. Just like Rip van Winkle. Maybe all the amazing times we had in that playhouse are rushing back to her and she'll suddenly remember how good things used to be. Maybe she'll—

"Good idea," she finally says, stepping away from the window and swinging her backpack onto her shoulder.

My brow furrows. "What?"

"Selling it," she says, and once again, her voice has that emotionless robot tone. Then, before I can even react, she disappears out the front door, mumbling something about seeing me tomorrow.

TWO TEXT MESSAGES AND A VLOG

Later that night, an alarm goes off on my phone, reminding me that I'm supposed to be at Clementine's house in ten minutes to film our next vlog. I don't really want to go. For starters, I'm really mad at her for laughing at the video of me on YouTube (which unfortunately is still up and now has over five hundred views). But mostly, I've been working on our English project for the past few hours and I'm really getting into it. I'm finding so many fun old pictures from when we were kids.

But I also know I've been avoiding Clementine, and I don't want to just completely blow her off. Especially when I promised I'd be there. I can tell the vlog is very important to her—and to me. Well, at least to sixteen-year-old me.

So I go.

Reluctantly.

When Clementine opens the front door of her house, she looks really surprised to see me. Like she didn't expect me to show up at all. She jabs her tongue into the side of her cheek as she gives me a cold once-over. "Oh, look, you showed up," she says in the most sarcastic tone ever.

"Sorry, I've been kind of preoccupied the last few days."

"I know," she intones. "I saw the video."

I try to ignore her jab. "Can I come in?"

"Whatever." She turns and I follow her inside, closing the door behind me.

I've never actually been *in* the Dumonts' house before. I mean, sixteen-year-old me has, obviously, but I have no recollection of it. It's *amazing.* It has these high ceilings and fancy chandeliers and a kitchen that looks big enough to land a plane in. I try not to let my reaction show, since I'm supposed to hang out here all the time, but when Clementine leads me into the basement and I see that she has basically an entire movie studio set up down there, with professional-looking lights and cameras and different backdrops, I just can't help myself. The word comes tumbling out of my mouth.

"Wow!" I say, in awe.

"What?" she asks, looking around to try to locate what I'm so excited about.

I rein in my reaction. "It . . . looks great. That's all."

She narrows her eyes. "It hasn't changed since our last episode."

I shrug, playing it off. "I know. I just think it looks great."

Clementine shakes her head. "Whatever," she mumbles again. "Let's just get this over with."

She's really mad. I can feel it. And I guess I can't blame her. I've basically been ignoring her since Saturday.

"Clementine," I begin cautiously. "I'm sorry about—"

"Where were you all weekend?" she interrupts. The sudden hostility in her voice makes me flinch.

"I . . . I told you. I wasn't feeling well. I pretty much stayed in bed."

I feel bad about lying to the girl who's supposed to be my best friend. But if I told her the truth—that I was hanging out with Jacob Tucker and Lily Harrington all weekend—I think her head might explode.

She takes a step closer to me. For a second, I'm kind of scared of her. She looks pretty frightening right now with her body all rigid and her eyes squinty. "Oh, really?" she challenges. "You were *sick*?"

"Yeah," I say, taking a tiny step back.

"Are you sure?"

I chuckle, hoping it doesn't sound as fake and anxious as it does in my head. "Yes. I'm sure. I think I would remember. I felt horrible."

She presses her lips together, like she's thinking really

hard. And then, in an instant, the whole scary monster face just vanishes. Poof. Gone. Like a light switch has been turned off.

"Okay," she says in a light, airy voice. "Whatever you say." Then she turns around to start setting up the camera. "Let's start with the nail art. Did you bring your kit?"

Um, no. I didn't even know that I *had* a kit.

"Uh . . ." I hesitate. "I forgot it. Maybe we can use yours?"

If Clementine is mad about this, she doesn't show it. She just smiles and says, "Sure, no problem."

By the time we're halfway through filming the tutorial, I'm starting to get suspicious. Clementine has been completely chill and chipper this whole time. Possibly a little *too* chipper. Even when I totally mess up the daisy-print design on my nails because, let's face it, I've never done nail art before and my hands are shaking like jackhammers when I try to hold the dotting tool. I expect her nostrils to flare and fire to come out of her mouth, but she just calmly takes the polish from me and says, "That's okay. I'll do it. You film."

That's when I *know* something is up. She's being way too nice. I don't even remember her being this nice to me *before* I ditched her all weekend.

Something is definitely going on.

But I don't really have time to think about it, or try to analyze Clementine's weird behavior, because by the time we finish filming the nail-art tutorial and then the makeup tutorial and then the hair tutorial, it's almost eleven o'clock and I'm exhausted.

When I finally get home and crash into bed, I check my phone to find text messages from two different numbers I don't recognize. They aren't linked to any names in my contacts.

The first says:

Unknown: I had fun on Saturday. Should we do it again on Friday night? Maybe a movie?

My heart practically pounds right out of my chest.

Jacob Tucker?

He's the only person I saw on Saturday, besides Clementine. Well, and Jeff, my hairstylist, but I really don't think *he* would be texting me to see a movie.

It has to be from Jacob!

Oh my gosh. Jacob Tucker is asking me out. A *boy* is asking me out on a date. Like an official date. At the *movies*! It doesn't get more official than that.

Rory used to go on tons of dates to the movies. One weekend she actually saw the same movie three times with three different guys! It was crazy.

I don't need three different guys. Just the thought of going to the movies with one guy is enough to make my stomach churn. And it's Jacob! Which I still can't get over. I mean, four years ago the thought of sitting in the dark with Jacob Tucker would have made my stomach churn, too. But with nausea. Not with excitement like it's doing now.

He's so cute. And so funny.

AND HE LIKES ME!

He has to, right? Boys don't ask out girls they don't like.

Do they?

I don't know. After that whole flirting lesson Clementine gave me right before my disastrous dance with Connor, I'm totally confused on how the whole boy/girl-courting thing works. Am I supposed to text him back right away? Or am I supposed to wait?

Oh, who cares!

I quickly tap out a response.

Me: Yes! That sounds like so much fun! I can't wait!

Oh my gosh, what will I wear?

I'm already sorting through my closet, quickly ruling out options, when I remember there was a second text message on my phone from an unidentified number.

I pick it up again and read.

Unknown: Finding the best pics for our project. I think this is gonna be great. See you tomorrow!!! 😊

I nearly let out a sob of joy. It's from Grace. She texted me. With three exclamation points *and* a smiley face. This morning she would barely even look at me and now she's sending me emojis!

I save both numbers to my phone, trying to ignore the flash of annoyance that my sixteen-year-old self didn't even bother to *have* Grace's number stored. But that doesn't matter. That materialistic, rude, vapid version of me is gone, quickly being replaced by this new and improved version.

I sink to the floor next to my bed and hug the phone to my chest, feeling relief and happiness spread through every inch of my body.

Finally, *finally,* things are turning around.

LAUGHTER
NEVER CHANGES

When I walk into school the next morning, I immediately know something is wrong. Like that feeling you get in a scary movie, right before something horrible and grotesque jumps out from a closet. The hairs on my arm even stick up a little.

Last week, when I walked into this very same hallway for the first time in my new sixteen-year-old body, about twenty people either waved or stopped to say hi or blew up my phone with text messages.

Now it's absolutely silent.

Well, obviously the hallway itself isn't silent. There are tons of people bustling about, opening and closing locker doors, calling out to one another, talking on phones, but not *one* person seems to notice I'm here.

Is this about the YouTube video?

No, it can't be. If anything, I would think people would be laughing at me. Not ignoring me.

I got a text from Clementine this morning telling me she wasn't feeling well and I should go to school without her. I was actually kind of relieved to get it. Not because I wish her ill or anything, but because, I don't know, hanging out with her sometimes feels like so much work. Like I have to say all the right things and look the right way and pretend to be this person who I don't even really like.

I was grateful to be able to drive to school on my own. Plus, I'm getting really good at this whole driving thing. I got up to thirty-five miles per hour today! It was exhilarating! But now, I kind of wish I had her by my side. For moral support or something. Or maybe just so I can ask her what's going on, since she always seems to know.

I try to assure myself that I'm just being paranoid. Nothing is going on. I just happened to walk into school at a moment when no one I knew was there. No big deal. I'm sure everything will fall into place by the end of first period.

❋

Except it doesn't.

After trig, I pass at least five people I recognize from our lunch table, and not one of them acknowledges me. In fact, they kind of act like I'm not even there. And when I wave to Annabelle in the hallway, she doesn't wave back. She just gives me a blank look, like she doesn't know me and is trying to figure out why I'm doing this strange spastic movement with my hand.

But it isn't until I get to my second-period French class that I know, without a shadow of a doubt, that something is definitely wrong, because Clementine is sitting in her usual seat, looking *very* healthy. Her hair and makeup are especially awesome, like she spent *extra* time getting ready today.

"Hi," I say numbly as I slide into the seat next to her. "I thought you said you were sick."

She gives me a huge smile that never reaches her eyes. I immediately know it's fake because I've seen her give the exact same smile to about a dozen people. People she would soon after call "losers."

My stomach swoops.

"I guess I'm feeling better," Clementine chirps in an extra-fake, sugary tone. "Isn't that amazing? How you can tell someone you're sick and then . . ." She shrugs and gives her hair a toss. "I don't know, just *not* be?"

I stare at her in confusion. "Are you mad at me or something?"

She tilts her head, like she's talking to a lost child. "No. Why would I be mad at you?"

Okay, I've watched enough high school movies to know that when a girl like Clementine says something like that, it has at least twenty hidden meanings layered underneath.

I'm about to ask her another question, but then the

bell rings and the teacher starts blabbing in incomprehensible French again. And when class is over, Clementine jumps out of her seat so fast, I barely even have time to make eye contact, let alone talk to her.

I would try to track her down, but I don't know her class schedule. Or her locker number. And when I find her at her usual lunch table and try to sit down, Annabelle turns to me and says, "I'm sorry. This table is full today." Then she rejoins the conversation and Clementine doesn't even look up.

I'm so confused my head hurts.

What is *Annabelle* doing there? I thought Clementine was boycotting her for stealing her parking space. Now they're chatting and giggling like besties.

And why is Clementine so mad at me?

Is it because I screwed up the nail-art tutorial yesterday? Or maybe because I've been acting so strange? Did she finally just give up on me?

I carry my tray around the cafeteria, looking for a place to sit. I see Grace sitting with some of her marching-band friends, but the table seems really packed and I don't want to press my luck with her.

I finally find a completely empty table near the back and plop down by myself. I guess I'm eating alone today.

I grab a french fry from my tray—for the record, high school food is *so* much better than middle school food!—and stuff it into my mouth.

So Clementine is mad at me? Do I really care? What-ever it is, I'm sure she'll get over it soon enough and we'll go back to being friends.

Friends.

The word echoes in my brain like a ball bouncing down a long, empty hallway.

Why *are* we friends? It's still a mystery that I haven't managed to solve yet. Sure, we run a successful vlog to-gether and seem to hang out together all the time, but she's not really that nice. Especially not to people she doesn't deem worthy of being in her circle.

Why do I even hang out with her?

What does sixteen-year-old me see in her?

A tray plops down in front of me, startling me out of my thoughts, and I look up to see Jacob climbing into the empty bench across from me. My face instantly lights up.

"Hi!"

"Hi," he says, but his tone is more cautious than mine. "What are you doing way over here all by yourself? Don't you normally eat with Clementine and her minions?"

I choke out a laugh. Minions. That's the perfect word for those girls. They follow her around, doing everything she says in an effort to get her attention.

And then it hits me. *That's* why no one has talked to me today! Clementine must have told them not to.

"I think I've been given a time-out," I say, rolling my eyes and taking a sip of my fruit punch.

Jacob cracks open his soda. "That sounds so middle school."

I laugh. "Right?"

He takes a sip from the can. "So, what horrific, unforgivable sin did you commit? Did you wear the same outfit as her? Or say that her bracelet made her wrist look fat? No, no, I know!" He holds up a finger. "You insulted the shoes. Tsk, tsk. You should know better."

I'm laughing so hard, I'm surprised fruit punch doesn't squirt out of my nose.

"So which is it?" Jacob asks.

"That's the thing! I don't even know what I did."

He glances over at Clementine's table and I follow his gaze. I catch Clementine looking at us before quickly turning back to her conversation, letting out a loud, obnoxious giggle at something Annabelle just said.

"Well, whatever," Jacob says. "Forget her. You can do way better."

My gaze automatically drifts over to Grace's table. She's laughing, too. But her laugh seems so much more real. In fact, I immediately notice that it's the exact same laugh she's had all her life. I used to call it her Chip 'n' Dale impersonation because it reminded me of the way a cartoon chipmunk would laugh. It's so infectious. I can't remember a time when Grace started laughing that I didn't eventually join in.

Even now, watching her from across the cafeteria, I feel my cheeks quiver.

Is that one of those things that my mom was talking about? Something that stays the same no matter how much changes around you?

As I watch Grace chatting with her new friends, I suddenly find myself wondering if *my* laugh has stayed the same after four years.

Somehow I doubt it. And that makes me the saddest of all.

CLOSING DOORS

Grace and I meet every day after school in the library to work on our nostalgia project and by Thursday we've nearly finished our presentation. It has so much good stuff in it. In addition to all the things we loved when we were younger—toys and fairy tales and tea parties—Grace also included pictures of herself in more recent years. She has a great photo from her first concert. She went to see a band I've never heard of, but she looks pretty happy about it. There's also a photo of her at one of her marching-band competitions, all dressed up in her fancy blue-and-white uniform. But I especially love the picture of her taken at her first homecoming dance, posing in her dress next to a really cute boy with floppy hair. She admitted that the boy ended up breaking her heart a few months later, but she wanted to include the picture in our presentation because, at the time the picture was taken, she was happy.

And when she thinks about him, she's nostalgic for that time.

Of course, I don't know this boy. Grace said he goes to a neighboring high school. But as she told me the story of their breakup, I soon realized that by skipping over the past four years, I haven't just missed out on stuff in my *own* life. I've missed out on stuff in Grace's life, too.

I try not to think about that, though. I try to focus on the fact that Grace and I have made excellent progress this week. Not just on the presentation, but on our friendship, too. Every time we've gotten together, it's been like old times again.

Well, almost. I can still feel Grace holding back somewhat. She still won't talk about what happened in seventh grade. And she still insisted that we crop each other out of all the photos we're in together, which made me incredibly depressed for a while, but it's all good. We've still come a long way since the night of the dance.

On Thursday afternoon, after we've edited and pasted in the final pictures and put the finishing touches on our script, Grace clicks Save and closes the lid of her laptop. "Well, that's it. I think we're done."

I smile. "I like it."

She grins back. "I like it, too. I think Mr. Heath will give us a good grade."

I feel my smile fading. "But besides the good grade, you had fun this week, right?"

Grace looks away and starts packing up her stuff. "Yeah, sure," she says breezily.

"Grace—" I begin, but I'm cut off when I hear footsteps approaching our table.

I look up to see Clementine towering over us with her hands on her hips and a really annoyed expression on her face. "So this is my replacement, huh? This is who you've been ditching me for all week? A loser band geek?"

I notice the pain flash over Grace's face as she quickly finishes packing up her things. "I better go," she mumbles.

I, on the other hand, am completely speechless. I can't believe Clementine would say that. And right to Grace's face! It's the final straw.

"She's not a loser band geek!" I fire back, fully aware that I'm not using my library voice. But I don't care. "She's my friend!"

Clementine snorts. "Yeah, you pick real winners, Adeline. Annabelle said she saw you hanging out with a middle schooler at the Human Bean this weekend. When you *claimed* to be sick."

I wince. She's right. I did lie about that.

So *that's* why Clementine's been so mad at me. Annabelle ratted me out. Is that why Clementine lifted the boycott on her? Because she sold me out? Gosh, I can't keep up with all this drama. It's like a reality show in these hallways.

"It's not like you have any right to be mad," I retort. "You're the one who's been ignoring me all week! *And* you got all of your little . . . minions to ignore me, too!"

Clementine wrinkles her nose. "I'm sorry. Did you say *minions*?"

"Yes! They follow you around and do whatever you say. Like little puppets. But you know what? I'm sick and tired of being your minion. I'm not going to do it anymore. I don't need you to tell me where to go or what to say or how to do my makeup. I'm my own person, and—"

"You are *not* your own person," Clementine harshly cuts me off. "I *made* you. You were nothing before me. You were a loser just like her."

Grace zips up her bag and stands up. I can tell she's desperate to get out of here. I don't blame her. I'm desperate to get out of here, too.

"Grace, wait," I say, but she shakes her head and bolts out of the library.

I hastily stuff all my things into my bag and start to follow her. Clementine grabs me by the arm. "Do you want to tell me what on earth is your problem? You've been acting crazy all week."

"No," I snap, glaring down at her hand on my arm. "I've finally been acting *sane*." Then I break loose from her grasp and head for the door, leaving Clementine fuming and alone in the middle of the science fiction section.

As soon as I get outside, I scan the parking lot for

Grace. I spot her hurrying down the center aisle to her car. I run to catch up to her. "Grace! Wait!" I call out.

But she doesn't slow until she reaches her car and presses a button on the key to unlock it. "Addie, just leave me alone," she calls over her shoulder.

"No," I say sternly. "I won't. I'm so sorry for what she said back there. She's . . . a horrible person."

"Who *you* hang out with," Grace reminds me as she opens the car door and tosses her backpack inside.

I grab her shoulder and turn her around. "Who I *used* to hang out with," I correct her, pleading with my eyes for her to listen to me. To believe me. To forgive me.

"But I'm done," I whisper, my voice cracking. "I'm done with Clementine. I don't know why we were friends. I don't even know how we got to *be* friends."

Grace narrows her eyes at me, like she's trying to figure out if I'm joking or not. "Wasn't it after your stupid *Romeo and Juliet* music video?"

A rock sinks into the bottom of my stomach and lands with a thud.

Suddenly it makes so much sense.

Too much sense.

I ditched Grace and left her to fend for herself on our seventh-grade project. I filmed a music video starring my cool and popular older sister and her drop-dead gorgeous boyfriend. Clementine must have liked it and started hanging out with me after that.

I lost one friend but gained another. On the very same day. With the very same project.

I feel physically sick. Like I might actually throw up all over the hood of Grace's car.

I was so obsessed with doing something cool and mature, I was so obsessed with growing up, that it cost me the best thing in my life: my friendship with Grace.

Tears well up in my eyes. "Grace, I'm so sorry about what I did. I was an idiot. I was a horrible friend."

Grace doesn't respond. She looks down and fiddles with the keys in her hand.

"I just want to be friends again," I go on. "That's why I stole the six of hearts card, so we could—"

Her head pops up and she glares at me. "You did what?"

"I stole the card from my neighbor."

"You mean you didn't *pick* the six of hearts?"

I shake my head. Why is she getting so wrapped up in this one little detail? "No. I picked the seven of spades. I pretended to trip and fall so I could swap my card with the guy sitting next to me."

"You cheated," she says coldly.

"Maybe a little," I admit, "but it was only because you wouldn't talk to me and I was so desperate to hang out again and try to fix things. Grace, I want to be your best friend again."

Grace's face is unreadable for a moment. She stares at

me with a stony expression and I have no idea what she's thinking. Clearly, she can't still be focused on this stupid technicality. Clearly, she has to understand what I'm trying to say. I did this for *her*. For us.

"Grace," I say gently. "You can't keep getting so hung up on the rules."

"And you can't keep *breaking* the rules!" she snaps, her face turning red, just like it used to do when she was a kid. "You're always doing that. You're always trying to find a way around things. You never want to do any of the hard work. You're always looking for the easiest way to get somewhere."

"You think this is the easy way?" I can't hold the tears back any longer. "You have no idea how hard this has been for me. You have no idea what it's like to wake up and realize that you've lost your best friend, the most important thing in your life, and not be able to fix it. Trust me, this *isn't* the easy way. There's no way it could be. This is the hardest possible way I've ever gone. And I wish you would just let me fix it."

Grace stares at me for a long time, her gaze hard and unforgiving. Finally, she shakes her head. "I'm sorry, Addie. But it's too late. You already threw it all away."

She gets into her car and I desperately grab for the door handle, to keep her from closing it. "Please," I say, tears choking the word. "Don't leave."

Grace bites her lip, like she's trying to fight back

tears of her own. Then, once she's regained control of her voice, she says, "Stop banging on a door that's already closed."

Then she pulls the car door from my grip and slams it shut.

THE INFAMOUS
HAIR FLIP

I stand in the parking lot for a long time, just staring at the empty space where Grace's car used to be. My phone vibrates in my bag, jolting me from my trance. I pull it out and look at the screen.

Jacob: Hey! At the Human Bean! Come hang w/me?
😉 ☕ 🍪

I let out a sigh and close my eyes. I don't really feel like being social right now. I just want to go home. But then I think about exactly what's waiting for me when I get there. An empty house, a closet full of sparkly clothes that have lost their sparkle, an old playhouse that my mom wants to sell, and a dog who might be cute but who fails miserably in the field of giving sage advice. And I could definitely use some of that right now. Plus, the idea of seeing a friendly face is very tempting.

I just lost two best friends in the span of an hour.

I open my eyes and type out a reply.

Me: Okay.

The parking lot at the Human Bean is full so I have to park two streets away and walk. When I get inside, the place is hopping. It looks like an extension of the high school hallway. Everyone talking loudly, playing on their phones, and sipping lattes like they're in a commercial for coffee.

It's funny how I used to want nothing more than to come here and just hang out. Just be one of the cool kids. But now this place makes me feel queasy. Like I'm an imposter who doesn't fit in.

No matter how grown-up I might look on the outside, I still feel like I'm twelve years old.

I spot Jacob right away. He's sitting on one of the couches in the corner. I start to make my way over to him but slow when I notice that he's not alone. Sitting right next to him is a girl with long, wavy blond hair. Her back is to me, but strangely enough, she looks a lot like Clementine.

Of course, I know it's *not* Clementine. She has made it quite clear she doesn't want anything to do with Jacob Tucker, and Jacob has made it pretty clear he doesn't think too highly of her either.

But as I approach the table, I hear a familiar voice coming from the couch. It sounds *exactly* like Clementine.

"You are too funny! How did I never know you were this funny?" The girl squeals with laughter and then tosses a long lock of hair over her shoulder.

I freeze on the spot.

I know that voice.

I know that laugh.

I know that hair flip.

It's her. It has to be her. No one else can rock a hair flip like Clementine Dumont.

But *why*?

Why is she here with Jacob? She thinks he's a big loser. She told me so!

I stare in stunned silence as she cuddles up close to him, like she's trying to climb right into his lap, and plants a kiss on his cheek.

Then she turns and looks me right in the eye, giving me the most menacing smile I've ever seen. Jacob turns to see who she's looking at and his face drains of color. His eyes widen as he quickly pushes himself off the couch, nearly knocking Clementine onto the floor in the process.

He starts moving toward me, but it's too late. I'm already running out the door. I don't stop when I get to the sidewalk. I keep running. My heart is thudding in my chest; my breathing is strained but I don't dare stop.

How could she?

How could he?

I thought he liked me. I thought he had a crush on

me! Isn't that what he implied at the dance? Isn't that why he asked me out on a date? We're supposed to go to the movies tomorrow night. So why is he cozying up to Clementine at the Human Bean? And why would he text me to come hang out with him if he was already here with *her*? What kind of awful person does that?

Maybe he never liked me at all. Maybe he was just using me to get to Clementine.

I'm halfway to my car when I hear him shout behind me. "Addie! Slow down! Wait!"

But I don't slow down. I don't wait. I just run faster.

SLOBBERY
SWAMP BALL

When I get behind the wheel of the car, tears are already streaming down my face. I turn the key in the ignition and drive as fast as I can (a reckless forty-five miles per hour) back home. I park the car in the driveway, run into the house, and slam the front door behind me. Then I just collapse against the wall. I'm crying so hard I can't see straight and I can't breathe.

Why would Clementine do that to me? I thought she was my friend. Grace would never do anything like that. Ever. Because Grace was a real friend. Clementine is . . . Well, I don't even know what she is.

I don't know what anything is!

What is this life? Who have I become?

Sixteen was supposed to be amazing. It was supposed to be perfect. There weren't supposed to be sloppy

"What?" I ask. "Go ahead. Go outside. You don't have to ask my permission."

But she doesn't move. She just watches me, her big brown eyes pleading and pathetic.

I let out a sigh. "Okay. Let's go."

I open the door and she runs out, checking three times to make sure I'm following her. As I step outside, I try to ignore the yellow-and-white playhouse at the far side of the backyard, but it's so big it's like trying to ignore an elephant in a minivan. This backyard *is* that playhouse. It's so crammed full of memories. It's so painful to look at, knowing that what I had inside those walls I will never have again.

Buttercup finds a tattered tennis ball in the grass (which was probably yellow at some point but now looks like the color of a swamp) and scoops it into her mouth before dropping it at my feet.

"You're right," I say, "I need the distraction." I pick up the ball, cringing at how slobbery and slimy it feels. I throw it as hard as I can across the lawn. She darts away and is back in an instant, dropping it in front of me again. I throw it and she's off, but this time she doesn't come back right away, and when I follow after to figure out what's taking so long, I spot her standing upright with her paws on the windowsill of the Hideaway, whimpering. That's when I notice that the window of the playhouse is open. The ball must have landed inside.

Well, there's no way I'm going in there after it.

I walk up to Buttercup and grab her by the collar, pulling her down from the windowsill. "C'mon," I urge. "Let's go back inside."

She immediately wrenches free from my grasp and jumps back up onto the window, letting out a pathetic little cry.

"I'm not going in there," I tell her.

She turns her head to me and pants, begging with her dark eyes.

"Just forget it. Let it go! It's gone, Buttercup. It's . . ." My voice shatters and I start sobbing all over again. "It's gone," I whisper through my tears.

I step up to the window and pull her back down again. As I do, I can just make out a sliver of the Hideaway's interior through the open window. There's a Summer Crush poster on the wall. It's dusty and slanted. One of the pushpins probably fell out. It makes me cry even harder.

Buttercup must sense my distress, because she finally gives up on the ball and jumps down, trotting eagerly to the house.

"I know what we need," I say as I follow her. "A Summer Crush marathon. That will definitely make us feel better."

I grab my phone and trudge up the stairs to my room. Buttercup jumps on the bed and lies down next to me, ready for the party to begin. I search my phone's music library, disappointed when I find there's nothing in here that I recognize. And not a single Summer Crush song.

"No wonder I'm such a miserable person at age sixteen," I tell Buttercup. "I don't have any good songs to cheer me up!"

I navigate to the music store app and search "Summer Crush." To my confusion, the only albums that show up are the four I already own.

Huh. That's weird.

Why hasn't Summer Crush released a single new album in the past four years?

I click open the Web browser and type their name into a Google search.

That's when the final jagged pieces of my already-shattered world come crumbling down around me. That's when it feels like my life really is *over.*

Summer Crush broke up two years ago.

RETURN OF
THE STARFISH DRESS!

I lie in my bed and cry for what feels like hours. I watch the YouTube video of me attempting to dodge the marching feet of a hundred musicians over and over and over. It's up to seven hundred views now. Although to be fair, a bunch of those are mine.

I suppose I could email YouTube and ask them to take it down. But I find the video strangely fitting. There I am, trying to survive in a jungle that I don't fit into. Trying to avoid being crushed to death by a world that I don't understand.

Grace wants nothing to do with me. Clementine betrayed me. The whole school is ignoring me. My life has fallen apart. And according to the article I read online, after Summer Crush broke up, Berrin released a solo album that everyone hated, Maddox started a line of designer cologne, and Donovan and Cole both ended up on bad reality shows.

Life can't get much worse than that.

The house is so quiet. My parents aren't home from work yet.

It's just me and Buttercup. She lies on my bed like the loyal friend she is. My *only* friend now.

When my tears are all dried up, I peer around my bedroom. My new, fancy, sixteen-year-old bedroom with its black-and-white motifs and hot pink accents and framed photographs on the wall. I wonder when I decided to redecorate. I wonder if Clementine helped me pick things out. I wonder how different this room would have been if Grace and I had decorated it together.

At first glance, it seems like the bedroom of my dreams. With a closet full of amazing clothes and a drawer full of makeup and a reflection in the mirror that embodies everything I've always wanted.

And yet the room feels so terribly empty. It was decorated by a stranger. And now I feel like a foreigner living in it. A trespasser.

I get up and open my closet door, sighing when I see all the beautiful clothes inside. Cute tops and short skirts and dresses that don't have glittery marine life on them. And suddenly, all I want is to step into my old closet. To put on my old clothes. All I want is that stupid blue-and-white striped starfish dress.

I'm about to shut the door again when something sparkly on the top shelf catches my eye. I glance up and my hopes instantly rise.

La Boîte aux Rêves Cachés.

I'd almost forgotten all about it! Why didn't I think of this before? The answer is so easy!

If locking the wish inside is how I got into this mess, then unlocking the wish should get me out of it.

Carefully, I pull the box down and carry it over to my bed. With a deep breath, I lift the lid. But it won't budge. I yank harder. Nothing.

Then I remember the last thing Mrs. Toodles said to me before I left that night.

"Be sure to hide the key in the safest place you can think of. If you lose it, your wish will be locked inside the box forever."

The key! I need to find that key! I try desperately to recollect the last time I saw it. I distinctly remember leaving it in the lock the night of my twelfth birthday and vowing to find a safe place to hide it the next morning.

But the next morning I woke up here. In this body. With this life. And a *huge* gap in my memory.

Which means, sometime in the past four years, I hid that key.

But just like with everything else that's happened in those four years, I have no hope of remembering it.

With determination, I march into my closet and start tearing everything from the shelves. I search every pocket of every pair of pants and every sweatshirt. I search boxes and bags and old backpacks. I empty every drawer in my nightstand and desk and dresser. I even check all my eye shadow palettes, thinking I might have hidden the key inside one of them.

By six o'clock, my room looks like it's been ransacked by the bad guys in a spy movie. And I still don't have the key. I sit on my bed (which I've torn all the sheets and covers from and even flipped the mattress of) and try to catch my breath. Buttercup left a long time ago, obviously not wanting to get involved. Smart dog.

I stare at the piles of clothes littering my carpet and consider checking all the pockets again. Then, suddenly, I realize something and slap myself in the forehead.

Of course the key wouldn't be in *those* clothes. I didn't have those clothes when I was twelve!

I jump to my feet, grab the jewelry box, and run down the stairs to the basement, where Mom keeps our old stuff. After scouring all the boxes, I finally find one labeled "Addie's Clothes" and pull it down. It's heavy, and I nearly fall over from the weight of it. Once I wrestle it to the ground, I rip it open and start pulling out all my old clothes. Jeans that I thought were too childish because they had pink stitching on the back pocket, a sweater I never wore because it had a frilly lace trim, and . . .

Oh my gosh!

I nearly start bawling all over again when I shake out the blue-and-white starfish dress. I hug it to my chest and bury my face in it. It smells old and musty but I don't care. It's suddenly the most special thing in the world.

I check every item of clothing that has a pocket but there's still no key. And now I've just made another mess.

Where would I have put it?

"Be sure to hide the key in the safest place you can think of. If you lose it, your wish will be locked inside the box forever."

I rack my brain, trying to come up with the safest place I would have thought of at age twelve. Which shouldn't be that hard. I'm technically still twelve now.

What's the safest place I can think of?

A bank? A vault? A secret government compound?

Gah!

This is hopeless!

I leap to my feet and pick up the jewelry box again, staring it down like I'm staring down an enemy in a duel. I try one last time to pry the lid open but it's like it's superglued shut. This is so stupid. The thing is hundreds of years old. It shouldn't be this hard to break open.

Break open . . .

The thought nearly knocks me onto my butt.

I can't do that. This is an antique. Mrs. Toodles's family heirloom. Not to mention, a box with magic powers! I can't just destroy it.

But honestly, what choice do I have? I'm running out of options. I have no idea where else I would have hidden that key, just like I have no idea how to pronounce Trigostronomy. Or speak French. Or write text messages in top-secret emoji code. All that knowledge is lost in the giant black hole in my brain.

For all I know, I could have thrown the key away years ago!

No. This is my only option.

With a deep breath, I cradle the jewelry box close to my chest and walk over to my dad's workbench. I gently set the box down and grab a hammer from the rack on the wall.

"I'm sorry, Mrs. Toodles," I say softly. "I'm sorry, Starlit Lady."

Then I close my eyes, raise the hammer back, and send it flying.

SEEING GHOSTS

I keep my eyes shut tight, afraid of the carnage that lies before me. When I finally get the courage to open them, I hold my breath.

The box is still in one piece.

Actually, it doesn't appear to have even a single dent in it.

Did I miss?

I glance around for something else that might have been smashed with my bad aim, but everything looks exactly as it was.

That's weird.

I inhale a huge breath and try again. This time, I keep my eyes open. I pull the hammer way over my head, gripping it sturdily with both hands. Then I bring it crashing down toward the bench. It's a direct hit. I actually *see* it smash straight into the top of the jewelry box.

And yet, I might as well have brushed it with a feather. *La Boîte aux Rêves Cachés* doesn't even have a scratch. Frustration boils inside me. I grab the box and angrily hurl it toward the cement wall. It bounces off like a Ping-Pong ball and lands on the ground, completely unharmed.

But I do notice a small scuff mark on the wall.

How is this even possible? Does the box have an ancient spell on it? Is it made from some eighteenth-century indestructible material that I've never heard of? Antique jewelry boxes shouldn't be this durable. There's got to be a way to bust it open.

I grab the Box of Hidden Dreams and the starfish dress for good luck and run back upstairs to my room. I plop down in front of my laptop and search:

"Box of Hidden Dreams Starlit Lady"

No results.

I try it in French, checking my spelling in an online French dictionary as I go.

"La boîte aux rêves cachés dame étoilée"

Nothing.

Which, I suppose, makes sense. Mrs. Toodles said it was a secret that's been passed down for generations. She said no one knew about the jewelry box or its magical powers. But wouldn't there at least be something about the Starlit Lady? If she was arrested and executed, wouldn't there be a historical record of that?

Someone *has* to know more about this!

I let out a sudden gasp, close my laptop, and sprint down the stairs, crashing right into my mom, who's coming in from the garage looking tired and cranky.

"Whoa!" she says, steadying me by the shoulders. "Where's the fire?" She studies my face. "Have you been crying?"

I hastily wipe at my cheeks. "I'm going to see Mrs. Toodles. I have to talk to her."

Mom stares at me for a long moment. Her expression changes from confusion to concern.

"Adeline," she says, and I don't miss the way her grip on my shoulders tightens. "Are you okay? Do you have a temperature?" She holds her hand against my forehead.

I brush it away. "I'm fine. I'm just going to run over there really quickly. I'll be right back."

Mom releases my shoulders and presses her fingertips into her eyelids. When she finally looks at me again, her face is pale and ashen. Like she's just seen a ghost.

"I'm worried about you, sweetie," Mom says. "You've been acting so strange lately. Are you getting enough sleep? Are your classes too stressful this semester? Maybe we should—"

"Mom," I interrupt impatiently, trying to step past her. "I said, I'm fine."

But I don't get very far. My mom's hand whips out like a ninja's and grabs me by the elbow. "Clearly you're not fine!" she snaps, and I startle at her tone. She sounds stressed and agitated.

"Adeline," Mom says, regaining her composure. She gently guides me into the kitchen. For a long time, she just stares at me with that same anxious look in her eyes, and I worry that she's not going to say anything else.

That I'll be waiting the rest of my life for her to finish that sentence.

Then she says, "Mrs. Toodles died last year."

CHEATER, CHEATER, GREEN-SLIME EATER!

I lie in my bed on Friday morning, unable to get up. I can't feel my legs. I'm so cold. My whole body is so cold.

I never got to say goodbye.

I'll never see her again.

That's why no one answered the door. That's why there were blinds in the window instead of curtains.

I never got to say goodbye.

Well, maybe sixteen-year-old me said goodbye. Maybe sixteen-year-old me went to visit Mrs. Toodles every week just like I used to. But that doesn't make me feel any better. And somehow I find it hard to believe that's true.

Sixteen-year-old me was probably too busy being cool and popular and filming makeup tutorials with her shallow best friend to bother visiting a senile old lady with dementia.

Mrs. Toodles was probably just another "unimportant" thing to fall off her list.

"You don't have to go," Mom says to me for the third time that morning. She's sitting on my bed, pushing hair back from my face to check my temperature again. Her frown tells me I still don't have one and that confuses her. She thinks I'm sick. Like really sick. She thinks that's why I've been acting so weird.

And who knows? Maybe she's right. Maybe I *am* really, really sick.

Maybe this whole thing has been nothing more than a feverish delusion while I lie in a hospital bed, dying from malaria or smallpox or the plague.

Maybe none of it is actually happening.

Wouldn't that be nice?

"I'm sure your teachers would understand," Mom says. "I'll call the front office. I'll even call in sick too so I can stay with you."

"No," I tell her, finally finding the strength to push the covers from my body. It's even colder out there than it is in here. "I have to go. I have to give a presentation in English."

Today is the big day, when Grace and I present our nostalgia project to the class, and I won't abandon her again.

I roll out of bed and drag myself to the bathroom.

"Are you sure?" Mom calls after me.

"I'm one hundred percent positive," I call back. Then I shut the door.

I stare into the mirror. That strange, unfamiliar

sixteen-year-old reflection stares back at me. Funnily enough, I'm starting to get used to seeing her. She's starting to feel a bit more normal.

I don't know if she'll ever fully feel like me. But for now, we're in this together. We have to make it work.

"You can do this," I tell myself and the girl in the mirror. "*We* can do this. You may not look like me and I may not feel like you but we're all we've got now. So let's just try to make the most of it, okay?"

She gives me a weak smile in return. I figure that's the most I'm going to get right now, but I'll take it.

With a reluctant sigh, I turn away from my reflection and start the shower.

I admit that the idea of facing Clementine again and seeing Jacob Tucker and all those people makes my knees almost give out, but I'm doing this. I'm doing what I should have done four years ago.

For Grace.

❋

I pick out something simple to wear: a pair of jeans and a baby-pink T-shirt. I'm sure Clementine would highly disapprove. I'm sure it's not nearly up to snuff by her standards, but I don't care. It doesn't matter. Clementine and I aren't friends anymore. She doesn't get to comment on my clothes.

I brush out my wet hair, tie it into a simple braid over my left shoulder, and skip the makeup drawer, mostly because I'm just too lazy to bother with it. But also because I'm still not sure what I'm doing with all that stuff.

When I walk into the kitchen, Mom is blending her power smoothie. She's dressed in one of her smart suits again, obviously having decided to go to work now that I've decided to go to school.

She shuts off the noisy blender when she sees me. "Hi, sweetie. How are you feeling?"

I shrug. "Fine."

It's a lie. I don't feel fine. I feel empty and cold and sad. I feel like someone pulled a giant rug right out from under me. Except instead of it being a rug, it was my whole life.

I collapse into one of the chairs at the kitchen table. "Actually, that's not true," I admit, tears threatening to flow again. "I feel horrible."

Mom pours her green goo into a glass and comes over to the table. She pulls out the chair next to mine and sits. "Do you want to talk about it?"

I lift my head and glance out the window into the backyard. From here, I'm just able to see the roof of the Hideaway. It used to be my favorite place in the world. Now it just stands there, abandoned. Left behind to gather dust and memories.

"I cheated," I whisper toward the house.

But it's my mom who hears. She rests a reassuring hand on top of mine. "Like on a test?"

"On everything."

Mom frowns. "I'm afraid I'm not following."

I think about what Grace told me yesterday, after she found out I'd switched the playing cards so that I could be her partner for the project.

She's right. I do always look for the easiest way to get places.

That's exactly how I got here. In this mess. Because I cheated. I wanted a shortcut to growing up. I wanted to be sixteen so badly, I didn't care how I got there, or what I'd miss along the way. Rory's graduation and my first day of high school and my first kiss and the day I got my cell phone and my sixteenth birthday and Buttercup as a puppy.

I don't want to skip over all those things. I want to *live* those things.

I don't want to take the shortcut. I don't want to take the easy way. I want to go back and do it right.

But I can't. The indestructible jewelry box is locked and the only other person who even knows about it is gone.

"I grew up too fast," I finally admit to my mom.

Concern flashes over her face. "What do you mean? Are you in some kind of trouble?"

"No," I mumble. "Never mind."

She pulls me into a hug and I let her. I rest my cheek on her chest like I used to do when I was little and she strokes my wet hair. It may not solve all my problems but, I admit, it feels good.

"I know what you need," Mom says, kissing my head.

"I doubt that," I tell her.

But then a second later her voice deepens, her body stiffens, and a low growl rumbles in the back of her throat. "The Yeti Forgetti *always* knows what you need."

I let out a girly shriek as her hands dig into my sides and she starts tickling me. I squirm and laugh and try to get away. But my mom is still as strong as ever and she keeps me trapped in her arms, tickling relentlessly.

"Mom!" I squeal. "Stop!"

"Who is Mom?" the Yeti Forgetti booms.

"Yeti Forgetti!" I plead. "Stop!"

"The Yeti Forgetti can't stop! The Yeti Forgetti needs more tickles!"

By the time I manage to wriggle away, I'm breathless and red-faced and Buttercup is barking relentlessly, wanting to get in on the game.

I may not have forgotten everything that was bothering me, but she was right. It was exactly what I needed.

Mom laughs and stands up, smoothing down her hair, which has gotten totally disheveled. "Here," she says, pushing her green sludge smoothie toward me. "You can have this one. I'll make another."

I sniff it and take a tentative sip.

It's not half bad. I down it in two gulps.

"You should get going," Mom says, pouring more ingredients into the blender. "Or you'll be late."

I stand up and toss my schoolbag over my shoulder. "Thanks, Mom," I say.

I'm not really talking about the smoothie. But I think she knows that.

She smiles. "Anytime."

THE WINKY-FACE
CONSPIRACY

When I get to school, Jacob is waiting for me on the front steps. Seeing him there all alone, looking kind of lost, I get a strange sense of déjà vu. For the first time since I woke up in this life, he looks like the Jacob Tucker I remember from Sky View Middle School. Not because he's magically shrunk or regained all his baby fat. It's something in his eyes I can't pinpoint. A piece of him that hasn't changed.

Then I notice he's holding a can of Grape Crush.

I crack the tiniest of smiles but then recall that the last time I saw him he was cuddling with Clementine in the middle of the Human Bean and I quickly banish that expression.

He sees me and comes rushing over. "Addie," he says breathlessly. "We have to talk."

I push past him and start to climb the steps. "I have nothing to talk to you about. You were using me to get to Clementine. It's fine."

"What?" He nearly croaks the word. "No! That's not what happened at all." He leaps in front of me, forcing me to stop. "Please, just listen."

I fold my arms across my chest, willing myself not to cry. But every time I think of Clementine leaning over to kiss his cheek, my eyes sting.

He takes a deep breath before he begins talking a mile a minute. "It was all her. I swear! I was just sitting there reading and she came over and started talking to me. I tried to get her to leave but she wouldn't take a hint. And then she wouldn't stop flirting with me and trying to kiss me. It was so weird!"

"So," I say, still suspicious. "You didn't text me to come meet you for coffee just to make me jealous?"

"Text you?" Jacob looks confused. "I didn't text you anything about coffee."

With a sigh, I take my phone out of my bag and show him the message I received from him yesterday. He squints at it, eyebrows furrowed, and then like a bolt of electricity hitting his brain, he suddenly jerks upright.

"I can't believe it," he mutters under his breath. "She is so manipulative!"

"What?"

"She set us up!" he cries. "She asked to borrow my phone to look something up. She said hers was dead. She must have sent this and then erased it so I wouldn't see it. Don't you see? She *wanted* you to see me with her."

Huh?

It takes a moment for my brain to catch up. Would Clementine really do that? Would she really try to hurt me like that? I bite my lip and stare at him, still unsure whether or not to believe him.

"C'mon," Jacob says teasingly. "Do you really think I would put a winky face in a text?"

I turn the phone back around and look at the message.

Jacob: Hey! At the Human Bean! Come hang w/me?
😉 ☕ 🍪

And then the lightning bolt hits my head, too. I don't know why I didn't see it before. It's full of emojis. The very language of Clementine Dumont.

I scroll back to the text message he sent me earlier in the week, asking if I wanted to go to the movies. Not a single cartoon picture to be found.

"So you didn't write this?" I confirm, feeling the joy and relief rise up in my chest.

Jacob barks out a laugh. "No. I mean, yes, I would have wanted to hang out with you. But I didn't lure you there so you could watch Clementine Dumont crawl all over me."

That makes me laugh, too. It's a weak one, but it's still a laugh. "So you don't like her?"

"No way." He shakes his head adamantly, then takes

a step closer, reaching toward my face. It isn't until his fingertip brushes against my cheek that I realize he's brushing away one of my tears. Looks like I'm crying. *Again.*

He hands me the can of grape soda. "I like *you*," he says.

A small shiver runs through me.

He likes me!

A cute boy likes me!

"Wait a minute," I say, feigning suspicion. "Is this safe to drink?"

He laughs, takes the can from me, and pops the top himself. It fizzes and sighs but there's no purple explosion in his face. Then he hands it back to me and I take a sip.

It tastes delicious.

"So you like me?" I ask in a teasing voice.

He gives me the most adorable half smile. "Isn't it obvious?"

I shake my head. "I guess not to me."

He clears his throat. "Well, then either I have a lot to learn about girls or you have a lot to learn about guys."

I bite my lip to stifle a burst of laughter. "Maybe a little of both?"

His half smile turns into a full-blown, beaming, ear-to-ear grin. "Maybe a little of both," he agrees.

CLICK

Clementine and her minions ignore me all day. No surprise there. I sit as far away from them as possible in both French class and lunch. I don't care what they think. All I care about right now is rocking this English project and proving to Grace that I can still be a good, reliable friend.

"Are you ready?" Grace asks curtly when I meet her outside our English classroom before final period. I can tell she's still upset about yesterday.

"Yes!" I reply, trying to sound bright and upbeat.

She doesn't smile. She just hands me the script she's printed out for our project. "Good. Then let's get this over with."

I sit anxiously through the rest of the presentations while we wait for our turn. One pair performs a little skit. Jacob and his partner do a rap that's so adorable, I can't stop smiling through the entire thing. And another group filmed a really awesome movie.

When it's finally time for us to present, Grace plugs the small flash drive into Mr. Heath's computer and our presentation appears on the big screen in the front of the classroom. She begins her part, clicking through pictures of herself with her favorite childhood toys, and her very first trumpet, and her first marching-band competition.

She recites her lines flawlessly, just like we rehearsed. Then, after she reaches her final slide—the picture of her at her first concert—she hands the small clicking device to me and steps aside.

I swallow and stare at the screen, clicking the button in my hand to get to the next slide.

I've started with a photograph of me at age five. I'm sitting in the back of a convertible with Rory, the wind whipping our hair into our faces. I remember when my dad came home in that car and we freaked out, thinking he had bought it. It turned out he had borrowed it from a friend at work who was letting us take it for a joyride. My dad drove, my mom sat in the passenger seat, and Rory and I giggled in the back. We drove all around town, stopping only to eat. There was something about that day that always stuck with me. We all had so much fun. Maybe it was because we all knew it was temporary. Soon we would have to give the car back. So we knew we had to make the most of it.

"Nostalgia," I begin, glancing down at the script that Grace and I wrote, "is defined by the dictionary as 'pleasure or sadness caused by remembering something from the past and wishing that you could experience it again.' "

I click the button and the photo changes. The next picture is of me at age seven. It was taken right after my parents completely surprised me by redecorating my whole bedroom with the princess theme, complete with the castle in the clouds painted onto my ceiling by a guy from my dad's construction crew. I'm standing next to the white dresser and pink chiffon curtains with a huge grin on my face. My two front teeth are missing.

"There are certain moments in our lives that stay with us," I go on, glancing down at my script. "That get saved in our mind like a photograph saved to a hard drive."

I click to the next slide. It's me at age fourteen. The day my parents brought home Buttercup to surprise me. I'm sitting on the carpet in the family room, laughing while I try (and fail) to wrangle the bouncy golden puppy who's crawling all over my lap.

Looking at the photo now, I remember what my mom told me the other day. How they got Buttercup to help me deal with Rory leaving for college. So even though I look absolutely elated in the picture, deep down, beneath the surface, there was a hole inside of me. A hole left behind by an older sister who moved over two thousand miles away. And I never got to say goodbye. At least, not the part of me that remembers.

"These are the moments that we look back on with

a sense of longing, wishing we could store them as more than just photographs," I say to the class. "Wishing we could save them as locations in a GPS device. Destinations that we can just hop in our cars and visit whenever we want."

I can feel my voice starting to break but I command myself to keep it together. Just a few more pictures and then it'll all be over.

I click to the next slide. This one is a picture of me at age six, standing in front of the yellow-and-white play-house that would soon become our Hideaway. It was right after my father finished building it. Before Grace and I moved in and made it our own.

I stare at the photograph of six-year-old me and, suddenly, I can't breathe or speak. She looks so happy. So perfectly content to be right there in that moment. She's not thinking about the future or the past. She's thinking about how awesome that playhouse is. How amazing her father is for building it. She's thinking how lucky she is to be living in that life.

I don't realize how long I've been just standing there wordlessly staring at the screen until Grace clears her throat. I blink and look over at her. She gestures for me to get on with it. I force a smile and look to Mr. Heath and the audience, who are all sitting quietly, waiting for me to continue.

I glance down at the piece of paper in my hands. The

script of what I'm supposed to say about nostalgia. How it's like a warm blanket. How it comforts us when we're feeling sad or lonely. How it's a *good* thing. And maybe it is. But right now, I can't bring myself to say any of that.

I can only manage to speak the truth.

My truth.

A truth I'm not sure I fully realized until this very moment.

"But maybe . . . ," I begin, my voice quavering and my hands shaking. I lower the script and face my classmates. My peers. "Maybe we're just nostalgic for things because we're so focused on moving forward that we let the present moment completely pass us by. And then, by the time we blink and remember to look around at what's happening right *now,* the present moment is gone and everything that made us happy—everything we *loved* is in the past." I peer over at Grace, expecting to see that same look of betrayal that I saw the night of the dance. But she's just staring at me with her mouth hanging open.

I flip to the next slide. It's a picture of me at my sweet-sixteen birthday party. I'm dressed in an amazing strapless black dress with sequins, and my sleek, straight hair tumbles over my bare shoulders.

Of course I don't remember the picture being taken. I don't remember if I was truly happy in that photograph, but I know for a fact Grace wasn't there. So I can't imagine that I was.

I take a deep breath and keep talking. "You know, I used to think that if I was just older, everything would be better. My life would be perfect." I bite my lip. "But then I got older. I grew up. And I realized that things weren't better. They were just more complicated."

I click to the next slide. A picture I found on my phone of me posing with my adorable little green car. It was the day I got it. The smile on my sixteen-year-old face shows how excited I am, but the pain in my heart right now reminds me that it's a moment I completely missed out on.

"I used to think that growing up was a destination. A finish line to cross."

Click. Next slide. A selfie I took in the Human Bean.

"But it's not," I go on. "Growing up is a journey. It's not about getting somewhere. It's about what we do and see along the way."

I flip to the next slide. It's a photograph of me at age twelve. Grace and I were on the floor of the Hideaway in our sleeping bags, looking up at my mom, who was holding the camera. At Grace's request, she's been cropped out of the picture so it looks like I'm having a slumber party all by myself.

"Maybe if we weren't so obsessed with getting older and moving on to the next big thing, maybe if we started appreciating what we have *right* now at this very second, then we wouldn't *be* nostalgic for the past." I reach for the mouse on Mr. Heath's computer and click. A small box appears around the photograph. I drag the left side out until the entire original picture is revealed. Until Grace is back in the photo, smiling up from her sleeping bag right alongside me. "Then we would realize that everything we want, everything—and every*one*—that makes us happy, is already right here. Right now."

I look to Grace and she looks back. For just a brief moment, I can see something in her eyes. A glimmer. A flicker of forgiveness. And then the smallest hint of a smile.

It's not much, but I'll take it.

STARTING OVER

When I get home later that afternoon, I'm feeling a little lighter in my step. A little more hopeful about everything. Buttercup greets me at the door, almost as if to ask, "How'd it go?" I give her head a rub. "I think it went pretty well," I reply.

She runs into the kitchen and stares at her bowl. I sigh. "Wow. You really do have a one-track mind." I head into the pantry. "Okay, let's see what we can find for you today."

I sort through the contents of the shelves. "Instant rice? No. Pancake mix? Probably not. Chicken and noodle soup? Sure, why not."

I grab the can of soup and bring it over to the counter. Just as I'm about to pop off the top, I hear a strange *whirring* sound. Like an electronic fan that's just turned on. I glance over at Buttercup's bowl. She's still staring at it intently. And that's when I notice something strange about the futuristic dog dish.

It's moving.

Not the entire thing. Just the plate on the top. The weird V-shaped opening is rotating to the left. I take a curious step toward it, studying it just as intently as Buttercup has been doing for the past week.

After a few seconds the whirring sound halts and the dish stops rotating, revealing a brand-new, untouched, perfectly portioned supply of dog food. Buttercup immediately attacks it, wolfing it down like she hasn't eaten in years.

"Oh my gosh!" I exclaim. "You little sneak!"

She wags her tail in response but doesn't look up from her meal.

"That thing has been automatically feeding you every day and you've been acting like you're starving to death?"

Her tail wags again. I take that as a yes.

Well, that certainly explains why I could never find the dog food. It was hiding *inside* her dish!

That just goes to show, you should never trust a dog when it tells you it's hungry.

I'm about to return the can of soup to the pantry when a text message dings on my phone. I race over to my schoolbag and dig it out, hoping it's from Grace.

It's not.

Mom: Just got an email from a woman who wants to buy the playhouse. Have you cleaned it out yet?

I slouch in defeat. I forgot she was selling the Hideaway. I haven't even been inside it since this whole fiasco began.

But I guess it's time.

I find some large trash bags under the sink and some empty boxes in the basement, and I trudge into the backyard. Buttercup follows excitedly after me, thinking we're going to play ball.

"Sorry," I tell her, with a sad shake of my head. "This is something I just have to do."

Buttercup lies down in a sunny spot on the grass while I step reluctantly onto the Hideaway's white wraparound porch. The house lets out a soft creak. Like it's grumbling about being woken up after such a nice four-year slumber.

I open the door and am immediately shoved back by the cloud of dust that blows into my face. I cough and swat at the air with one hand while the other searches for the light switch. Thankfully, it still works.

The small antique lamps on the walls illuminate the room, bathing the house in a soft glow.

It's a total mess. Cobwebs and dirt everywhere.

Did I ever come back in here after the fight?

It certainly doesn't look like it.

I glance around the small room. It's filled with so many memories that hit me all at once, making it hard to breathe.

So many reminders of the life I had. With Grace as my best friend.

There's the small table in the corner with the remnants of our play tea set and the little plastic teapot where Grace and I used to hide secret messages to each other. There are the Summer Crush posters lining the walls, half of them falling down and curled at the edges. There's the soft pink carpeted floor under my feet that Grace and I used to hop around on in our sleeping bags. There's the green paint stain on the wall from our failed mural. Even the little black chalkboard is still here. The one that Grace and I used to write our business names on. Like Graddie Productions and Graddie's Buttercup Bakery and Dolly Day Care.

Now it's lying abandoned on the floor by the window.

How can such a small space hold so many memories?

It's like they've all been locked up in here, just waiting for someone to let them out. For someone to set them free.

I guess that's what I'm here to do.

With a heavy sigh, I pick up my trash bag and get to work. Maybe Mom's right. Maybe it's time to let this house go so another little girl can build amazing memories in it.

I start with the Summer Crush posters, carefully removing the pushpins holding them to the walls and tossing them into the bag. There are four posters of the whole group. One of them—my favorite one—is a picture taken from above. The camera is pointed down at the boys and they're smiling up at it. Then there's one poster of just Berrin—my favorite. He's leaning against a wall with his hands in his pockets, looking kind of lost and thoughtful. And finally there's the poster of Cole—Grace's favorite. I remember the arguments we used to get into about who was the cutest member. Who was the most talented. Who was the best dancer. There was never a resolution. We both stuck to our Summer Crush crushes with an unwavering loyalty.

With a sad smile, I unpin the poster of Cole and begin to stuff it into the bag. But a voice from behind startles me to a stop.

"Cole was always the cutest one."

I spin around to find Grace standing in the doorway of the playhouse, her hands stuffed into her back pockets.

"No way," I counter without missing a beat. "Berrin has the eyes. You can't compete with the eyes."

"But Cole has the killer smile. With the best teeth."

"Sure," I allow, peering down at the poster I'm still holding. "If you like *buck*teeth."

She laughs and takes a step into the house, glancing around. "So your mom is really selling it?"

I nod, following her gaze to the clothing rack full of costumes. "Yeah."

"Probably for the best," she murmurs.

"Yeah," I agree, trying to make myself believe it. And I do. *Almost.*

I watch Grace silently take in all the memories. The same way I did when I first walked in here.

"Wait," I say, with sudden realization. "How did you know I was back here?"

She shrugs. "Just a hunch."

"A hunch?"

She looks at me and cracks a smile. "Yeah. I got a very strong Hideaway vibe when I was driving over here."

I can't help but grin. Grace and I could always count on our psychic abilities when we needed them most. It's not the kind of magic that requires an antique jewelry box bewitched by an eighteenth-century mystic. It's the kind of magic that happens between two best friends.

It's comforting to know that connection still exists somewhere between us.

It's even more comforting to believe that maybe it always will.

"Grace," I begin, my voice trembling again. "I'm sorry about swapping out the playing cards. I'm sorry I cheated. You have to know that I only did it because—"

"Because you wanted to try to rekindle our friendship," she finishes. "I know."

"Yes! Exactly! And I'm so sorry about what happened on my twelfth birthday. And every day after that. I've been such a mean, insensitive turd."

Grace looks away, hiding a smile. Then, after a moment, she asks, "Did you really mean what you said to me at the dance? About waking up to discover you were magically sixteen?"

I look down and scuff the carpet with the toe of my shoe. "Sometimes it feels that way. Like I skipped over my entire life and I'm just now realizing what was important to me." I take a deep breath and look at her. *"You,"* I say with all the conviction that I have. "You were important to me. You still are. I just want my friend back. We can dance to Summer Crush and hop around in our sleeping bags and eat junk food until our stomachs hurt. We can even have a tea party!" I fling my arms wildly toward the teapot and saucers on the little table. "Whatever you want to do. I just want things to be the way they were."

Grace presses her lips together, not saying anything. And the longer she stands there, the more I fear that this is not going to end well. That I'm never going to get her back.

Finally, after what feels like hours of painful silence, Grace sadly shakes her head and I feel my chest squeeze.

"But they can't," she says softly, almost like she's talking to herself. "You were right. What you said today during our presentation was right. We can't keep looking backward and being nostalgic for moments that are gone or things that don't exist anymore. We have to stop trying to live in the past and just live now."

I feel a sob rising in my throat. I try to swallow it but just end up hiccupping instead.

"Things can't be the way they were," Grace continues, "because we're not the same people anymore. Too much time has passed. We've grown up. We've moved on. We've found new friends and new interests and new music to dance to." She nods to the poster still in my hands. "We're not twelve years old anymore, Addie. You can't just turn back time and erase four years."

"But—" I begin to argue.

Grace raises her hand to stop me. I sniffle and hiccup again.

"*But,*" she echoes, her expression pensive. "It might be nice to start over. You know, get to know each other as we are *now.*"

The knot in my chest instantly starts to unravel and I wipe my nose.

"Do you think that would be okay?" she asks in a near whisper.

I nod over and over again. "Yes," I squeak. "Yes. Definitely. I'd like that."

"Cool. How about we hang out tomorrow?"

I bite my lip. "Okay."

Grace takes one last look around the Hideaway and flashes me a playful smile. "But not here. We're way too old for this place."

THE SAFEST PLACE

I remove the last costume from the clothing rack and stuff it into the trash bag. Then I move on to the kitchen. I empty all the cabinets—dusty plates, stuffed animals, a few dolls left over from the days of the day care—and toss those in the bag, too.

Grace is right. We're too old for this place now. We've grown up, moved on, made new friends (or lost new friends, in my case). Things are different. I'm sixteen. This is my life now. I'm just going to have to accept that. I'm going to have to learn how to put on makeup and speak French and pronounce Trigonostrophy and dance to new music.

But it makes me happy knowing that Grace and I will be friends again.

It may not be the same as it once was. We may not bounce around in sleeping bags or choreograph routines to Summer Crush songs or have tea parties, but we'll find new things to do together. We can go to movies and hang out at the Human Bean and talk about older, more mature things like books and politics and the news. Maybe I'll even start taking trumpet lessons again so I can join the marching band.

Okay, maybe not that.

The point is, everything is going to be fine. Because for the first time since I woke up in this life, I feel like myself again. Or some variation of myself. I'm not the twelve-year-old girl who made a wish on a magic jewelry box anymore. But I'm also not the sixteen-year-old girl I woke up to find in the mirror.

I'm someone completely new. And, hopefully, improved.

I move to the small table in the corner and pick up two cups and saucers from our old tea set, tossing them haphazardly into the bag. Everything must go. The house needs to be empty. A blank slate for the next owner to create her own memories.

With a sigh, I scoop up the white floral teapot—the one Grace and I used to hide our secret messages in—and start to throw it into the trash bag. But I stop when I hear a soft rattling inside.

That's strange.

I gently shake the teapot. There it is again. But it's definitely not paper. It's more of a *jingling* sound. Almost like a . . .

I lift the top of the teapot, peer inside, and let out a loud gasp.

I can't believe it.

It's been here all along. Waiting for me. In the safest place I can think of.

In the home that Grace and I built together. In the heart of our friendship.

I tip the teapot over and shake the ornate brass key into my hand. For the longest time I just stare at it, like I'm trying to figure out if it's real or not.

But I know it is.

Nothing has ever felt more real in my life. No choice has ever felt bigger.

I drop the trash bag onto the floor and immediately dart into the house. I run up the stairs, Buttercup galloping eagerly behind me, trying to keep up. I head straight to my bedroom and screech to a halt when I burst through the door.

It's still there. Sitting on my desk.

La Boîte aux Rêves Cachés.

The Box of Hidden Dreams.

The prison that holds my wish captive.

"Be sure to hide the key in the safest place you can think of. If you lose it, your wish will be locked inside the box forever."

I'm breathing so hard. Either because of my mad dash up the stairs or because of what I'm about to do. Maybe a little of both.

With trembling hands, I slowly insert the key into the lock. It fits perfectly.

I suck in a huge breath and turn it until I hear a faint click as the lock disengages. I open the lid, once again hearing that distant, ethereal sound of a woman singing. And there it is.

My wish.

I wish I was sixteen.

The ink hasn't faded. The paper hasn't yellowed or crumpled with time. The box has been keeping it preserved all these years. Keeping it safe.

I run my fingertips over my messy twelve-year-old handwriting.

This is exactly what I wanted. I wanted to be sixteen. I wanted to be in high school. I wanted to wear makeup and have a cell phone and get dressed up for dances and dates with boys and hang out at the Human Bean.

And now I have all those things. A cell phone with all the best apps. A drawer full of makeup. A closet full of beautiful clothes. Even a date with a cute boy. Tonight!

And to top it all off, Grace is finally back in my life. Which means everything is perfect. Everything is exactly as I imagined it.

But then I think about the presentation we gave today. All those memories I didn't recognize. All those pictures I don't remember taking. All the things I never really did. A life I didn't really live.

I grip the wish tightly between my fingers. It's so light. Almost weightless. It's amazing how something so significant can feel like nothing but air in my hand.

It's amazing how four years can feel like a whole life-time.

I close my eyes and focus all my thoughts on one single thing.

One single thought.

A new wish.

A new beginning.

A new choice.

Then, in one swift motion, I rip the paper in half. Again and again and again. I keep ripping until the pieces are so small, I can't rip them anymore.

I don't want to take the shortcut. I don't want to skip over all those things. I want to *live* them.

CASTLES
IN THE SKY

I dream I'm flying through clouds. I soar higher and higher until I reach a magnificent castle. I float down to the drawbridge and knock on the door. It opens and I walk through only to find there's no floor on the other side and suddenly I'm falling, plummeting through the clouds to the ground below. I try to fly again, but it's like I've lost my wings. Lost my magic. Just before I hit the ground, I wake up with a jolt.

I blink up at the castle above me. It looks identical to the one I just fell through.

Why is there a castle on the ceiling?

I blink again, but it's still there.

Then, finally, my brain catches up and I sit upright so fast, the room spins a little. Even through my temporary blurry vision, I can see the pink comforter and white dresser and pink chiffon curtains.

My hands immediately fly to my head, expecting to feel the soft, sleek strands of my sixteen-year-old hair, but instead I feel thick, bumpy locks tied up in a bun.

A bun!

I jump out of bed and run to the mirror, grinning like a crazy person when I see my reflection.

My reflection. Freckle-faced, curly-haired, four-foot-six *Addie* Bell.

I leap onto my pink princess bed and start jumping up and down, shouting, "It worked! It worked! It worked!"

Mom comes bursting into my room a few moments later. She's dressed in yoga pants and a tank top, her hair pulled back in a ponytail. She looks like herself again.

"What's going on?" she asks, eyeing me suspiciously.

"Mom!" I bounce off the bed and run to her, wrapping my arms around her waist and squeezing so tightly. She seems a bit taken aback by my attack hug, but eventually she squeezes me back.

"Everything okay?" she asks.

"Yes!" I shout. "Everything is *perfect!*" She gives me another quizzical look. "I just . . . ," I begin, trying to come up with a good excuse for my strange behavior. "I had the craziest dream!"

Mom sits down on my unmade bed. "Tell me about it."

"I dreamed I was sixteen and in high school!"

She smiles. "Wow. You must have loved that dream."

I giggle. "I did! At first. I mean, it was cool. I got to

wear makeup and have a cell phone and drive a car and go to high school dances! But then it turned into kind of a nightmare pretty quickly."

Mom cocks an eyebrow, suddenly super-interested. "Why's that?"

I sigh. "Because I realized that high school was actually superhard. I was in French class but I barely spoke French."

Mom laughs. "That sounds terrifying."

I laugh, too. "Yeah. It was. And I had to take this weird math class called trigonometry and . . ."

I sputter to a halt. Wait a second. Did I just pronounce that right?

I think I did!

"Yes," Mom prompts. "Trigonometry and . . . ?"

I let out a guffaw. "Yeah. Trigonometry. Trigo*nom*etry. Trigo*nom*etry. Huh. It's so easy! I don't know why I had so much trouble before."

Mom tilts her head curiously and I realize I'm probably not making the most sense. "Anyway, then I discovered that Grace and I weren't friends anymore and . . ." I have to stop because my throat starts to burn.

As soon as I mention Grace's name, Mom's expression darkens. "Speaking of," she says, in a serious tone. "I got a call from Grace's mother this morning."

I feel a sense of dread. It sounds like I'm about to get in trouble.

"I'm not happy about the way you treated her last night."

Last night?

Hang on a sec. What day is it?

"I really think you should apologize to her at your party today."

My party is *today*? It's the very next day?

It's like I never left!

And that means I have a chance to do it all over again. The party is where everything went wrong. Grace and I had the big fight over the gift she gave me, which led to me abandoning her during our school project. But now, I can fix it. I can steer this ship back on course.

"Yes!" I yell, skipping wildly around my room. "Yes! Yes! Yes!"

"Addie?" Mom says, still looking at me like I'm crazy.

I stop skipping and put on a serious face. "You're absolutely right, Mom. I behaved horribly toward Grace. I will definitely apologize today and I'm sure we'll have an uproarious time."

"Uproarious?" Mom echoes with a frown.

"Yes," I reply. "It means superfun."

Mom laughs. "I know what it means. I'm just surprised . . . You know what? Never mind." She stands and walks toward the door. "You should get dressed, Addie. The guests will be arriving in a few hours."

"Okay," I tell her. "Mom?"

She turns around. "Yeah?"

"Don't ever stop calling me Addie, okay?"

Mom squints at me. "Why would I stop calling you by your name?"

"I mean my nickname. Addie."

Mom looks more confused than ever. "Yesterday, at the restaurant, you told me you hated your nickname. You said it was babyish."

I bite my lip as the memory from the parking lot of JoJo's Pizza comes flooding back. "I know," I admit, fidgeting with the edge of my comforter. "But it's kind of growing on me."

THE NEW
(AND IMPROVED)
ADDIE BELL

As soon as my mom leaves, I bound off my bed and open my closet door. Everything is here! All my old clothes, which somehow feel new again. After much deliberation, I pick out a red-and-black plaid dress with a black satin ribbon belt.

I look in the mirror and my mouth falls into a frown.

Something isn't right.

Something is missing.

My freckles are back. My skin is clear of makeup. My cheeks are slightly fuller. And my hair is . . .

My hair!

I yank on the rubber band and my thick curls tumble around my shoulders. I run my fingers through them a few times to get out all the tangles and then I check my reflection again.

A smile immediately brightens up my entire face. I

don't know why I never wore my hair down before. It looks pretty good! It's so fun and bouncy.

I'm just about to close my closet door when something sparkly catches my eye in the mirror. I spin around and my gaze lands on *la Boîte aux Rêves Cachés*.

It's sitting on my desk, right where I left it after I made the wish to be sixteen. I tiptoe across my bedroom, as though I'm afraid walking too fast or too hard might scare away the magic spirits hidden inside.

I scoop the jewelry box into my hands and examine it from all sides.

I still can't believe that it worked. That Mrs. Toodles is really a descendent of an eighteenth-century witch.

And if I'm really back, that means Mrs. Toodles is alive!

Holding my breath, I lift the lid and peer inside.

I'm not sure what I'm expecting to see in there, but the sight still takes me by surprise.

The box is empty.

I already destroyed my wish. I ripped it into tiny pieces. There's nothing left inside.

Still, I somehow feel the need to keep the box safe. Keep it hidden. Just like Mrs. Toodles's long-lost relative did. I carry the box into my closet and store it on a high shelf, concealing it behind a bunch of extra pillows.

Just as I'm checking it from all angles to make sure it's invisible, I hear something in the hallway. My gaze whips to the door, fully expecting to see Buttercup come racing into my room, tail wagging and body wiggling.

Then I remember . . .

I don't have a dog when I'm twelve. Mom and Dad don't get me one until Rory leaves for college in two years.

My heart clenches as I think about her soft fur and adorable ears that perk up every time I ask her a question. I'm going to miss her waking me up with slimy kisses and greeting me at the door when I come home from school. But at least this way, I'll be able to see her as a puppy and watch her grow up. Not just in pictures. But in real life.

"No, I can't go," I hear a voice in the hallway whine. "I have to be here for my little sister's lame birthday party. My parents are forcing me. Like I want to spend my Saturday with a bunch of twelve-year-olds."

I let out a giddy yelp and sprint into the hallway. My sister is standing there with her phone pressed to her ear.

"Rory!" I dole out another attack hug. She drops her phone in surprise and nearly tumbles over.

"What the heck?" she says, her arms limp at her sides.

"I missed you so much!" I say, squeezing her tighter.

"You missed me?" she asks in a confused voice. "But I just saw you last night."

"I know. But I still did. Is that okay?"

It's kind of strange, but I can almost feel her body soften a bit. And then, a second later, she actually hugs me back. "Sure. Whatever," she mutters, but I can hear the smile in her voice. Even if I can't see it.

Maybe Rory will go to Rice University. Maybe there's nothing I can do about that. So I figure I better make the most of her last two years at home.

A moment later, her body suddenly stiffens again. She pulls back and glares suspiciously at me. "Oh, I know what this is about. You wanna use my makeup, don't you? Okay, maybe *just* a lip gloss, but if Mom asks, you didn't get it from me."

I shake my head. "No. I don't want to use your makeup."

Her eyes narrow. "Since when?"

I shrug. "Since now."

"Why are you being weird?"

"I'm not. I have plenty of time to wear makeup later. For now, I'm not sure I really need it, you know?"

She gives me a blank look as I do a little skip and prance to the stairs.

"Addie," she says, leaning over the railing.

I stop at the first landing and peer up at her. "Yeah?"

She twists her mouth to the side, like she wants to say something really big and important. But in the end, she just says, "Your hair looks supercute, by the way."

I beam. "Thanks!" And I continue down the stairs, taking the long way, through the dining room, to the kitchen.

When I get there, Mom is decorating cupcakes and Dad is eating sour-cream-and-onion potato chips out of the bag. I run and give him a hug.

"Happy birthday, the sequel!" he says, kissing the top of my head.

"Thanks!" I nudge my chin toward the bag in his hand. "Go easy on those chips," I tell him. "I hear onion can stay in your system and affect your breath for days."

Dad gives me a strange look, then glances down at the potato chips. He cups his hand over his mouth and blows, smelling his own breath. Then he crumples the top of the bag closed and returns it to the pantry.

"Did you cut through the living room with your shoes on?" Mom asks, peering at my feet.

"Nope!" I say, sticking my finger in the frosting bowl and licking off the yummy buttercream chocolate. Mom tries to slap my hand but I duck away just in time.

I check the clock on the microwave. The guests aren't scheduled to arrive for a few hours, but I still have one more thing to do before then.

Checking to make sure Mom and Dad are occupied in the kitchen, I sneak out the front door. I practically skip all the way down the block to the small cottage-style house at the end of the street. I bound up the front steps and ring the doorbell. Mrs. Toodles answers about two minutes later, looking exactly as I remember her. Jewelry covering her arms, neck, and fingers to the point that you can barely see her skin, and her long, silvery white hair tucked under one of her signature tiny hats. This one has a bluebird perched on the side. I don't tackle hug her like

I did to Mom, Dad, and Rory, for fear that I might break all her bones, but I'm so happy to see her again. And I have so much to tell her!

"Hi, Mrs. Toodles!" I sing, flashing her the biggest smile I can muster.

It takes a moment for her to figure out what's going on, and then she says in her usual rattling voice, "Adeline?"

"Yes! It's me!"

"Oh my! How good it is to see you! Would you like to come in?"

I shake my head. "I can't. My birthday party starts soon and I have to get back to my house, but I wanted to stop by to tell you that it worked! It really worked!"

She tilts her head. "What worked, dear?"

"The jewelry box. I made a wish to be sixteen and I woke up to find that four years had passed! Just like that! Rory was at college and Mom was working and I was in high school and you . . ."

I trail off. My voice tightens at the memory of my mother breaking the news that Mrs. Toodles had died. But I can't tell her that.

"You were off on another one of your adventures!" I finish, feeling confident it was the right thing to say. "And it was crazy. Because I lost the key and I couldn't open the box to get my wish out. But then I finally found the key. I had hidden it in the safest place I could think of, just like you said. So I unlocked the wish and now I'm back and it's like I never left. Except I did. Because everything has changed!"

I stop and think about what I just said. *Has* everything changed?

As far as I can tell, nothing's *actually* different. Rory is still talking on her phone nonstop. Mom is still obsessed with the living-room carpet. And I still live in a pink princess bedroom with a closet full of clothes purchased from the kids' department.

"I mean," I say, amending my last sentence, "I guess everything just seems different because *I've* changed."

Mrs. Toodles is silent for a long time and I wonder if she's fallen asleep with her eyes open.

"Mrs. Toodles?" I ask.

She startles. "Yes, dear?"

"I was just telling you about *la Boîte aux Rêves Cachés,*" I tell her.

She makes a *tsk, tsk* sound with her teeth. "Speak English, dear. You know I can't understand French."

Can't understand French?

But she's the one who told me that's what the jewelry box was called.

"The Box of Hidden Dreams," I repeat in English.

There's another long silence and I worry she's fallen into a trance. Then she says, "The what, dear?"

"The jewelry box," I tell her indignantly, getting frustrated. "The one that grants wishes."

"Oh, Abigail, that sounds like a lovely story."

"No, Mrs. Toodles. It's me. *Adeline*."

"Of course it is!" she trills after a pause.

Now I'm confused. What just happened?

"Maybe you can tell it to me sometime," she says gently.

"But you told *me* the story," I remind her. "About the Starlit Lady, who was the personal mystic to Marie Antoinette."

I'm hoping that if I just give her enough of the details, it'll jog her memory.

"Oh! That reminds me of a story I wanted to tell you," she says, completely ignoring my attempts. "Have you heard the one about the frog, the dog, and the fish?"

I can't believe it. She forgot. The dementia stole the story from her mind. Will it ever come back? Or is it gone forever? How exactly does dementia work?

Maybe it'll never come back. Maybe it really is gone.

But not forever.

Because now *I* know the story. And I guess it's my job to make sure it stays remembered.

"Mrs. Toodles," I interrupt her while she's in the middle of prattling on about three animals fighting over the rights to swim in a magic pond.

"Yes, dear?"

"I want to come visit you more often. Would that be okay?"

"Of course!" she says. "I love visitors. But you must

beware of my neighbors. They're running a money laundering scheme from their kitchen."

I sigh. I highly doubt that, but I don't argue with her. "Well, I'll make sure to avoid them. But really, I just want to see you. And I want to write down all of your stories."

"How nice!" she says. "What for?"

I swallow. "So no one ever forgets them."

BEST FRIENDS FOREVER

By one o'clock, the party is in full swing. Everyone is having a great time. Summer Crush plays on the speakers, the backyard is covered in streamers, and my mom's cupcakes are a huge hit.

But I'm starting to worry because Grace isn't here yet. It's not like her to be late. In fact, she's *never* late. Every time the doorbell rings, I run to answer it, only to find it isn't her.

What if she doesn't even come?

What if she's still so mad about our fight in the Hideaway last night that she decides to skip my party altogether?

But then I remind myself that she *has* to come. Jacob Tucker told me that we had a huge fight at my twelfth birthday party. She'll be here.

I try to busy myself by eating some of the snacks my

mom put out and joining in on a game of Egg and Spoon, during which you have to carry an egg balanced on a spoon across the lawn to your partner and then they have to carry it back. All without dropping the egg.

But I completely forfeit the game halfway through my turn when I hear the doorbell ring. I jump, causing my egg to roll off my spoon and splatter in the grass. "Sorry!" I call to my partner and run into the house, just beating my mom to the door.

"I'll get it," I tell her.

She laughs and walks back into the kitchen.

I swing the door open wide, ready with my smile and my apology. But my face drops when I find not Grace standing on the front porch, but a twelve-year-old Jacob Tucker. All the extra baby fat is back in his cheeks, his dark hair is messy and falling into his eyes, and he's only a few inches taller than me.

"Jacob!" I say, forcing myself to smile again. "Hi! Welcome!"

He stands there awkwardly, holding a six-pack of grape soda, which he thrusts at me. "I brought these for you," he mumbles, staring at his shoes. "Sorry about the exploding one yesterday."

"Thank you!" I beam back at him, even though he's still not looking at me.

Gosh, I forgot how awkward and shy he is!

"Grape soda is my favorite," I tell him.

"I know," he mumbles.

"It tastes especially good when it shoots up your nose."

He braves a glance away from the floor and looks up at me, probably to check that I'm joking. I smile to let him know that I am. "I mean," I go on, "you wouldn't think it would taste good, mixing with your boogers and all, but yesterday when that can exploded in my face, I was like, 'Mmm! Grape soda snot! Delish!'"

He chuckles. "I'll have to try that sometime."

"You really should."

He bites his lip and stares down at the ground again. "Happy birthday, Addie."

I lean forward and give him a kiss on the cheek. He nearly jumps backward in surprise, his face turning a bright crimson color. Then, after a short pause, he pulls his face into a grimace and whines, "Ewww! Gross! Why did you do that?"

I shrug. "Just 'cause."

He groans and wipes at his cheek. "Well, don't. Ick."

But as he pushes past me into the house, I swear I see him crack the tiniest of smiles.

It doesn't *really* count as a first kiss. Not yet, anyway.

With the six-pack of soda balanced in one hand, I reach out to close the door, but it doesn't shut all the way. It bounces off something and comes swinging back at me, nearly ramming me in the nose.

I look up to see what the door bounced off and come face to face with Grace. Exactly as I remember her. Her dark blond hair is woven into the most elaborate braid I've seen yet, and she's wearing an adorable navy wrap dress that ties at the waist.

"Wow!" she says, looking me up and down. "You look great! I love your hair!"

"Thanks!" I say, touching my curls. "I love yours, too!"

Then we stand there for a moment, staring at each other. Even though so much has happened for me, I have to remind myself that for Grace, our big fight was just last night.

"Look—" I start to say, just as Grace blurts out, "Sorry I was late!"

We both chuckle nervously and Grace holds out a small wrapped box. "I was wrapping this and I couldn't get it right. I wanted it to be perfect."

I feel my heart swell as I set the soda on the floor and take the gift from her.

"Thank you. Should I open it now?"

She shrugs. "If you want."

"I do," I tell her emphatically. "I really, really do."

I can't take the suspense any longer. This is the gift that launched the end of our friendship. I have to know what's inside. And I have to set it right.

But as I hold the small box in my hand, I also know that no matter what it is, I will love it. This is one of those things in life that I can be 100 percent certain of.

I rip off the wrapping paper to find a silver cardboard box. I lift the lid and gasp. Inside, lying on a bed of white foam, is the most gorgeous bracelet I've ever seen. It's gold with a little heart-shaped charm hanging off of it.

"It's a best-friend charm bracelet," Grace tells me. "I had it engraved with the word *Graddie*." She holds up her arm to reveal the exact same one dangling from her own wrist.

I'm speechless as I remove the bracelet from the box and examine the small charm. "I love it," I'm finally able to say. "I love it so much."

And I do.

I can't for the life of me figure out why I would have said anything else. Why I wouldn't have loved this.

That is, until Rory walks by and leans over my shoulder to look at the gift. "Aww," she coos. "How cute. Best-friend bracelets. I think I had one of those when I was like seven."

I know she doesn't intend for it to be mean, but I feel myself bristle at the comment. The thought that Rory finds the gift immature definitely stirs something. An old frustration that's buried deep inside me. The burning desire to be older and cooler in the eyes of my big sister.

Is this what happened? Is this how it all started? Did Rory make that same comment to me, causing me to lash out, blame Grace, and then go running to Clementine?

I stand up straighter.

Well, it's not going to happen this time.

I'm not ditching Grace on our English project. I'm not going to become BFFs with Clementine. In fact, I doubt I'll even say two words to her at school on Monday. Which, honestly, won't be much of a change.

"I think it's amazing," I tell Rory defensively as I clasp the bracelet around my wrist and hold it up next to Grace's. Grace beams at me while Rory just shrugs and starts tapping something into her phone.

"Whatever," she mumbles, walking away.

"You really love it?" Grace asks after my sister is gone.

I close the front door behind her and pick up the six-pack of soda again. "I really love it. And I'm sorry I was such a bad friend last night."

Grace tugs at her earlobe, suddenly looking uncomfortable. "That's okay. I'm sorry I overreacted."

And then the most amazing idea in the history of amazing ideas hits me. "How about a do-over?" I ask.

Grace furrows her brow at me. "What do you mean?"

"Another slumber party. Tonight. In the Hideaway. We can have a sleeping bag obstacle course, and work on our routine, or our English project, and maybe even have a tea party!"

I can tell instantly from Grace's reaction that it was the right thing to say. The *best* thing to say. She grins. "I'll be there!"

RETURN OF THE STARLIT LADY

"Five, six, seven, eight!" Grace calls out.

The first verse of "Love Is a Four-Letter Word," one of our favorite Summer Crush songs, kicks off and we start dancing.

Walk one, two, three, out four, head roll, ball change, kick.

Down one, hair flip, shoulder, shoulder, step, pause, and turn.

"Then I thought we could do something like this," Grace says, doing a swinging twirl kick.

"Awesome!" I try the move and nearly wipe out. We both break into laughter. "Then at the end," I say, righting myself, "we can do cool jazz hands." I fall to one knee, stick out my hands, and wiggle my fingers.

"Jazz hands?" Grace gives me a skeptical look. "Aren't those a *little* immature?"

I can't help but giggle. "Maybe."

We practice the routine five more times until we're both breathless and our legs are sore. Grace collapses on her sleeping bag and spreads her arms out like she's going to do a snow angel. "Gosh, I love Summer Crush so much. I can't *wait* for their next album! What do you think it'll be called?"

I don't have the heart to tell her that, unfortunately, this will be the last album. That our favorite band is breaking up. So I just plop down on my own sleeping bag and say, "I have no idea. But definitely something to do with stars. Or hearts. Or stars. Or maybe hearts."

Grace giggles. It's a little private joke between us. We once noticed that all four of the Summer Crush albums had either the word *star* or *heart* in the title. *Queen of My Heart, Stars and Stripes, Royal Heart Flush,* and finally the most recent, *In the Stars.*

"Or maybe they'll go with something completely new and different," Grace says. "Something like . . ."

"Moon!" we both shout at the exact same time. Then we do the thing we always do when we have one of our weird psychic moments. We point to each other with open mouths and start cackling like little old ladies.

"That was crazy!" Grace exclaims.

"The craziest," I agree, with a smile the size of Texas on my face.

Gosh, I missed this so much.

Lying here, on my sleeping bag next to Grace, I suddenly realize that I don't really care if Summer Crush breaks up. I don't care if Berrin releases the worst solo album in history, Maddox starts hawking perfume, and Donovan and Cole turn into bad reality TV stars. Because even though we'll never have another Summer Crush album to look forward to, even though we'll never again stay up until midnight waiting for the songs to release online, I know for sure now that Grace and I will never split up. We'll always be friends. And that's something even better to look forward to.

Even so, I *might* send a strongly worded fan letter to Summer Crush pleading with them to stay together, just in case.

"What do you want to do now?" I ask, rolling onto my stomach.

Grace shrugs. "How about we work on our English project?"

I pop up to my knees. "Yes! I actually had a great idea for that."

"You do?" Grace looks a little apprehensive, particularly after the disagreement we had yesterday. I'm sure she thinks I'm going to suggest we make a music video to an old rap song or something.

"A fairy tale!"

She frowns. "But I thought you said last night that you didn't want to do a fairy tale."

"I changed my mind! Plus, I came up with the best fairy tale!"

Grace's eyes grow as large as pancakes. "What is it?"

"It's actually a story Mrs. Toodles told me. About a woman with magical powers. She was called *la Dame Étoilée,* which in French means 'the Starlit Lady.'"

"Ooh, French," Grace says approvingly. "This is going to be good. Mrs. Toodles always has the best stories."

I smile and launch into the tale of *la Boîte aux Rêves Cachés.* I tell her about Marie Antoinette and her personal mystic, who was kept a secret until the revolution, when her identity was discovered and she was executed as a witch, all her belongings destroyed. I try to tell it as well as Mrs. Toodles did, inserting dramatic pauses and changing my voice at just the right times for just the right effect. It seems to be working. Grace is resting on her elbows, staring at me intently as I speak.

"So what happened to the box?" she asks when I finish.

I shrug. "That's the mystery. No one really knows. It was passed down from mother to daughter for generations and then it just . . . disappeared."

I think about the gem-encrusted jewelry box on the top shelf of my closet and smile. Probably better that no one knows about it. I wouldn't want it to fall into the wrong hands.

"This is great," Grace says. "We can film it like a movie."

"Yeah!"

"And you can play the Starlit Lady!"

"And you can play the daughter who finds the jewelry box!"

Grace jumps to her knees. "Yes!"

"And we can ask Rory to play Marie Antoinette."

Grace's smile falls right off her face. "Do you think she'll do it? She never seems to want to do anything with us."

I wave away her concern. "Trust me, she'll do it. We'll just remind her that Marie Antoinette had tons of shoes and makeup and she'll be in."

Grace giggles. "Cool. We can build the Box of Hidden Dreams out of cardboard and fabric. I saw a YouTube tutorial about it."

"Perfect!" I say, and we both jump to our feet to get started.

"This can be the Starlit Lady's cottage," I say, rolling up the sleeping bags and pushing them into a corner.

"Maybe we can have a scene of her drinking tea with her daughter before she's executed," Grace suggests, pointing to the teapot and teacups on the table.

"Great idea!"

Two hours later, we have our first shot all ready to go. Grace has constructed the most amazing jewelry box out of nothing but a cut-up Kleenex box, some old curtains my mom had in the basement, glue, and ribbon.

She places it on the table next to me and adjusts the

camcorder on the tripod. "Just a little to the left," she says, and I scoot my chair over. "Perfect."

Grace is so much better at manning the camera than I am. She's so meticulous and analytical; she always finds the best angles and lighting.

"Okay, ready?"

"Ready," I say, trying to get into character. I'm wearing a long evening gown that we found in the back of my mom's closet, a giant hat, and loads of jewelry. It's pretty over-the-top, but it looks great. The only problem is, every time I move, I jingle like crazy and Grace and I both crack up laughing. I hope we can get at least one take of this first scene without breaking into hysterical giggles, although I know that's probably impossible.

Grace is about to push record on the camera when she suddenly stops and frowns at the viewfinder.

"What?" I ask, adjusting my hat. The small motion makes all sorts of jangling noise.

"It's an interesting story," she says thoughtfully, and for a second, I almost feel like she's putting something together. Does she know what happened? Is she getting some weird reverse echo from the future?

No, that would be impossible.

She bites her lip in concentration.

"What's wrong?" I ask anxiously.

She shakes her head like she's coming out of a daydream. "Nothing. I just think it would be cool if the story were real. Like if the box really *did* grant wishes."

I let out a nervous stutter of a laugh. "Yeah, that would be pretty cool."

She stares at the cardboard jewelry box on the table. "What would you wish for?"

I glance around the Hideaway at the sleeping bags stuffed in the corner; the Summer Crush posters on the wall; the teapot, cups, and saucers set up in front of me; and Grace standing behind the camera, readying to push record. Then my eyes land on the small chalkboard sign in the window where we've written "Graddie Productions" for our new movie studio.

What would I wish for?

I look back at my friend—my *best* friend. Then I smile and say, "This."

ACKNOWLEDGMENTS

Special thanks to Jim McCarthy for believing in this book and to Wendy Loggia for turning that belief into a reality. I also must thank Cathy Berner from Blue Willow Bookshop, without whom I'm not sure this book would have ever been written. And to think it all started with the word *cheese*. (She knows what this means.) Also thanks to the wonderful people at Delacorte Press and Random House who brought this book to life. And to Nicole Gastonguay for making it look worthy of a shelf. Thank you to Joanne and Benny, the dynamic duo, for helping me take this nugget of an idea and shape it into something real. Thanks to Michelle Levy for choreographing the Graddie dance routine. And of course, as always, I am indebted to Terra Brody for her costuming prowess, to my parents for their love and support, to my dogs for somehow always knowing when I need them most, and to Charlie for reading anything and being *everything*.

But above all else, thanks to my readers, young and old(er). Whoever you are, wherever you live, whatever you do, never forget that *you* have magic in the heart. The *real* kind. ♥♥♥

ABOUT THE AUTHOR

JESSICA BRODY is the author of several books for teens and tweens, including *The Karma Club, 52 Reasons to Hate My Father,* and the Unremembered trilogy. She splits her time between California and Colorado, where she lives with her husband and four dogs. When she was twelve, she was convinced her life would be perfect if she was sixteen.

Visit Jessica at:

JessicaBrody.com

facebook.com/jessicabrodyfans

instagram.com/jessicabrody

@JessicaBrody